# The Temptation

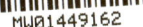

FILTHY RICH AMERICANS | BOOK FIVE

Vance is too tempting!

NIKKI SLOANE

Text copyright © 2021 by Nikki Sloane

Cover design © Shady Creek Designs

Cover Photography © Depositphotos, Inc.

All rights reserved. Except as permitted under the U.S. Copyright Act of 1976, no part of this publication may be reproduced, distributed, or transmitted in any form or by any means, or stored in a database or retrieval system, without the prior written permission of the publisher.

The characters and events portrayed in this book are fictitious. Any similarity to real persons, living or dead, is coincidental and not intended by the author.

Aboard Edition

ISBN 978-1-949409-12-3

For my husband

ONE

VANCE

Tension was something I was accustomed to in my life. I wore it effortlessly, the way my father wore a bespoke suit as a second skin, as he did now. He sat in the chair across from me in the formal living room, dressed in his standard three-piece black suit.

My gaze snagged on the colorful silk peeking out from his front breast pocket.

His girlfriend's doing, for sure. Macalister Hale had obsessed over tradition his whole life and embodied a classic look. He much preferred people's attention stay on him rather than his pocket square, but Sophia was pushing him to be fashion-forward. Or at least to join this century.

Any other time, I would have enjoyed the idea that a woman half his age had such power over him, but I was too distracted to focus on it. My father had shown up at the Hale estate and announced he had something important to discuss. He'd arrived without warning, likely because if I'd known he was coming, I'd have avoided him.

So, I'd reluctantly followed him into the front room of the

house which had once been his and dropped down onto the couch my former stepmother had reupholstered the year before her death.

Of course, I immediately regretted my decision.

Alice loomed large between us, and the weight of unspoken words pressed down on my chest, making it difficult to breathe in my father's presence. He already knew what I'd done, but it did nothing to ease my guilt.

"This will only take a minute," he said.

His tone was full of his usual commanding indifference, the one that was so effective at telling you only his opinion mattered. His posture was rigid and straight, as if he were perched in a throne and not a chair, but again—this was normal. He was an imposing figure to the rest of the world. He made other people uncomfortable with a simple look.

But I saw through it today, and this was what had me so distracted.

Whatever he wanted to discuss, it gave him hesitation. In fact, the great and powerful Macalister Hale seemed . . .

Nervous.

My stomach churned with unease. My father didn't do nervous. I swallowed thickly. Fuck, was he going to bring up Alice? Was this the conversation we desperately needed to have—the one I *still* wasn't prepared for?

My father's gaze shifted away from mine. "I'm planning to ask Sophia to be my wife."

I blinked in my lack of surprise. My family had its fair share of secrets, but the way my father felt about Sophia? That wasn't one of them. The entire town of Cape Hill knew, thanks to my father's proclamation five months ago at Damon Lynch's disastrous campaign dinner. The only thing surprising to me was that my father hadn't proposed already. We

Hale men were nothing if not decisive, and I was sure his mind was set. Once his decision had been made, what was the point in waiting?

He wanted her.

And he'd raised me to understand Hales took what they wanted.

"All right." I was unsure what I was supposed to do with this information. "You wanting me to wish you luck?"

"No, I don't need luck." His cold blue eyes snapped back to me. "I would, however, like your permission."

I was suddenly grateful to be sitting because the floor threatened to swallow me whole. "What?"

He drew in a deep breath, making his shoulders lift. "She's the same age as you, so it's understandable if that gives you unease." He had one arm draped over the armrest of his chair, his fingers tensed in a fist, and his thumb brushed back and forth over his knuckles. "I don't need to tell you how much I care for her. You heard what I said that night, which wouldn't have been possible without your help. I'll always be grateful for that."

My brain was still stuck on the part where he'd ask for my permission. It ranked right up there with him admitting defeat.

It was something he never, *ever* did.

"It was no big deal," I said automatically.

He ignored my statement. "I've spoken to Royce already, but I'd like your approval as well."

He hadn't asked my opinion about marrying Alice, but then again, that had been fifteen years and a lifetime ago. Had he ever asked for permission in his life? Until recently, he had no need for anyone else's approval.

God, he'd changed so much.

He hadn't exactly softened—his edges were still sharp

and exact. But there was a thoughtfulness in him now. An awareness that the world might not always turn at his command. That people did not have to bend to his will.

His fall from grace included time behind bars, and it had been one of the most difficult things we'd had to endure. Like my mother's death, the consequences he'd faced had been a turning point in his life.

Only, instead of receding into himself, this time he'd grown. He'd begun to open the doors he'd used to close himself off, and the man he'd once been started to reemerge. At least, that was what Royce said. I'd been seven when our mother had passed away and barely remembered either of my parents before that event.

I was off-balance now but did my best not to show it. Being caught off guard meant I was at a disadvantage, and that wasn't allowed in this house, even if he no longer lived here. I drew in a breath and sat back in my chair, pretending to be uninterested in giving him permission. "I appreciate the gesture," I said, "but it's not needed."

"I assure you it is." His hesitation dried up, and his voice filled with conviction. "I won't ask her for her hand without it."

I cocked my head. This had to be a bluff, but what game was he playing at?

Whatever expression I was making, it must have prompted him to explain. "You are my son, and you have a say in who becomes part of this family."

Distrust moved through me like the blade of an oar cutting through still water. "Yeah? So, if I say no, that you don't have my approval—what happens then?"

His eyebrow arched. "I work to try to change your mind."

That did nothing to ease my distrust. "Why do you care?"

"I believe I just explained that. You're my son, and your

opinion matters."

I narrowed my eyes. "Never did before."

"I know." He shifted awkwardly in his seat. "And I'm . . . sorry. I'm trying to be better."

If I wasn't so shocked at hearing an apology, I might have appreciated the way he acknowledged the truth. But I was too stunned to do anything but simply stare at him, contributing to the stillness of the space between us.

The elegant sitting room we occupied was rarely used. Like me, it was curated. Designed to serve a purpose. Its task was to be a lavish display of our wealth, but this room didn't make the house a home any more than my existence made me part of the Hale family.

But things *were* changing.

We'd both made awful mistakes, but tearing the family apart came with a surprising upside. It cleared a space for us to build something new, and he seemed willing to rise to the challenge.

I was less sure.

Scared, my mind corrected.

My father had a relentless gaze, but it warmed as it focused in on me, and his voice went uneven. "I love you, Vance."

I sucked in a sharp breath.

He'd never said it before, and my mind reeled. After my mother's death, no one in the Hale family knew how to care for anyone else. Under my father's brutal regime, the best chance at emotional survival was to not have feelings at all. Royce and I had learned all about self-preservation, and quickly, too.

And I wondered if the absence of love between us allowed space for something else to grow in its place. He was a difficult man to love.

For years I found him much easier to hate.

Things were far more complicated now, but my knee-jerk reaction to him saying he loved me was pure instinct. "You can't."

Disappointment and displeasure glanced through his expression. "Why not?"

My heart banged in my chest. It was what made me speak without thinking. "Because I had an affair with your wife."

The second my confession was out, I would have done anything to take it back. My affair with Alice wasn't news to him, but my father recoiled anyway. At least I'd returned the favor, and now he was the one caught off guard.

Weakness. It was whispered through my head, spoken in his voice.

But I was the one who felt weak, and my guilt was so acute, I could barely look at him.

"Vance," he started, unsure where he was going with it, "that's . . . irrelevant."

I repeated the word in disbelief. "Irrelevant?"

"You're my son regardless, and therefore I will always love you."

Faint, hurried footsteps outside the room grew louder as they approached, but he seemed unaware. His focus was fixed on me.

"I have done a great number of things," he continued, "that I am not proud of. I hope you're able to look beyond them and feel the same way for me as I do for you and your brother."

There wasn't time to contemplate what he'd said because Elliot, the head of our household staff, appeared in the doorway. His normally calm eyes were wide, setting me on edge.

"Forgive the interruption," he said quickly, "but two police detectives are here and would like to speak with Mr. Hale."

My father drew in a deep, preparing breath. Whatever

this was about, he wasn't expecting it, and he was resigned as he rose to his feet. "I'll speak with them in here." His voice returned to his cool, confident one. "Please show them in."

Elliot's eyebrows tugged together, and he struggled with how to respond. "Actually, I believe they're interested in questioning the younger Mr. Hale."

What? My heart skittered as I processed what he'd said, but my body moved instinctively. As I stood, I kept my gaze locked on Elliot, and felt my father's attention snap toward me. It burned with unease and perhaps . . . protectiveness? His curiosity wanted to know what I'd done to bring police to our doorstep, but I didn't have an answer for that.

I kept my nose clean, both figuratively and literally. A lot of the people in my social circle did drugs, and everyone knew Richard Shaunessy was a cokehead, but me? I'd never strayed into the hard stuff.

And certainly not anything to put me on anyone's radar.

"All right," I said. "Can you show them in, please?"

There was a tightness in my chest when the two men were ushered into the room. Their gazes briefly wandered over the lavish furnishings and snagged for a moment on my father, before settling on me.

"Mr. Hale," the taller of the two men said, taking a step my direction, "I'm Detective Hawkins, and this is my partner, Detective Lewis." They both wore suits with their gold department badges hanging from their breast pockets. "We have some questions for you."

My father's tone was brusque. "Don't say anything without a lawyer." He pulled out his phone and scrolled through his contacts, likely looking for his attorney's number.

My whole life, I'd done what he wanted. The path of least resistance was usually the fastest, and when you fell in line, you often got overlooked. It meant I could get away with things and gave me freedoms Royce never had.

No one looked too closely at the younger Hale boy.

And, yes, it was smart for my father to be cautious, but had he forgotten *I* was an attorney? Not that I was stupid enough to represent myself, but I hadn't done anything wrong. I could listen and always lawyer up if I didn't like the line their questioning took.

Detective Lewis, the older, rougher-looking cop, rested a hand on his hip and studied me critically. "Do you *feel* like you need a lawyer?"

His partner scowled. "We're not here to charge you. We just want to have a conversation." He tacked it on to the end as a threat. "For now."

A challenge rose in Lewis's small eyes. "If you'd rather we do this at the precinct, we can make that happen, but let's save us all the time, yeah?"

I swallowed dryly. "What's this about?"

Hawkins nodded, satisfied. "When was the last time you were in contact with Jillian Lambert?"

Concern welled inside me. "Why? What's happened?"

"Please answer the question, sir."

"A few days ago." I searched my mind for the specifics. "Friday. We spoke on the phone." Which was odd, now that I thought about it. I was twenty-seven. Like everyone else my age, I was phone adverse, and all my conversations were done via text.

"What did you talk about?"

I paused. "Stuff."

Irritation heated Hawkins's face. "What kind of *stuff*?"

"Personal stuff," I answered with a clipped voice. "What's this about?"

When my question went ignored, it made worry spike further in me. Had Jillian done something?

"What is the nature of your relationship with Ms. Lambert?"

My gaze darted to my father. "It's complicated."

The detectives exchanged a knowing look before Lewis's attention swung back to me. "I bet two smart guys like us can figure it out, plus we've got the time for you to explain it."

I took in a breath, causing my chest to lift. "We're friends."

He didn't believe me. "Like the kind of friends who sleep with each other?"

"No." Not that it was any of their business. "Not anymore."

"Was that what you talked about? Did she end things with you?"

"No, we stopped dating a while ago, and it was mutual." Abruptly, my pulse jumped, and my concern grew exponentially larger. I didn't bother to disguise the worry in my voice. "Has something happened to Jillian?"

Years ago, it was decided it would be advantageous to align our family with the Lamberts. Wayne Lambert was an enormous asshole, but he was also tight with the president, and my father had political aspirations. I'd been instructed to seduce the oldest daughter, and like the dutiful son I was, I'd done it.

I'd been forced into a relationship, only to discover the same was true for Jillian. Her father wanted to see her married off to a Hale. So, I wasn't lying when I said we were friends. The pressure we both felt gave us a kinship I'd never had with anyone before. Plus, she was attractive, easy to hang out with, and the sex was solid. We dated to appease our families, and if Alice hadn't gone over the balcony railing and died, it was likely Jillian would have become my wife.

But then my father went to prison, and the tarnish on the

Hale name was enough to release her from her obligation. We were both relieved. Our future together would have been an empty, fabricated marriage where we'd likely have grown to resent each other.

Hawkins tilted his head. "What makes you think something's happened to her?"

"Because you could easily ask her these questions and not me . . . unless there's a reason you *can't* ask her."

Once again, the cops exchanged a look. They seemed to come to an agreement, and Lewis's shoulders shifted, giving up the tough act. His face softened. "Ms. Lambert took her father's boat out on Friday afternoon without permission and—"

"Which one?"

My interruption threw him. "What?"

"Which boat?" Like us, the Lamberts had several in the marina.

"*The Trident.*"

I smirked. "Wayne Lambert got bent out of shape over her borrowing *The Trident*? She's better at captaining it than he is."

Crewing one of her father's elite keelboats in the Constitution Regatta had brought Jillian and me together, and what sustained our friendship after the relationship ended.

"She didn't have permission when she left port," Hawkins's tone was ominous, "or anyone else with her."

My heart thudded to a stop. Single-handing *The Trident* was possible, but sailing alone was always dangerous. A boat that size would be a lot of work, and a beast if the weather were anything less than perfect. Oh, shit. Hadn't there been a storm Friday evening?

I tried to convince myself as much as I did them. "She's an accomplished sailor."

The air in the room turned heavy as neither man said anything. The painful silence dragged on, winding tension tighter inside me.

For the first time ever, I'd forgotten my father's presence, so it jarred me back to life when he spoke, even when his voice was quiet and somber. "What happened?"

"A fishing vessel found *The Trident* adrift this morning," Lewis said. "Ms. Lambert wasn't aboard."

For a moment, I couldn't process what that meant. She'd gotten off her boat while it was at sea?

I blinked slowly as cold realization moved in.

"No." My mind refused to accept it. Jillian was too smart to make a mistake and go overboard. "There was a storm on Friday. She must have been forced to abandon ship."

The sadness in the cop's eyes was hard to take, and his gentle voice was worse. "There doesn't appear to be any damage to *The Trident,* and the life raft was still onboard," he hesitated, "along with her wallet and cell phone."

No.

There weren't many good people in Cape Hill. Jillian was one of the few, and my only real friend. She couldn't be . . . *gone.*

"We're still waiting on the phone records," the cop added, "but it appears you were the last person to speak with her before she boarded that boat. So, I ask you again, Mr. Hale—what exactly did you talk about?"

TWO

VANCE

Sleep would not come, and I sighed when I checked the screen of my phone and discovered it was nearly two in the morning. My father suffered from insomnia. Was I developing it, too? Fuck, I didn't want to be like him any more than I already was. It was already too much.

I lay in my darkened bedroom, staring at the chandelier suspended from the vaulted ceiling, and did what I'd done for the last two days—I spent it replaying the conversation I'd had with Jillian.

She'd sounded normal. Maybe even happy for once. I'd escaped my familial pressure, but hers had only intensified since, and the last year had been incredibly rough for her. We ran into each other often at social events, and like me, her smile was always fabricated. All for show. Inside she was deeply unhappy.

Jillian Lambert was instructed who to date, where she should work, what she could wear. Every aspect of her life was dictated to the point she was told who she was allowed to be.

Bottling up who you were and what you wanted would

eventually lead to catastrophe, and all the terrible choices I'd made were the proof of that.

When she'd called, she'd caught me during my lunch break on Friday while I'd been tucked away in a back corner of a restaurant. She'd started off by apologizing for pulling out of the upcoming regatta. Her schedule was too tight, she'd said. And then she'd shifted over to her favorite subject, which was teasing me about how, for the most part, I'd gotten out. I could be with whomever I wanted, and despite this, I was still single.

She brought it up so often, I wondered if she wanted to live vicariously through me.

"I don't need a relationship," I said.

"Yeah," her tone was dry. "Why do that when you can get the sex for free?"

I shrugged, even though she couldn't see. She wasn't wrong. "Sex is easy. When you add in all the other stuff? Then it gets complicated, and I'm not interested in that. My life is complicated enough."

"Oh, you poor, little rich boy," she patronized, and I allowed it because, again, she wasn't wrong. I didn't know the struggle most people did, and my problems were self-inflicted. Her voice was matter-of-fact. "Most people see it the other way around, you know. Sex is what complicates things."

Irritation flashed through me. "I thought you felt the same way I did."

"That sex is meaningless?"

It had been for us. As enjoyable as it was, it hadn't brought us closer emotionally, and I was glad. It made the break-up easier on both of us. "Yeah. It doesn't have to be a big deal."

"You're so full of shit, Vance." She laughed. "Sex is a *huge* deal for you."

"No, it's not." I looked at sex the same way as sleeping and eating. It was a basic need to be fulfilled and nothing more.

"Right. Then, you'd have no problem going without it." Excitement filled her voice. "Oh, my God, I bet you wouldn't even last a week."

My irritation grew to full-out annoyance. "What are you talking about? Of course I would."

Her laugh announced she didn't believe me. "Sure."

It came out without thought. "You want to put money on it?"

She paused, and I pictured a surprised grin on her lips. "I have money. What would I do with more of yours?"

"Not money, then." I didn't know why I was even entertaining the idea.

Well, that wasn't true. I was a Hale, and I'd been conditioned to not only accept every challenge thrown my way, but to succeed at it.

It was win at all costs.

"Okay," she sounded as if she were merely humoring me, "let's say I'm interested. What would you want to play for?"

I wracked my brain for what we each had that was of value to the other. If I were my father, I'd have asked for help networking or a political 'in' with her family. But the ambitions for me to enter politics weren't mine. I didn't want to hold office, and the thought of an eventual presidential run made my stomach turn.

The idea took shape, and a smile widened on my lips. "I want the boat you'll use for the Cape Hill Cup."

"Why? Don't you win that, like, every time?"

I did, but last year I'd narrowly beaten her to the buoys. "We both know you're the only real competition for me."

She made a sound that was too short to be called a laugh, and I imagined her on the other end shaking her head with a smile. "Isn't it less fun when it's a cakewalk?"

"Nope. Winning is winning."

She let out a sigh. "Okay, if I'm giving up my boat, this thing needs to be a serious challenge. One month isn't long enough. I'm thinking more like six."

My mind emptied at the unwinnable challenge. "Fuck, no." Was she crazy? "I'm not going six months without sex. Be reasonable."

Her laugh was deep and, Jesus, when was the last time I'd heard her do that?

"Plus, the race is in August," I added.

"Okay, three months," she amended. "You can do that, right?" She didn't wait for my answer. "If you go ninety days without sticking your dick in someone, then I'll tie my boat up to your dock myself." She paused only long enough to draw in a breath. "But if you can't abstain . . . then I get *your* boat and presumably the trophy."

All of Cape Hill knew my boat was the fastest in the marina. If Jillian had it? She'd win the race for sure.

But that wasn't going to happen because I wouldn't lose this bet. A lot of my problems could have been avoided if I'd just kept my dick to myself, so a sex hiatus actually wasn't a bad idea. Three months was a bit longer than I wanted, but I could cope.

"Okay, deal. But I want clarification." I glanced around the restaurant to make sure no one was listening. "Does oral count?"

"You mean, oral *sex*? Yeah, that counts. It's right there in the name." Her tone turned playful. "You know what? I'll be nice. As long as you're giving and not receiving, I'll say it doesn't count. If I remember correctly, you weren't half-bad at it. I'd hate to deprive the ladies of Cape Hill."

I laughed because I wasn't good with my tongue—I was

fantastic. She'd been a big fan of how I went down on her when we'd been together, and I saw right through what she was doing now. Getting a girl off with my tongue was a lot of fun, but if I got the opportunity to do that, it'd be really hard not to want to do more.

Jillian hoped to tempt me into losing.

"Well, as I remember it," I said, "you were just okay at blowing me."

Now it was her turn to laugh at my outright lie. She knew my claim was bullshit.

"Whatever," she scoffed. "I don't hear complaints from my boyfriend."

My smile froze, and the mood shifted abruptly. Her attempt at a joke landed like a dropped anchor.

Of course she didn't hear complaints from her boyfriend Ansel. She was probably the first girl who'd ever touched his dick, and he was hopelessly in love with her. When—not *if*—he got down on one knee and proposed, she'd say yes and pretend to be excited, but I suspected she'd die inside.

Ansel Farber was an okay guy, but he was awkward in every sense of the word. The only attractive part of him was his pedigree. Like the Hales, the Farbers were old money, and Jillian's father thought he could buy that kind of clout if he married his daughters into it.

I sat up straighter in my seat and let seriousness fill my voice. "You need to break it off with him before things go too far."

I'd brought this up a few times before, and at this point in the conversation, she usually told me to mind my business or that it was already too late. The deal was done in both of their families' eyes. She would eventually be Mrs. Jillian Farber.

But today her tone was light and airy. "Don't worry, I'm

handling it."

I perked up in surprise. "You are? How?"

"Forget about it. I'm taking care of it." Her tone made it clear this was something she couldn't talk about. Perhaps Ansel or her sister were nearby. "Back to our wager," she said. "Can I trust you to tell me if you lose the bet?"

"I'm not going to lose, but, yeah. You can trust me." Sometimes I wondered if we were the only people in Cape Hill we could trust.

"Okay, good," she said. "So, if you fall off the celibacy wagon into a pile of women, I'll hear it from you first before Sophia."

Because Sophia Alby was all-seeing, all-knowing. Gossip traveled fast through our small town, and all of it seemed to flow through her. Concealing anything from her was hard before, but impossible now that she was dating my father.

"Yes," I confirmed.

"Good luck, Vance. You're going to need it," she teased. Then she announced she had to run, and the call ended.

I'd relayed the entire conversation to the police, only watering-down the specifics about the bet I'd made with her. They'd focused on Jillian's state of mind during the call and pressed me about her cryptic comments regarding Ansel, but I wasn't much help.

Sophia hadn't heard a word about them breaking up, and he'd been a wreck since the discovery of *The Trident*. So, tonight I lay in my bed and speculated what she'd meant when she'd said she was 'handling' breaking up with her boyfriend. Why had she sounded so carefree and happy? It was like the weight of her family's expectations were no longer crushing her.

Maybe she'd planned her escape.

The thought made ice crawl along my spine, and I refused to consider it. There were a dozen ways out that didn't end with her willingly stepping off the bow of her father's boat and into the deep.

I was your friend. You could have come to me.

Jillian and I weren't in love and had never been, but we cared about each other. I would have found a way to make it work if I were her only option. Didn't she know that?

I needed someone to talk to. With Jillian gone, Royce was my first choice, and Marist my second, but they weren't here at the house this week. Marist was six months pregnant, and Royce had surprised her with a babymoon to Fiji.

I couldn't bother them with this.

I glanced at the screen of my phone again. It was possible my insomniac father was awake at this hour, but what the fuck would I say to him? I'd been avoiding talking to him for so long, reaching out felt . . . impossible.

Not to mention, selfish. He'd made attempts, and I'd brushed them all off.

Despite that, my thumb swiped over the screen, bringing up his name in my contacts. I held my breath as I readied to tap the button—

A high-pitched wail shattered the air.

It was so loud, the sound of it hurt my ears and made my mind go blank. A notification popped up on my phone, alerting me that the house alarm had been triggered.

"No shit," I yelled, but couldn't hear my voice over the painful siren.

My pulse spiked as I launched up out of my bed. What had set off the alarm? Had someone tried to break in? My gaze flew to the door. There could be intruders in the house. It took a moment to remember there was a panic room concealed behind a false wall in my father's old room. Should I head there?

Fuck, it was hard to think over the ear-bleeding sound.

I scrolled to the security app on my phone and stabbed a finger on the notification to bring up the details, then stared at the screen with disbelief. A window sensor had registered the sound of breaking glass, which tripped the alarm, but it was clearly in error. Not only was it a window on the second floor, but it was in the room I was currently standing in. If glass had broken in my room, I definitely would have noticed.

I flipped on the lights and peered at the offending window, confirming it wasn't broken, and as soon as I disabled the alarm, my phone rang.

It was Elliot, who wanted to know if I was all right and told me security at the back gate was on their way. In the absence of the alarm, it felt like cotton had been jammed in my ears, but I explained it was just a malfunction and a security guy didn't need to bother coming up to the house.

It took forever to settle down afterward, which I really needed to do. I hadn't slept well the last two nights and was beyond tired. If I fell asleep soon, at least I could get a few hours in before I had to be up for work.

I'd nearly drifted off when the alarm blared again.

Same issue, even down to the same window.

"I'm going to rip the goddamn thing off the wall," I told Elliot when he called again.

"Don't. It's tied to the whole system. If you try to disable the unit, it'll trigger a fail-safe and we won't be able to disable the alarm at all."

It wasn't his fault, but I was exhausted. "What am I supposed to do? The fucking thing's broken, and you know it's going to go off again. It's four in the morning." It was too late to move elsewhere, like a hotel, and even though Royce and Marist weren't home, we weren't the only ones who lived here. Staff quarters were in the east wing, which meant everyone was having a sleepless night. "Just turn it off."

Elliot sounded as tired as I felt. "You want to disarm the whole thing?"

I didn't see any other solution. On top of the sophisticated technology, the house was a fortress. There was a scale-resistant fence all along the perimeter of the sprawling grounds, motion-activated lights, and both gates had round-the-clock manned security.

"We still have the exterior cameras and lights," I said. "They're on a separate system." It was plenty of protection even with the alarm system off, plus that would be temporary. "We only need it down for a few hours. After you've turned it off, you'll call the company and have them send someone over." I didn't mean to channel my father—it just happened. "When the technician gets here, send him straight up to my room. I want this addressed before I leave for work."

Elliot barely contained his irritation, but he was a professional. "Yes, sir."

I jarred awake from my deep sleep and blinked against the light that abruptly filled my room. *What the hell?*

Deliberate footsteps carried a slender figure across the floor and straight to the window. No attention was paid to me, the owner of the room. I didn't have my contacts in yet, so I snatched up my glasses from the bedside table and readied to unleash my fury on the serviceman who'd rudely barged in without permission, or so much as a knock on my door.

Except . . . the serviceman wasn't a man.

I slipped on my frames and watched the woman as she gazed up at the window sensor. She must not have known I was in here. Maybe Elliot had conveniently 'forgotten' to warn her because he was pissed about my demand last night and wanted to punish me. He'd worked for my father for years, and now Royce was the owner of our family estate, so technically Elliot didn't have to take orders from me.

The woman's back was turned, and I was grateful, because dear God, she had a great ass. She wore a fitted dress shirt, a straight skirt that ended just below her knees, and sexy heels. My irritation with Elliot faded somewhat. Whatever he'd said to the security company, it'd put enough fear in them to send a sales rep to try to smooth things over with one of their premiere clients.

A young sales rep, too.

I sat up in bed and leaned back on my hands, allowing the covers to coast down my bare chest and hang around my waist.

"Excuse me."

I said it softly, but the woman yelped anyway and spun to face me, her startled eyes wide.

Well, shit.

I'd planned to shock her, and I'd succeeded, but I hadn't expected her to do the same to me. My confidence stumbled momentarily as I gazed at her. Her cocoa-colored hair was parted to one side and sleek, falling as a long curtain several inches past her shoulders. Bright, sparkling eyes were precisely lined with black, and her smoky eyeshadow walked right up to the edge of what was considered professional. My father would say it was too much, but I found it incredibly appealing.

My mouth went dry. She might have been the sexiest girl packaged in business appropriate clothing I'd ever seen.

As her charcoal-rimmed eyes scanned over me, I

continued to stare back at her. The apples of her cheeks had the faintest hint of freckles. As if they'd been sprinkled on her skin in powder form and then softly blown away. Her watermelon-pink lips parted, showing off their glossy sheen as she drew in a preparing breath.

Damn. My family liked having beautiful things in this house, so this girl fit right in.

Woman, my mind corrected because she looked to be in her late twenties. Maybe even a year older than I was.

Her posture stiffened as she became acutely aware of our situation. How she'd barged into a bedroom unannounced, and there was now a possibility the client sleeping inside was naked beneath his sheets. She certainly knew I was shirtless, and even though she attempted to disguise her interest, I could tell she appreciated what she saw.

It burst from her in a rush. "I'm so sorry, sir. I didn't realize anyone was in here."

Her voice was strong, yet feminine, and I liked the sound. Normally, I would have enjoyed how the sight of my bare chest left her flustered, but the truth was she had me just as affected—and she was fully clothed.

I still felt confident, but also weirdly vulnerable.

"It's all right." My voice was tight. "I take it you're from the security company?"

She lifted her chin in a quick nod and stepped forward, ignoring the fact I was still in bed. "Yes, I'm with Sovereign Systems." She thrust her hand out. "Emery Mendenhall."

I peered at her offered handshake with skepticism, but she stayed firm, patiently waiting.

"Vance Hale."

She subtly pressed her lips together when I accepted her offered handshake, and I had to fight the corner of my mouth from lifting into a smile. She was trying so hard to maintain professionalism despite the awkward situation. Was she wondering what lay beneath the covers across my waist? I had to make sure they didn't shift any lower, or I'd be even more vulnerable.

Typically, I wasn't the tiniest bit shy, and by no means tiny. In fact, I kind of enjoyed showing off my body.

She retreated from the handshake first and straightened. "I understand the sensor on the north-facing window gave you issues last night."

"More like this morning," I bit out.

Ms. Mendenhall pressed on. "I've cleared out the error and rebooted the system. All that's left is for me to manually reset the unit." She hesitated, unsure how to proceed. "Is it all right if I do that now? It will only take a moment."

I tossed a hand toward the window. "Sure, go ahead."

Her heels tapped across the hardwood as she moved to complete her task. Did she feel my gaze on her while she pushed the curtain back out of her way and examined the plastic box at the top of the window frame?

She wasn't short, but the window was tall and narrow, and when she pushed onto her tiptoes and reached up to remove the cover, it was just a fingertip's grasp too high. She lowered back the scant inch onto her heels, seemed to regroup, and tried again, but it was still out of her reach.

I yanked the bottom of the sheet free from where it was tucked in, wrapped it closed around my waist, and stood up. She was distracted, perhaps looking for a chair to pull over to stand on, so she didn't notice my approach until I was abruptly right beside her.

I had a fist clamped on my hip to keep the sheet draped around me and my gaze fixed on her, and I savored the way she froze, trapped by me. All she could do was suck in a sharp breath.

Because I was standing so close.

Maybe *too* close. Like her makeup, I skirted the line of what was professional, and her gaze slid across my muscles, tracing a line from my bicep to my eyes when I lifted a hand and flipped up the plastic cover for her.

The air around us thickened with intimacy. I was essentially naked and in her space, and she was very aware of that. It was interesting and pleasing that she didn't retreat.

Her voice fell to a hush, and her eyes hazed. "The chip."

"What?"

She attempted to blink away the fog. "If you could take the chip out and then reseat it . . ."

It wasn't any bigger than a postage stamp and came out of its clip easily. And as soon as that was done, I snapped it back into its slot with a quiet click. "Like this?"

"That's it." She tucked a lock of hair behind an ear. "You're all set."

I flipped the cover back down, lowered my arm, but otherwise didn't move. She was the perfect mixture of classically beautiful and smoking hot. Her eyes were a deep blue, reminding me of the Atlantic on a perfect day for sailing.

The moment between us grew more intense the longer we remained, and for a split second, I entertained the idiotic idea of letting the sheet 'accidentally' slip from my grasp.

I couldn't tell if she hoped for that to happen . . . or if I just *wanted* her to.

Desire wasn't new to me. In the past, I followed it wherever it led. But the lust coiling inside me now? It was more powerful than anything I'd had in a long time. It nearly knocked me sideways. Was it the same for her?

"I'm sorry," she whispered.

Was she apologizing for how sexy she was? Confusion washed through me. "For what?"

"The sensor malfunction. On behalf of Sovereign Systems, I'd like to formally apologize for the inconvenience. It never should have happened, and we'd like the opportunity to—"

The strange spell between us broke and dissipated as she withdrew into her professionalism, and I waved my hand to brush it off. "Thanks, I appreciate that."

Ms. Mendenhall's expression hung like I'd pulled the rug out from under her. She'd probably expected me to be angry and ream her out. And while I was exhausted and irritated, none of that was her fault. Yelling wasn't going to undo last night, nor would it make me feel better.

"I get it," I added. "Sometimes things break. You came as soon as you could and corrected it. That's all I could ask for."

Had I grown a second head? Because she peered at me like I had, and her tone was barely masked disbelief. "Right. Well, then," she bent and retrieved the purse she'd set on the floor by the window, "we're very grateful for your understanding, and your business."

For a moment, she hesitated. Then she fished out a pen and pulled a business card from her wallet. I watched as she hurried to scribble something on the back side of the card.

I straightened. "Thanks for coming out so quickly, Ms. Mendenhall."

Her pen was clicked closed and the card passed to me. "If you have any issues, or you need anything at all . . . my personal number is on the back." Her eyes charged with heat, leaving little doubt what she was implying. Her voice softened and wavered. "And it's Emery."

She was nervous, and her shy smile was sexy as hell. It

was incredibly risky for her to hit on a client, but she'd done it anyway, and I respected her game. I opened my mouth to reward her, only for the words to die on my tongue because Jillian's voice crashed through my head.

I bet you wouldn't even last a week.

The woman before me was the very definition of temptation; I could barely look at her without thinking about sex. If she'd shown up in my room a week ago, I'd have tossed her business card on my nightstand and done everything I could right then to convince her to join me in my bed.

But instead, I accepted the card and flashed a polite smile. "Thank you, Emery." I let my gaze drift toward the door in a clear dismissal. "Have a nice day."

Her lips parted in surprise, and her expression hung awkwardly. She hadn't expected a rejection, and she swallowed hard as she recovered. As soon as that was done, she gave a curt nod and strode swiftly from the room.

I felt bad, but I'd made a deal with Jillian, and fucking hell—I was going to honor it.

No matter what.

THREE

EMERY

Vance Hale's phone number was printed neatly in my notebook, and I glared at the nine digits. It'd been five days since I'd appeared in his bedroom, inappropriately fawned over him, and delivered the clear signal I was interested.

He didn't have a girlfriend, and the attraction he felt for me was obvious. Yet he hadn't taken the bait that morning. I'd chalked it up to him being tired and caught off guard. Except enough time had passed since . . . so why the hell hadn't he called?

Time forced my hand. I couldn't wait any longer.

I sucked in a deep breath and entered his number into my phone's contacts, then composed a text message.

> **Me: Hello, Mr. Hale. This is Emery Mendenhall. We met earlier this week. Are you free for lunch today?**

It didn't take him long to reply.

> **Vance: How'd you get this number?**

Me: I'd rather explain in person. I need to talk to you.

I sank the edge of my teeth into my bottom lip and waited for his response, but when it didn't come, I typed out another message.

Me: It's about Jillian Lambert.

He took less time to compose his reply.

Vance: Okay. I'll be at Franklin's at 12:30 and put your name in at the door. Do you need directions?

I knew the place and let out a sigh of relief.

Me: No. I'll see you there.

I'd only been to Franklin's once before. Jillian had taken me to the upscale, exclusive restaurant with bay views and entrée prices that were comparable to what I spent on a week's worth of groceries. Today, I would suck it up and pretend the cost didn't faze me, nor was I approaching my credit limit. I wasn't going to blow this opportunity, especially since it'd be my only one.

Vance was seated at a U-shaped booth that faced the windows, and when I appeared tableside, he dropped his menu and stood. The gentlemanly gesture was formal and foreign, and it made warmth bloom in my chest.

I liked how he welcomed me, even though I didn't want to. His cobalt blue suit was cut perfectly to show off his body and match his striking eyes, and I pretended not to care about either of those things.

"Hi. Thanks for seeing me." I slid into the other side of the booth.

He nodded and took his seat. It was strange to sit side by side and not across from him. We looked like a couple, rather than two people trying to conduct business.

Was that what this was? *Business?*

I pushed the thought away and focused on what I needed. He was a means to an end, nothing more but—shit. It wasn't helpful that he was so damn attractive. At least he knew it. There was a fine line between confidence and arrogance, and I imagined he crossed it more often than not.

Wait a minute.

Was it possible I'd played him wrong?

Instead of appealing to his ego, I could have taken him down a notch. Maybe he was one of those guys who fell apart when a woman blew him off. I bet that rarely happened.

Perhaps it never had.

He seemed like a hard man to say no to.

His brown hair was dark and wavy on top, with wayward ends that curled and yet didn't stray enough to be considered messy. His pale blue eyes appeared carefree until you looked deeper and saw the turmoil lurking inside, even as he tried to hide it. Like his intimidating father, he had a strong jawline and high cheekbones, but he was a modern, streamlined version of Macalister Hale.

Despite this, Vance didn't set me quite on edge like the rest of Cape Hill's royalty did. Something lurked inside him, something undeniably . . . relatable. Like he was trying very hard to be someone he was not.

He didn't bother looking at his menu. His focus drilled

into me. "You wanted to talk about Jillian."

I swallowed a breath. "Yes." I'd rehearsed this several times, but now the moment was here, and I wasn't sure how to start. "We were friends." I frowned. "We *are* friends."

Because I hoped to God Jillian was alive and okay.

His lips parted to say something, but I knew what was coming and cut him off.

"You're going to say you're friends with her and you've never heard of me," I announced. "It's because I don't travel in the sort of social circles Wayne approves of." I feigned bitterness, even though her father's likely disapproval actually helped my agenda. I needed to fly below the radar. "My friendship with her is kind of new, and she's been keeping it on the down-low."

His eyes sharpened and studied me. He wasn't sure if my answer was true, but he was willing to accept it for now. "How'd you become friends?"

"Through Sovereign." There was a goblet of water at my place setting and I took it. The cold condensation made the glass slippery in my fingertips, but I held on and tried to look casual. "I was onsite when the Lamberts were upgrading their system. We got to talking, and she invited me to join her for lunch."

I left out the important details, such as how one of the Sovereign Systems workmen had approached Jillian in her room and come on to her. He'd been both lewd and incessant, crossing the line so far, he couldn't even see it anymore. When I found out, I apologized profusely and fired him on the spot.

The workman hadn't liked that at all and caused a scene. He'd called me all sorts of names and threatened my career, but I'd stood strong and maintained my professionalism throughout.

Jillian hadn't just been understanding about the ordeal—she'd been surprisingly selfless. Sure, she was relieved when he was gone, but she'd been more focused on me. She worried about how I might lose my job, even when I was a total stranger to her.

She was the first halfway decent person I'd met in Cape Hill.

And still, I didn't mention there was no need to worry about my job. It was because my friend Eddie had never been a Sovereign Systems employee. I didn't tell her how we'd discussed the job beforehand or that I'd been the one to lend him a workman's uniform.

It was a means to an end, I'd reminded myself.

I'd become her friend under false pretenses, but the friendship itself was real.

The waiter appeared to take our order. I picked a salad, not just because it was the cheapest thing on the menu, but because I wasn't hungry. As soon as the guy was gone, Vance waited quietly for me to get to the part he wanted to hear—the reason I'd called this meeting.

I swallowed thickly, and my voice fell to a hush. "I think Jillian's alive."

Surprise coated his handsome face, but then a skeptical look swept through and washed it away. He wanted to believe, but he was wary of hope. "What makes you say that?"

"Jillian had a lot of friends, but her younger sister Tiffany is her *best* friend. They aren't just close, they're inseparable. If anything was wrong, Tiffany would know about it, and if Jillian was planning something, well... she'd tell her sister." I focused in on the faint dark blue line that ringed his irises. "As we sit here, the Lamberts are planning Jillian's memorial service. Everyone is devastated, especially her parents. Ansel's a mess. But you know the one person who isn't falling apart right now?" I paused for effect. "Tiffany."

His eyes clouded. "That doesn't mean anything. She could still be in shock or processing it." He tacked it on under his breath. "People deal with grief in different ways, trust me."

A strange pang flitted through my heart, reminding me this man was no stranger to grief. He'd lost both his mother when he was young and then his stepmother only a few years ago.

"Can I?" I asked. "Trust you?"

Maybe he leaned closer so he could hear better, or perhaps he'd done it to provide reassurance, but his proximity made the booth feel intimate, and my heart beat quicker.

"Because most of the people in Cape Hill can't be trusted," I added, "and I'm about to go out on a limb here, Mr. Hale."

He considered my statement thoughtfully before speaking. "You can trust me. If it helps, Jillian did." His voice was steady and quiet and genuine. "And it's Vance."

I nodded in acknowledgment and opened my mouth to speak, but his face abruptly contorted.

"I mean, I thought she did," he said.

The tightness in my chest waned a single degree. "I know what you mean." He'd been as blindsided by her disappearance as I'd been. "She didn't tell me everything, but I thought something like this . . . I'd know."

"Yeah."

We sat in our shared silence for a long moment, and I found it oddly comforting. It was nice not to be alone in this sadness.

It came from me in an uneven voice. "I heard you were the last person to speak to her. Can I ask what you talked about?"

He scrubbed a hand over his face, his fingertips tracing

the sharp angles of his jaw. "Nothing important, and nothing to give me any idea what she was planning. She sounded . . . happy."

But he'd said it with dread, like her being happy was a bad thing—

Oh, no. He thought she'd sounded relieved. Like a difficult decision had been made and her struggle was about to be over. It sat as a heavy stone in my stomach, weighing me down so badly I wondered if the booth would collapse beneath me.

I barely had enough breath to push it out. "I need to know exactly what you talked about."

Distrust made him cold. "Why?"

Because I need to know if this is all my fault.

"Wayne Lambert has a safe," I blurted. "And Jillian hired me to get inside it."

His eyes went wide. "What?"

"I don't know how you feel about him, but Mr. Lambert is—"

"An asshole." Vance stated it like it was common knowledge. "He's loud and rude, and thinks he owns everyone in this town." The look that flashed through his eyes was superiority. "Which, I can assure you, he does not."

While I shouldn't like it, I found his arrogance undeniably sexy. In fact, I found everything about him unfortunately appealing. But I wasn't interested in a dick measuring contest between two of the wealthiest families in the state, if not the country. The Hales were old money and used to have considerable power, but everything changed when Macalister went to prison.

In his absence, Wayne Lambert had tried to fill the void, and he'd been rather successful at it. It meant his already overinflated ego grew even larger.

"He *is* an asshole," I agreed. "He acts like his family is his property, and nobody has it worse than Jillian."

The man beside me stiffened with what seemed to be anger. "Yeah, I'm aware."

"She does exactly what her father tells her to do, and then he has the balls to say she has it so easy. He came from nothing, pulled himself up by the bootstraps, and built an empire." My tone turned as cold and sharp as a knife. "She'd *never* be able to do something like that, what he did."

"He won't let her," he said. "She tried once and applied for a showing at Fashion Week, but Wayne swooped in and put a stop to it."

"How?"

"He threatened to cut her off if she went through with it. He was sure she was going to embarrass the family."

Anger flickered through me. I hated Wayne Lambert with a rage that burned hotter than the fires of hell. And I was certain that if Jillian had been given a choice, she'd have become a designer, and an excellent one at that.

Years ago, her father had reluctantly let her turn one of the spare rooms in their mansion into a studio, but he refused to see her dream as anything more than a frivolous hobby. Instead, she worked at Barlowe Pharmaceutical during the day and hovered over her sewing machine every night.

"You know what?" I couldn't stop myself. "Fuck that guy. Her stuff is great, and he wouldn't—"

I froze.

I doubted Vance would care about my language, but we were seated at the most expensive restaurant I'd ever eaten at in my life, and I wondered if dropping an F bomb might shatter the delicate china before us.

Instead, he grinned, and all the air inside my body disappeared. Jesus, his smile had an unnatural power on me. It stunned me senseless and wiped all the thoughts from my brain. I kind of forgot how to breathe.

"I told Jillian the same thing every chance I got," he said.

I felt both relief and unease at the same time. This would be easier if his personality sucked. He was supposed to be a spoiled, rich playboy, which meant hopping in and out of his bed would require minimal effort from me.

The last thing I needed was for him to be a decent guy. Or worse—for me to get attached.

My gaze swung away to look out the window and drift over the deep blue water stretching across the horizon. "She got tired of him telling her she'd never amount to anything, and . . . well, she decided to get some leverage." Beyond the glass, seagulls floated in the wind. "She hoped there'd be some inside Lambert's safe."

"Was there?"

I pressed my lips together. "I don't know. Once I cracked it, I left the room. It's standard policy to leave the client alone because the contents are private." I set my focus back on him. "Not to mention, what I did was illegal. Jillian isn't the owner of the safe, and we figured it'd be better if I had deniability."

He pulled his chin back in surprise. "You *cracked* it? You didn't just get the combination?"

"Getting locked safes open is sort of my specialty. I'm a licensed and certified master safecracker." I took a deep breath. "And I'll lose that license if it gets out what I did."

He nodded in reassurance. "I get it, Emery. I'm good at keeping secrets."

He said it like he'd had a lifetime of practice.

So . . . how many secrets did he have locked inside him? I wanted to know. Safecracking was a game, and it ran through all other aspects of my life, which meant the desire to crack him open was immediate. My fingers longed to touch and learn what he was hiding, but I had to fight against the urge.

I'd come too far to get sidetracked. I needed to stay focused.

"When did this happen?" he asked.

"The night before she took *The Trident* sailing." My tone was serious, but hopefully not desperate, even though I was. "That's why I'm hoping you'll tell me what you two talked about."

He adjusted the collar of his shirt, then cast his hand up as if surrendering. "Sex, mostly."

Once again, he made thoughts evaporate from my brain, and the word came out with forced casualness. "Oh?"

She'd told me sex with Ansel wasn't great, but was she sleeping with Vance on the side? They'd dated once, but she'd acted like that was ancient history. They were only friends these days.

The spark of jealousy that ignited in me was fucking ridiculous. Why did I care if Jillian and Vance were still hooking up? I had no claim or interest in him other than my agenda.

Right?

His gaze slid over my face, studying me thoughtfully. "Jillian and I made a bet."

"A . . . sex bet?" I asked with heavy skepticism.

His shoulders fell as he sighed. "More like a 'lack of sex' bet. If I go ninety days without, she was going to give me the boat she races in the Cape Hill Cup. If I lose, she gets mine."

A needle scratched across a record in my mind. He'd be really freaking hard to seduce if he was trying to win a celibacy bet. "That's it? That's all you talked about?"

"I also told her to break up with her boyfriend." He tilted his head as if the thought occurred to him. "Not for me," he clarified. "We've been down that road, and it wasn't right for us. But Ansel's not right for her either."

"No," I agreed. "What'd she say to that?"

"It wasn't the first time I'd mentioned it to her. Usually, she tells me it's none of my business, but this time was different. She said she was handling it."

I perked up. "Handling it? How?"

"I asked, but she wouldn't elaborate."

"But it seemed like she had a plan?"

Sadness clouded his eyes. "Yeah."

I frowned and dropped my gaze to the tabletop. "Maybe this is part of it."

He asked it hesitantly, like he was cautious to put the idea out in the world. "You think she faked her death?"

"I don't know." It was better than the alternative. I returned my attention to him, and the rest of the restaurant faded away. "I told her to break up with Ansel, too, but I didn't stop there. I encouraged her to get out and start a new life, free from her father's control. I said, 'Show everyone you can do it on your own.'"

His broad chest expanded with his deep breath and perhaps a little hope too. "So, she took whatever was in that safe and used it to run?"

I shook my head. "Again, I don't know. It didn't seem like she brought anything out with her after she finished with the safe, but she was in there a long time. And when she came out, she seemed anxious."

Alarm widened his eyes. "Like she was scared?"

Jillian had come flying out of her father's bedroom with determination etched on her face, not fear. "It was more like whatever she discovered, she wanted to act on it right away."

"But no clue about what was inside?"

"No." I lifted my shoulders in a hopeless shrug to disguise my crushing disappointment. "It could be anything."

Because Wayne Lambert lived to hoard secrets and apply them at the right time to get whatever he wanted.

The conversation lulled, and as if he'd sensed it, the waiter appeared with our lunch order. I stared blankly at my salad, waiting for the man to move on so I'd be alone with Vance and could speak freely.

Except Vance beat me to it when the waiter was gone. "If she did plan it," he said, "then she had help."

I'd had the same thought, and up until today, Vance had been my biggest suspect. "But who? Tiffany?"

He considered it. "Maybe, but she couldn't do it alone. She doesn't know how to sail."

"A lot of Jillian's friends do, though. Her friends . . . and *your* friends."

He cut into his salmon and took a bite, but he seemed too lost in thought to enjoy his food. Was he running through a list of possible suspects?

"I can ask around." He paused abruptly. "Should we tell the police?"

Was he kidding? "Tell them what, exactly? That I broke into her father's safe?" I scowled. "Look, if Jillian went to such extreme measures and didn't tell us, then I have to think she doesn't want to be found."

His eyebrows tugged together. "I'm not sure what to do with that information."

"I am," I said. "I want to know what's inside Lambert's safe."

His blue eyes were clear and sharp as he evaluated me. It was obvious he was curious, but he was also cautious and smart, and maybe just as calculating as I'd been warned. Rumor had it the Hales didn't do anything unless it directly benefited them.

Vance didn't need money. The only thing I had to offer

him of value was my expertise.

Or your body.

I crossed my arms, leaned them on the table, and turned to give him a sultry look. "Don't you want to know?"

Rather than lean toward me, he straightened. "No, I don't." That was surprising, and whatever look was on my face, it forced him to elaborate. "Emery, this town is full of secrets, and I don't want to dig any of them up. Sometimes," he searched for the right way to express himself, "it's best if they stay in the dark where they belong."

Instinctively, my fingers curled into fists. He had no fucking idea what he was talking about. Secrets had taken *everything* from me, and now I demanded justice.

Or revenge.

At this point, I couldn't tell the difference.

"So, that's it?" My tone was pointed. "You don't care to know what happened?"

He scowled. "I'm not saying that."

"Right. Well, good news. Looks like you're off the hook with your little bet with Jillian."

He looked weirdly pained, and it gave me pause.

"Interesting," I said finally, but there was no warmth in my voice. "Still going through with it because you care that much about a stupid race?" Especially when he couldn't be bothered to learn what happened to his friend?

Darkness filled his expression, and it made my body go still. He was the picture-perfect playboy heir on the surface, but a wolf lingered beneath his façade. One with sharp teeth and a desire to eat his enemies.

"I don't care about her boat or winning a fucking race," his tone was resolute, "even though I probably will. I don't care about beating Jillian at our bet, or winning at all, for once in my damn life. What I *do* care about is that I made a promise to my friend—possibly the last one I'll ever get to make." His intensity sucked me in until I was drowning in his striking eyes and powerful voice. "I will keep it."

Air seeped out of my lungs in a heavy sweep. I believed every word he'd just said because his conviction was undeniable. He'd remain loyal to Jillian, even as she'd abandoned us without saying a word. It wasn't just admirable. It made me envious. I longed to have a friend like him.

The atmosphere shifted between us as he blinked and something like heat moved into his eyes. His voice was as smooth as the lacquered wood trimming his private yacht. "You should know, if you'd given me your number last week, I would have called you."

His statement set off a flurry of thoughts in my mind, but the loudest one was the first to come out of my mouth. "So, you're saying . . . since you can't have sex with me right now, you're not interested?"

His lips had turned up in a seductive smile, but now it froze. I wondered if his statement had sounded good in his head, and since it hadn't landed like he'd thought it would, he wished to take it back.

"That came out wrong," he said.

"Did it?" I challenged.

He didn't exactly squirm, but his confidence had taken a hit. "I'm not into dating, and I don't know if I've ever had a relationship that didn't include sex."

"So, it didn't come out wrong. You're saying there's no point in having a partner if fucking them isn't on the menu."

Frustration made the muscle along his jaw tick. "I'm *not* saying that. Just that I've never done it before."

Years of practice had taught me to think fast on my feet

and adapt when plans changed. The whole point of seducing him was so he'd bring me into his world, and then I could move undetected in his social circle. Maybe I could still get him to welcome me in without using sex.

I delivered my challenge with finality, like a gauntlet being thrown down. "You should try it. Hell, I'll even volunteer."

My statement caused his brain to temporarily go offline, and he blinked through the outage. "What?"

"It'll be easier to go ninety days without if you're not available."

"Eighty." His voice was uneven because he hadn't finished recovering. "It's eighty days now."

"Okay, eighty," I said.

His eyes narrowed and focused in as he tried to discover my hidden agenda. "You don't even know me, and you're . . . asking to be my girlfriend?"

I shifted in my seat, adjusting my posture so I looked confident. "It could be just for show. I can help you look like you're off the market. A rich, hot guy like you probably has women throwing themselves at him left and right."

It wasn't an attempt to flatter him—Jillian had told me as much.

My compliment didn't distract him either. "What would you get out of this arrangement?"

"Access to Jillian's friends."

He didn't buy it for a second. "You mean Wayne Lambert's safe."

I shrugged. "*Can* you get me access to that?"

He considered how to respond. It looked like he appreciated that I'd been honest, but he wasn't exactly comfortable with my goal. "Maybe, but that's not going to happen."

"Why not?"

"Because I've done the whole 'dating just for show' thing before, and I'm over it. If I'm with someone, it's because I want to be with them. No one else gets to decide for me."

"Didn't you just say you were interested? That you would have called me if not for the vow you made to Jillian?"

"Yeah, I did, but you need to understand. Having you pretend or actually be my girlfriend isn't going to help."

I stared at him. "Why's that?"

His gaze swept down my body, caressing each curve, and his expression was, for lack of a better word, scandalous. His gaze moved even slower as it slid back up and settled on my lips. Then he lifted an eyebrow, arching it up into a perfect upside-down V. "Because, Emery, I'm fairly certain you're the definition of temptation. I don't trust myself to make it a week with you around."

I sucked in a sharp breath, and goosebumps lifted on my arms. He gave me a different version of the wolf now, one that said he was considering eating me, enemy or not. And—fucking hell—I was sure I wouldn't mind that one bit.

"I can keep my hands to myself," I said, except my voice wavered and I sounded anything but convincing.

"Hmm." It announced he didn't believe me, but his eyes said how pleased he was to know his desire wasn't one-sided.

My body tightened. The pull toward him was sexual and as unavoidable as gravity. The booth closed in around us and the air went thin, leaving me breathless. This thing between us was unexpected. Shocking. And so powerful it was scary.

That meant it was *exciting*.

I'd come to this lunch with the goal of seducing him, and now I was disappointed I wouldn't get the opportunity. I bit down on my lip and struggled to find a new angle, but he tore his gaze away and glanced at his smartwatch to read the text message that had appeared onscreen. His mood darkened, making the chemistry between us dissipate and release the hold it had on my body.

"I need to go." He pulled the cloth napkin from his lap, dropped it on the table, and eyed my barely touched salad. "Feel free to stay and finish your lunch. I'll have Patrick put it on my tab."

My pulse skyrocketed as my window of opportunity began to close. "Vance, wait. Can we at least try?"

He ignored my question as he slid out of the booth and stood, casting his glance down on me. "It's good Jillian kept you a secret from me."

"She didn't," I said. "Where do you think I got your number?"

His smile only turned up the corners of his lips, but it made his eyes shine with mischief. "Be prepared to hear from me in about eighty days."

I pressed out a smile to mask what I was thinking.

If I had my way, he'd be hearing from me a lot sooner than that.

FOUR

VANCE

It seemed like all of Cape Hill had turned out for Jillian's memorial service today, and yet somehow there were even more people at the marina clubhouse for the reception this evening. It'd been three weeks since she'd gone missing, but people acted like it had been months.

Jillian would have liked the service. The speeches were touching and heartfelt. Memories were shared and tears shed. One of her cousins drew out a much-needed laugh from the mourners when she revealed seven-year-old Jillian had snuck down after bedtime to watch TV and landed on *Jurassic Park*. She'd had to sleep with the light on for weeks afterward.

It was loud in the clubhouse event space which sometimes served as a ballroom. If not for people's dark clothes, you'd never have guessed they'd come from a funeral. The wealthiest families in America mingled with each other, talking and laughing and occasionally grabbing an appetizer from the silver trays that waitstaff circulated.

Cape Hill's elite used any opportunity to climb the status ladder, strike deals, or make power moves. Even a funeral wasn't off limits. When I was young, I thought this was the way of the world, but my eyes were open now. Jillian was *gone*, one of their own . . . and they didn't care. The jovial atmosphere left an acrid taste in my mouth, and I polished off the remaining whiskey in my glass to try to wash it out.

I used my empty glass as an excuse to shuffle off from the group of people I'd been talking to, but instead of heading to the bar, I crossed the crowded room and went out the glass door that led to the back patio.

The large deck wasn't in use because it was early May. Tables and chairs were huddled together under canvas covers, and the chilly evening wind tried to get at me, making the tail of my black tie flap in the breeze. I grabbed the lapels of my suitcoat, pulled it tighter around my frame, and strode to the balcony railing.

The sun was setting, painting the horizon in yellows and oranges.

Below was the marina and its docks stretched out in perfect rows, decorated with boats and yachts tied at nearly every slip. My father's boat, *Checkmate*, was the largest sailing vessel in our family's fleet, and it drew my gaze. The water seemed smooth as glass tonight, but I was aware how looks could be deceiving.

It was supposed to be calm the day my father had gone sailing with Sophia last year.

He should probably sell it. He hadn't stepped foot on his boat since then.

The fact it didn't have a captain probably contributed as well. He'd fired Lucas Ridley after the accident, which was bullshit. Lucas didn't come from money, but his father was the headmaster of Cape Hill Prep, and we'd become friends our freshman year as members of the sailing club.

I'd gone off to college and then law school, while he'd stayed in town and worked his way up to captain of *Checkmate*. We didn't see much of each other since he'd been relieved from my family's staff, but that was to be expected. I'd heard he'd started chartering his boat for luxury trips out beyond the cape. A more elegant version of booze cruises.

I hadn't seen him at the service or at the reception, but there were a lot of people. Surely he was inside somewhere. He'd had more patience with Jillian than I did when she'd joined the sailing club.

An odd sensation trickled down my spine.

If Lucas were here, he would have sought me out. He didn't hold me responsible for my father firing him, and his friends at this reception would be limited. Once he'd graduated from our prestigious high school, he'd ceased to exist for a lot of our mutual friends. He was a townie, an 'other.'

The help, Richard Shaunessy called him behind his back.

Lucas's slip in the dock was empty.

Was he out on a chartered trip now? That didn't make much sense. All of Cape Hill was here.

So, why wasn't he?

Emery's accusatory voice wafted through my head. Lucas Ridley was probably Jillian's friend as much as he was mine. He owned a boat and certainly knew how to sail.

I scrolled through my contacts until I found his number and thumbed out a text.

> **Me: Hey. Did you go to Jillian's memorial service today?**

The three dots appeared on screen to tell me he was typing, but then disappeared. As I waited, my odd sensation prickled. Again, he began to type and then the dots disappeared. This wasn't that hard of a question to answer, and yet he struggled.

Lucas: No, I'm in the Caribbean. How was it?

Me: It was nice, but difficult. Are you working?

It took him even longer to respond.

Lucas: No. Just felt like getting away.

That made it sound spur of the moment, but sailing down the Atlantic coast was at least a five-day trip. One that would require planning and preparation.

Me: Let me know when you're back. We should grab lunch.

This time, there was no response.

Maybe I'd caught him at a bad time, or in a place where cell service was spotty, but my suspicion intensified. I didn't get a chance to dwell on it because the door behind me swung open with a creak and heavy footsteps announced someone's approach. I turned to see a man making his way toward me, who wore a black suit and a weary expression—one that was atypical for him.

Uncomfortableness stiffened my posture. "Wayne."

He tried to disguise his displeasure but failed. When Jillian and I had been together, he'd insisted I call him by his first name, claiming we were family. After the break-up, it was clear he'd prefer I go back to addressing him as Mr. Lambert. Today was the first time I didn't enjoy the irritation my supposed lack of respect caused him.

"Christ, it's cold out here," he muttered. He came to stand beside me at the railing, his gaze focused on the horizon. It was quiet as he stared at the sunset, but it wasn't peaceful. The tension in me was so tight, I found it difficult to breathe. I'd had a lot of practice in my lifetime, but I still felt uncomfortable around grief.

"I'm sorry for your loss," I said in a hush.

"Thank you."

Wayne was in his late fifties, and his hairline had retreated from the top of his head, exposing a shiny dome that was surrounded by a ring of graying dark hair. He was lean and in good shape for a man his age, but his face was puffy, like dough that had been overworked.

His surgeons had made his skin look unnaturally elastic.

I glanced at the large glass back wall of the clubhouse and to the reception still going on inside. Had he come out here to escape from them? Would he prefer to be alone? There wasn't a drink in his hand.

"Can I get you anything?" I asked.

He simply stared at the ocean, his cheeks pinking in the cold air. Like he was waiting for Jillian to emerge at any moment from the chilly water and his nightmare would be over.

Finally, he turned and set his attention on me, revealing I'd been so, *so* wrong about what he was thinking. There was calculation in his eyes, and something else I couldn't quite place.

Dark enjoyment?

"Yes, there is something you can get for me." His voice was sly. "Damon Lynch will be stepping down from HBHC's board soon, which means his seat will be available."

What he was implying was so shocking, it turned my spine into steel. We were at his daughter's funeral, and *this* was what he was focused on? Becoming a board member of Hale Banking and Holding Company? Fuck, he was worse than everyone else. Did he seriously look at Jillian's death as an opportunity?

"You're barking up the wrong Hale," I snapped. "I'm not on the board. If you're interested in a seat, you need to talk to Royce."

My brother had recently been promoted to chief operating officer of the company and was the only Hale currently seated.

Wayne wasn't fazed. "It'd be better coming from you."

"Yeah? Why's that?"

"Because you'd be my only real competition."

I froze. Yes, I was a significant shareholder in the company, but I'd been practicing corporate law for HBHC for less than a year. I was young and an unlikely candidate, plus this wasn't part of the plan my father had drafted for our family.

Of course, neither was him going to prison.

"No one's approached me about it," my tone was frosty, "because if they had, I would have told them I'm not interested."

He stared at me like I'd just confessed a crime. Then his expression shifted to a skeptical one. He thought I was bullshitting him—but I wasn't. I liked living in the middle, flying under the radar. Joining the board would invite all kinds of scrutiny, not to mention cries of nepotism, and it'd put a political target on my back.

"Prove it, then," Wayne demanded. "You can convince both Royce and Macalister that I'm the best option. While your father's not on the board anymore, he still holds significant sway over its members, and a recommendation from him would be persuasive."

It would be, but he was dreaming. My father *hated* him.

"I don't see that happening, *Wayne*." I put extra emphasis on his name before I turned toward the clubhouse. I didn't want to spend another moment with him.

"I bet you'll change your mind, Vance. Especially when I tell you your father's not the only one who likes to collect secrets." His tone was sinister and choked with malice. "It's been a hobby of mine for quite some time. And I believe your stepmother Alice enjoyed it as well."

My movements slowed to a halt, including my heart. I'd stopped halfway across the patio, so I had my gaze directed toward the door, but I couldn't actually see it.

It was because my attention was focused completely on the man at my back.

"I imagine," he continued, "you don't want that kind of scandal to get out. I think your whole family would prefer it didn't."

Oh, *shit*.

My affair with Alice. *He knew.*

My entire body tensed until I was unmovable stone. "You don't want to do this." My tone was as threatening as an approaching hurricane. "My father will come after you, and all you have is hearsay from a woman who—"

"Do I?" he patronized. "You're sure that's *all* I have?"

I turned to face him, and his victorious expression was a punch to my gut.

Fuck.

Fucking fuck!

I was twenty-two when Alice and I began hooking up, which meant I was young and dumb. Getting involved with her was only one of the many stupid choices I'd made back then. My affinity for documenting us together on my phone?

That was another.

And Wayne Lambert grinned at me now like he was in possession of something incredibly damning. Photos, or a video, or worst of all—both.

"What do you want?" I snarled.

He was so pleased with himself it turned my stomach, and now he looked at me like I was an idiot. "That seat on HBHC's board when it comes available. Make it happen, and this," he searched for the right word, "*unflattering* information will stay between us."

My hands tightened into fists, wanting to squeeze the life from the man across from me, but our father had drilled patience into Royce and me from birth. I'd learned the best strikes came from calculated strategy rather than being baited into an emotional reaction.

I could be smart about this. Let Wayne Lambert think he was in control of the situation while I planned my next move.

I spat the words out as if there was dirty seawater in my mouth. "I'll see what I can do."

I didn't wait to see his thrilled smile. Instead, I turned and strode as quickly as possible toward the door, desperate to get somewhere that I could be alone with my thoughts. My mind raced much faster than my feet did as they carried me through the crowd.

If word got out that I'd slept with my stepmother, it wouldn't just ruin my planned career in politics, it'd ruin my family. Alice hadn't been a great person, but she was gone now, and I didn't want to see her name dragged needlessly through the mud. And while my father already knew about the affair, the information could still hurt his reputation, not to mention, if he had to visually witness it . . .

That would hurt him far worse.

And I wasn't going to allow that to happen.

The sound of the people around me buzzed like noisy, irritating insects, and I sidestepped Chloe Penhurst when she moved into my path. She had a superpower ability for sensing when I was vulnerable, and even though I saw right through to her agenda, I'd still let my dick land me in trouble with her. She was fun and hot, but we weren't compatible anywhere outside of the back seat of her Bentley.

I was nearly to freedom when a feminine hand latched on my shoulder, and I groaned under my breath. I didn't want to get stuck in an awkward conversation that would end with me rejecting her tonight.

Only it wasn't Chloe.

"Vance," the woman said. "How are you doing?"

There was a kindness in Sophia's tone that was surprising. We'd been friends in high school, but not close, which meant her concern should have felt misplaced . . . but it didn't. It was genuine.

"I'm fine," I lied.

Her eyes were similar to my father's in the sense that they didn't miss much. "Really? You and Jillian stayed tight even after the break-up."

"Yeah," I wasn't sure what else to say, "we did."

She swept the curtain of her blonde hair back over her shoulder and then smoothed a hand down the side of her black dress, as if her palm was sweaty. "Look, I know he's not your first choice, but if you want someone to talk to—"

My eyes narrowed. "I'm *fine*."

I craned my neck, looking around for him. Had my father sent her? That would explain why he wasn't at her side. He disliked small talk almost as much as Wayne Lambert, so he usually stayed close and let his girlfriend handle it for him. It was one of the only times he ever relinquished control.

Sophia realized who I was looking for and assumed what I was thinking. "Macalister's getting me a drink," she said. "But you should know, he's worried about you."

"Oh?" I patronized. "He actually said that?"

"He didn't have to." She shifted on her heels and put a hand on her hip. "You Hales aren't great at expressing feelings, but I've learned how to translate him."

My tone was flat. "Great."

"You know you can't avoid him forever, right?"

"You sound like Royce," I muttered.

She pressed on, ignoring me. "And he doesn't give up when he wants something."

Inside my pocket, my phone vibrated with a text message, and I dug it out, grateful for the interruption.

Lucas: Not sure if I'm coming back to Cape Hill.

Hyperawareness needled up my spine.

Her question drew my gaze up from the screen. "Something wrong?"

"No." I paused, contemplating what this meant. "It was just a strange text." I slipped the phone back into my pocket, but she stared at me, wordlessly demanding I give her more information. I sighed. "I asked Lucas when he was coming home, and he just answered me. He said he wasn't sure if he was coming back to Cape Hill."

Her lips parted with surprise. "Like, ever?"

I shrugged, unsure.

"Wow," she said quietly. "He must be taking this really hard."

I blinked. "You think he left . . . because of Jillian?"

"They were spending a lot of time together."

"They were?" My heart beat a little faster. Jillian and Lucas? I couldn't picture them hooking up. "What did Ansel think about that?"

It was an interesting development, but I was saddened

Jillian had kept another secret from me. Lucas wasn't rich, meaning he was a man her family would never approve of. Had he helped her escape?

Holy shit. Was there a chance she'd run off to the Caribbean with him?

That thought left me with yet another question. How well had I really known my friend?

"I don't think she was cheating on him, if that's what you're asking," Sophia said. "Ansel knew she was taking sailing lessons from him." Her focus returned to me, and a sad smile crept on her lips. "I'd heard she was training to beat you."

Ah. That made sense why she'd hidden it from me. Plus, it was very "on brand" for her. I'd admired her competitive streak, which rivaled my own.

Movement behind Sophia caught my attention. My father had spotted us and was heading our way, meaning I needed to make a quick exit if I was going to avoid him. I didn't have an excuse to end the conversation, so I quickly surveyed the people around us, searching for a familiar face I could use. I'd say I had something important to discuss with them, and my father wouldn't be able stop me from leaving.

I believed I was in control of my destiny, but perhaps the universe thought otherwise, because the crowd happened to part at that exact moment. It created an aisle for my focus to travel down, and she stood at the other end of it all alone, wearing a black dress that did nothing to downplay her sexiness.

There was nowhere else to look, nowhere to hide. Emery Mendenhall looked like the answer to all my problems, plus a whole slew of new ones.

When her gaze found mine, she locked on and began her approach, but my father arrived first.

"Vance," he said in greeting.

He was formal and intimidating, and his word stopped Emery dead in her tracks. Her gaze swung away as she abandoned her plan of talking to me. Perhaps she thought she could try again later.

Instead of acknowledging my father, I directed an easy smile toward her and kept my tone light. "There you are."

It left her with no choice but to join the conversation, and it was stunning how quickly she reset back to her original plan. Her smile was soft and natural, but I saw the question hinting at her eyes.

"Here I am," she said, taking a final step toward me and closing the circle between the four of us.

"And this is?" Sophia's tone was pleasant, but unease edged across her expression. She knew everything and everyone in Cape Hill and did not like being in the dark about the woman standing beside me. My father had the same look, only amplified into distrust. He assessed Emery critically in a single glance, noting her dress was tight and how it flaunted her curves. I could hear the thought running through his mind.

Too much.

But it wasn't. She looked amazing and could wear whatever the fuck she wanted as far as I was concerned. Hell, I wouldn't object if she wanted to wear nothing at all—

Wait, no. That'd be a very bad idea.

And since I was already thinking about a bad idea, I let another take shape.

"This is Emery Mendenhall," I announced. "My girlfriend."

FIVE

VANCE

EMERY WAS MASTERFUL AT HIDING HER REACTION AND DIDN'T miss a beat, thrusting her hand out toward Sophia. "Nice to meet you."

Sophia stared back in disbelief. It was unfathomable to her how this stranger had made it deep into her circle without being discovered, and for a moment she looked completely lost. But then her shoulders relaxed, she pressed on a smile and accepted the handshake. "Sophia Alby."

As always, I could sense my father's focus on me, but I pretended to be oblivious. If I looked at him, he'd deliver his scathing judgment without uttering a word, and I didn't care to see it.

When the women were done with their greeting, Sophia tilted her head toward him. "This is my boyfriend, Macalister Hale."

Their age gap was nearly thirty years, but Emery didn't bat an eye. She simply accepted the information and offered another handshake. "You must be Vance's father. I see the resemblance."

He looked like he expected her to spring a subpoena on him. His calculating eyes narrowed on her extended hand, but otherwise he didn't move. When it was clear he wasn't going to take her offered handshake, rather than be offended, she seemed to let the slight roll right off her. Emery moved closer and slipped her hand beneath my arm.

I drew in a breath.

It was stupid, this immediate urge to flex my bicep and remind her there was muscle beneath the black wool of my suit sleeve. I shouldn't care about trying to impress her; not to mention, she'd already seen me shirtless. And I definitely shouldn't like the way it felt to have her at my side, holding on to me. We barely knew each other.

Sophia attempted to sound casual, but it was stilted. "Where'd you two meet?"

Emery's smile was wide. "In his bedroom."

My father's voice was sharp and demanding. "Excuse me?"

I couldn't stop the grin that peeled back my lips. He valued efficient and direct conversation . . . but only on his terms. Also, he was old fashioned and did not like discussing anything inappropriate in public.

"Emery works for Sovereign," I said, "the security company we use for the house. She fixed a faulty sensor in my room, and I took her out for lunch afterward." Technically, all of that was true, even if dating her were a lie.

She turned to look up at me, and goddamn, her soft smile was so convincing, I nearly believed her feelings for me were real. She looked hopelessly enamored, and I swallowed hard. It was appealing, this idea I could make a woman fall under my spell. And it was especially appealing with *this* woman.

But my father had never been a trusting man, and he peered at us with such intensity, I instinctively pulled her closer and shifted my shoulders to put myself between them, like I could somehow protect her from his scrutiny.

Sophia visibly struggled to figure out how this relationship had happened under her nose, and I felt weirdly compelled to help her out.

"It's new," I said.

Like, only ninety seconds *new*.

Emery exchanged a playful look with me, and it was seriously hot. It set off alarms in my head. I was only twenty-two days into my bet. It was fucking ridiculous to feel like I was starving, and yet . . . here I was, craving her. If I was going to make it to the other side of this bet, I needed to think of Emery as a business partner and nothing more.

My father's scowl abruptly evaporated, and it caused my pulse to kick. He was plotting something, and whatever it was, I was sure I wouldn't like it.

He sprung his trap in a cool voice. "I assume you'll be taking this new girlfriend with you to Monaco?"

"Monaco?" Emery repeated.

"The Formula One Grand Prix in two weeks," I said.

"Vance is a sponsor ambassador for HBHC," my father added.

While our family didn't own a team, our bank was one of Mercedes's top sponsors, and the week-long event was one I looked forward to all year.

Irritation wound around me like a tight band. I understood what he was doing. I hadn't sought his approval on dating Emery, so he thought this 'relationship' wasn't anything serious. Bringing up Monaco was his way to call my bluff. Escalation was my only option.

"Taking Emery is a great idea." My smile matched the one he gave when presented with a challenge. "I'm supposed to leave next weekend, though, so that's not much notice for her employer."

He lifted his chest, pushed his shoulders back, and power flared in his eyes. It was as close to a victory dance as my father got. "I'm sure something can be arranged. Between Royce's house and my own, we are Sovereign's biggest client." He leaned forward, going in for the kill. "The Hale name should be all you need, but if you'd like me to speak to someone on your behalf and have her schedule cleared, I can accommodate."

"That's not necessary." My voice was calm, not revealing how screwed I was. A full week with Emery at my side during each event and pretending to be my girlfriend was a recipe for disaster. But I was locked in now. If I backtracked, I'd lose, and it was win at all costs in my family.

Emery was unaware of the tension radiating from me. She set her other hand on my forearm, so she was hugging my arm to her body, and it diffused me in an instant. My focus swung to her, and I had to force the awareness of her hold from my mind.

"I'd love to go," she said softly, "and I don't think my work will have a problem with it." She buried meaning in her words. "I can be convincing."

My father stiffened. "Excellent. I'm sure Vance will enjoy your company."

"Yes." I clenched my teeth beneath my smile. I'd face temptation with every breath she took.

With that settled, the conversation lapsed, and I worried about the topic we'd move on to next. I didn't want to talk about Jillian, or my feelings, or let my father corner me into setting up a time to meet with him. We'd been interrupted by the police before I'd been able to give him my blessing on marrying Sophia, and I'd successfully avoided being alone with him since.

It wasn't that I didn't approve. I liked Sophia well enough, and it was clear she was good for him. He'd been happier this last year, quicker to forgive or to find a smile. He was also better at communicating and trying to express his feelings . . . which filled me with dread. Emotion made me uncomfortable in general, and it seemed perilous to discuss feelings with him.

"I didn't mean to interrupt you," Emery said to my father and Sophia, "but do you mind if I borrow Vance for a moment?"

Relief coasted through me. I was grateful for the escape, and I didn't protest when her hand slipped down into mine, lacing our fingers together. It was an innocent gesture, barely a display of affection, but electricity surged from our connection. Touching her, even in such an innocent way, was nice.

When was the last time I'd held a girl's hand?

Fuck me. Had I ever done it?

We were already on the move when she whispered it to me. "Is there somewhere we can talk? Like, privately?"

"Yeah." I gently tightened my grip, guiding her out into the hall.

The front of the marina clubhouse was filled with the offices and the pro shop, and behind them lay the restaurant. It was closed tonight due to the event going on in the ballroom, but I knew we could sneak in. It was a great place to hide out when you didn't want to be around your parents, to hang with friends, or if you needed a secluded place to hook up with a girl.

The restaurant was dark except for the emergency exit sign, which cast an eerie glow on the empty chairs and tables. Emery had let go of my hand, followed me in through the door, and then gazed at the space with interest. I'd eaten here at least a hundred times and never paid much attention to the décor, but she strolled around the room like she wanted to take in the ambiance. The nautical theme was understated and nice.

Her roaming gaze finally settled on me, and she tilted her head. "So, *boyfriend*, how was the service?"

She was softly lit by the ambient light, and it exaggerated her perfect silhouette wrapped in black. She looked so goddamn appealing, it made me stupid. "Service?"

"Jillian's memorial?" Her voice lost some of its power. "My name wasn't on the list, so I couldn't get in."

Tightness squeezed my lungs. "If I'd accepted your offer last week, that wouldn't have happened. I'm sorry." I smoothed a palm down the front of my tie like I could wipe away the regret inside me. "The service was fine." I shook my head at my poor word choice. "It was nice," I amended.

She looked pleased by that. "What changed your mind about my offer?"

I swallowed thickly. Whatever evidence Lambert had to use against me, there was at least a chance it was in his private safe. I couldn't tell her about his attempt to blackmail me, because then she might ask with what, and I wasn't ready to confess that to her.

And I worried if I refused to tell her, she'd keep digging. She struck me as the type of person who didn't give up easily.

"I realized dating you would piss my father off."

A dubious look slid down her face. "Why? Because I don't come from money?"

There was a time that would have been a factor, but no. Royce had married a Northcott girl, uniting our families as my mother had wanted. It meant I was off the hook when it came to love. "It's because you're too . . . sexy."

She jolted with surprise. "Uh, what?"

I tossed a hand toward her. "Have you seen yourself? You're fucking gorgeous, and that dress flaunts it." I said it like

I was mad at her. "Who comes to a funeral looking that hot?"

My words literally knocked her back, and she ripped her gaze away from me. It flew toward the door as she considered bolting through it.

But she didn't.

She remained, taking in shallow breaths. "Jillian designed this for me, and it's black, so I thought . . ."

"Don't misunderstand, he's the one who has a problem with it." I didn't intend for it to come out seductive, but old habits died hard. "*I* fucking don't."

For effect, I let my gaze sweep over her appreciatively. Her lips parted so she could pull in a sip of air, and color flashed across her cheeks. Heat stirred inside me, intensifying the craving for her.

Shit, I was already failing at thinking of Emery as nothing more than a partner.

"I didn't want to talk to my father tonight. So, when I saw you, wearing that dress that he probably thinks is inappropriate, I saw an opportunity."

She didn't exactly like hearing that. "That's it?"

"No." I walked to the bar, set my hands on top, and leaned forward to look behind it. "I think your theory about Jillian has merit," I snagged the top of the bottle I was looking for, "and I want to help you find out if it's true."

She watched me with suspicion as I pulled the pour spout out of the top of the premium vodka, and she lifted an eyebrow as I took a long swig straight from the bottle.

But rather than sound shocked, she was faintly amused. "That's stealing."

"They're used to bottles going missing at these events, trust me." It would have been easy to lock them away, yet they never did. Staff would probably bill Lambert three times what this bottle was worth, and I kind of enjoyed that idea. "You don't really care, do you?" I teased. "You don't seem like much of a rule follower."

"Because I broke into Lambert's safe?"

I held her gaze for a long moment. "And because you set the alarm off at my house."

She didn't even flinch. She barely blinked, and there was no denial in her eyes. Instead, she considered her response carefully. "I needed to talk to you, and that was my way in."

I wasn't as paranoid as my father, but I wasn't stupid either and didn't believe in coincidences. Since our lunch together, I'd suspected the faulty sensor in my room had been orchestrated.

"You took a huge risk doing it. I could have you fired."

She didn't look nervous. She laughed like I was being ridiculous. "Sovereign might slap me on the wrist, but they won't fire me."

"Oh?" What she'd done was a massive pain in the ass, and my family was powerful. We were used to getting our way. "Why's that?"

Her smug smile was seriously hot. "Because I'm too fucking good."

Surprise washed through me. Whatever expression I held, it made her feel like she needed to defend her statement, to argue her case. Her posture stiffened, and she put a hand on her hip.

"I'm a two-time Vegas Vault champion, the one people call when everyone else has failed. And I'm not talking about cheap hotel safes that any idiot with a magnet or an admin code can get into." Her voice dripped with confidence. "I'm talking about banks. Embassies. The FBI."

I stood utterly still in my fascination, the bottle of vodka in my hand ignored.

"So," she continued, "I'm sorry I inconvenienced you and your staff by setting off the alarm a few times, but I'm not sorry for the outcome. Sometimes rules need to be bent to get what you need, and I'm okay with that."

"Win at all costs," I uttered.

"Yeah, I guess."

I'd never been turned on so fast in my goddamn life. Every inch of this girl was sexy and intriguing, and it pumped desire in my veins. To stop myself from telling her as much, I took another sip of the vodka and focused on the subtle burn of the alcohol. It allowed me to reorganize my thoughts.

"Thank you for being honest," I said. "If you'd lied to me, then I'd have to break up with you."

The corner of her mouth tugged up into a smile. "I see." Her eyes widened abruptly, and she over-exaggerated her enthusiasm. "Does this mean you're taking me to Monaco?"

I knew it was a terrible idea, especially because I hoped she'd say yes. "If you want to go."

She nodded, and . . . was all her enthusiasm fake? Because the excitement lighting her eyes seemed real.

"As partners," I added. Was that the right word? I found a better one. "Friends."

To seal the deal, I thrust the vodka toward her. She eyed the clear bottle with the blue label, then took it from me and pressed the mouth to her lips. There was something innately sexual about it. My lips had been on that glass just a minute ago, and now hers. I wondered if any of my taste lingered there, and if so, did she like that?

The sexy bob of her throat as she swallowed made my blood run south of my belt. God, I was weak. Getting half-hard over watching her take a drink was unacceptable.

It burst from me without warning. "I'm allowed to kiss you."

What the fuck?

That was the thought running through both of our minds, judging by the way she slowly lowered the bottle and stared at me.

I raked a hand through my hair. "What I mean is, that's not against the rules."

She angled her head. "Rules?"

I needed to get control and put this conversation back on track, so I rushed through it. "Jillian and I talked about what was and wasn't off limits. I was just letting you know because if we're going to sell this relationship, we'll need to kiss at some point." The room seemed suddenly hot and uncomfortable. "When we're in public. Not when we're alone."

Her amused expression was downright evil. "You're saying you don't want to kiss me when we're alone?"

I glanced up at the ceiling and pinched the bridge of my nose. "I'm not saying that, but it'd be better if I didn't."

She brushed her thumb over the stem of the bottle, and I mentally begged her to stop. All I could picture was her hand on me and her wicked thumb trailing over the head of my dick. The temperature in the room skyrocketed until I was sweating beneath my dress shirt. I was so off my game, everything felt upside down with her.

"Let me give you some helpful advice," she said. "Don't tell me I'm sexy. Or hot. Or *fucking* gorgeous, because that shit is going to get in my head. If you don't want to be tempted, then don't tempt me." Her tone softened. "Don't make me like you, Vance."

"That's easy. There's not much to like."

It was meant to be glib and offhanded, but it came out

sounding far too real, and I grimaced. I projected myself as a confident, carefree man who had everything he wanted, when the truth was anything but that. Alice had seen the real me and exploited it to her advantage. I wasn't going to make that mistake again.

Sure, Jillian had caught a glimpse once or twice, but I'd avoided showing her the worst of it. How sometimes I'd hated myself even more than I'd hated my father.

It was impossible to tell if she meant it or if she were simply trying to be polite. "I'm sure that's not true."

To recover, I pushed out the most dazzling smile I had in my arsenal. "We can check back after a week in Monaco and see if you feel the same way."

SIX

EMERY

Clouds blanketed the sky and threatened rain, but Vance wore sunglasses as he stood on the tarmac beside his family's private jet. He was deep in conversation on his phone as I climbed out of the back seat of the Rolls Royce he'd sent to pick me up.

God, if my parents could see me now.

I should have gawked at the sleek, luxury airplane I'd spend the next nine hours on with him, but instead my gaze was drawn to the man. Vance wore a navy cashmere sweater and jeans. His clothes were casual and normal, yet he looked anything but average. There was an otherworldly sense about him, like the air parted and moved differently around him in a more respectful way.

Too much money, my father used to say, *will make good people unrecognizable.*

It wasn't Vance's fault he'd been born into wealth any more than it was my fault I'd come from a family that was broke. But as he stood there, looking like the world was at his fingertips, I felt both jealousy and admiration. I wanted a life like his.

When he spotted me lingering beside the Rolls Royce, he stopped talking mid-sentence. I couldn't see his gorgeous blue eyes behind the dark lenses, but I imagined them studying and evaluating me.

I'd struggled with what to wear today, and finally settled on comfort over style. I wore a black motorcycle jacket over a gray t-shirt and fitted black sweatpants. His head tilted down in the direction of my black low-top Converses.

I'd made a conscious effort not to dress too sexy, but when his sunglasses came off, it looked as if I'd failed.

Shit, I *wanted* him.

And he stared back like he wanted me, too.

The tension between us grew until it became unbearable, and I broke, turning to watch the driver of the car pull my suitcase from the trunk. I would have offered to help, but I doubted he'd let me, plus it was one tiny bag. I hadn't a fucking clue what to pack for this trip, and when I'd told Vance, he'd said not to worry. He'd handle it.

Whatever that meant.

I jammed my hands into the pockets of my jacket and tried not to look awkward as Vance finished his call.

"I don't know, Royce." His tone was sharp with irritation. "Probably when I get back. Look, I need to go. Emery's here." He paused as he listened to his older brother, then pressed a hand to his chest and grinned. "I had no idea you cared so much about my love life. I'm touched."

Once he said goodbye, he slipped his phone into the back pocket of his jeans and strolled toward me.

"Wow, you look hideous."

I froze. "What?"

Breath hung in my lungs, but I had no idea if the cause

was what he'd just said, or how he leaned in and brushed a kiss on my cheek. The warmth of his lips on my skin remained even after he straightened away from me. He gauged my reaction and tilted his head, delivering a playfully stern look.

"You're going to have to do better than that to convince people you like me. You know there will be media there, right?"

I resisted the urge to touch the spot on my cheek that continued to heat from the presence of him. "You just told me I look hideous."

His smile was full of sin. "Yeah, because I'm not allowed to say you look hot." He jerked his head toward the stairs of the plane. "Come on. We can try again once we're on our way."

Oh, hell.

When we reached the base of the stairs, he held out a hand, gesturing for me to go up first. I latched my fingers around the metal railing and began to climb, keeping my mind focused on the steps rather than the billionaire heir I wasn't supposed to entice.

The interior of the plane was even nicer than I imagined. Spacious pairs of seats were wrapped in creamy white leather, and the partitioning walls were rich mahogany. I took the first available chair by a window and pretended flying on a private jet was as normal for me as it was for him. I didn't look around or marvel at how comfortable the seat was.

I had to fake that I lived in his world now, so he'd see me as an equal.

He dropped down into the seat beside me, nodded to the flight attendant when she handed us both glasses of ice water, and then turned his full attention on me.

"I forgot to ask," he said. "How was your trip?"

I set my glass in the cupholder of the chair's armrest. "It was good."

Two days after Jillian's memorial, Sovereign had sent me out to California. One of their clients had lost everything in a wildfire . . . everything except what was in their fireproof Cunningham safe. "It was quick. The internals weren't damaged, so I was able to manipulate the open without having to drill."

The door to the plane was pulled closed with a heavy thud.

"Did you get to see what was inside?"

I nodded. "Some documents, a few guns, some family photos. It was an older couple, and they both cried. It was a nice change of pace." He shot me a dubious look, prompting me to clarify. "Tears of relief for once, instead of disappointment. I try not to look, but a lot of the time there's nothing inside, or at least nothing of value. That's hard for some people."

"You've never cracked one full of gold bars or stacks of cash like in the movies?" he teased.

"If it counts, I've done a few high-end jewelry store vaults. It's amazing how many people, in our digital age, scribble the code on a Post-It note and then lose it. That's a really expensive lesson to learn."

The flight attendant had to interrupt to confirm the catering with Vance and then gave us the safety briefing. Afterward, she took her seat behind the partition at the front, and my heartrate ticked up a notch. I was nervous. Not just about the flight, but the whole trip, and hoped to distract myself by keeping the conversation going.

"Probably the most memorable open I've done so far was in Chicago," I babbled. "This wealthy Russian guy had died, and his last will and testament was locked in the safe. I flew in the afternoon of the funeral, and the family asked I come straight to the house. No one trusted anyone else, so they all demanded to be in the room—with their lawyers—while

I worked."

Outside, the engines warmed up.

"I'm sitting on the floor in front of this safe while everyone around me is dressed in black and breathing down my neck. Some of them were arguing, others were crying, and it was so freaking hard to hear the wheel clicks even with my amp. And when I cracked it, his widow literally pushes me out of the way to get inside."

I was fairly certain they were mafia and the heart attack that had killed the guy might not have been the true cause of death. Completing that job had been the longest thirty minutes of my life.

He gazed at me with interest, and for once it wasn't sexual. His navy sweater really brought out the color of his eyes, and they were like topaz—multi-faceted and sky blue. They sucked me in, demanding more, and I worried if I stared at them long enough, he'd pull every last secret from me. It left me with no choice but to look away.

"How'd you get into your line of work?"

We were moving now, taxiing toward the runway, and I watched the signal lights outside roll by. "My father."

"He cracks safes, too?"

"Yes, he could, but he passed away ten years ago."

Even with my attention out the window, I sensed the drop in mood in the man seated beside me. "Oh. I'm sorry to hear that."

"Thanks." I'd already taken a few risks with Vance, and he'd proven trustworthy. It was time to deepen that trust. "My dad grew up kind of rough, but still, he was charismatic. My mom said he was always the most charming person in the room. He'd learned to be a jack of all trades, someone who knew how to, like, *get* things from people. Or for people." I swallowed a breath and faced him. "Before he died, he taught me everything he knew, and some of those things weren't necessarily legal."

Distrust clouded over him. "Meaning?"

"When I was sixteen, I got busted for petty larceny."

Surprisingly, there wasn't a hint of judgment in him. "Shoplifting?"

"No. I picked pockets at the subway station closest to Times Square." I fiddled with the zipper on my jacket. "I'd been doing it nearly a year when the cop caught me."

He was unsure what to say. "Okay, wow, I—"

"It's not something I'm proud of, but," I glanced at our surroundings, "we can't all own private planes." My voice dipped down into a hush. "Sometimes we didn't even have a roof over our heads." I straightened in my seat, not wanting to see any pity from him. "Lifting wallets and watches was easy, and I was good at it. I just thought you should know."

The engines ramped up and the plane accelerated, rocketing us down the runway. I enjoyed the way it pressed me back into the seat and held me together. The friends I'd grown up with knew about my arrest, but I'd lost contact with them after high school, and hadn't told anyone since. I'd reinvented myself over the last ten years, and it was easy to pretend this new version of Emery didn't have a record.

It was a calculated gamble telling him the truth, but I hoped it'd bring us closer, and it was nice not to have it hanging over me. His gaze was turned forward as the plane climbed, and he took a sip of his water, perhaps considering what to do with this information I'd just dropped on him.

He set his glass back in the cupholder and turned his shoulders to me, leaning over the armrest. "Show me."

"What?"

He was so relaxed, how was it he also looked so powerful? "You said you're good at it. I want to see."

My half laugh was more surprise than humor. "I'm out of practice because I haven't done it in years." That wasn't *exactly* true. "Well . . . other than that one time."

"Oh, yeah?"

I weighed the pros and cons of telling him the story and decided it was all right. "I went on this date last year, and the guy was an asshole, so I decided I had the time to let him know. Like, I literally had the time because I took the Rolex right off his wrist."

A smile broke out on Vance's handsome face. "You stole his watch?"

"I *borrowed* it," I corrected. "Look, the guy was one of those Wall Street douches. He spent the first thirty minutes of our dinner irate that the bartender had screwed up the *ridiculously specific* directions for the drink he'd ordered, and the next thirty minutes lecturing me about how awesome he was. I barely got a word in."

"But you got his watch off without him noticing."

"Watches are easy for me. It was the first thing my father showed me." Some of my favorite memories were practicing with my dad, using the same gold watch he'd learned from with his father. "The guy was fucking clueless, so I excused myself for a minute. He thought I was going to the restroom, but I doubled back and went to the bar and ordered him another one of his stupid, fancy Manhattans. I paid for it, gave the bartender a big tip, and asked if it could be delivered to my table. When the drink was ready, I dropped the douche's watch inside."

The splash and the way it made the ice slosh had been oh-so-satisfying.

I didn't stick around to see how the drink delivery played out, but I'd imagined the moment afterward. I pictured the tumbler with the guy's Rolex resting at the bottom of the glass as it was set down before him, and then heard the bartender's smug voice. *"From the lady, sir."*

Vance looked—for lack of a better word—delighted. "Well, now you *have* to show me."

Hales were used to getting what they wanted, and it was clear he wasn't going to let it go. I threw my hands up in casual surrender. "Okay, whatever, but not right now. You'd be too suspicious of any move I made."

He was willing to accept that and nodded. "You hear from the guy again?"

"Thankfully, no. He made me want to swear off dating altogether."

"Well, that's not true." His sly smile was sexy. "Because now you have me."

Did I? We were in this weird gray area where I couldn't tell what was real. While we were both sexually attracted to each other, we couldn't act on it. And he said he didn't date—but we were currently jetting off on a week-long trip together. The line separating our relationship from fact and fiction was blurry.

He moved abruptly.

Warmth flooded down through me, and my breath went shallow as he reached out and traced his fingertips over the curve of my cheek. It was featherlight, just a hint of a touch, but goosebumps showered down my arms.

My voice was a whisper, and I doubted he could hear it over the roar of the engines as we continued our ascent. "What are you doing?"

His word was thick, heavy with desire. "Practicing."

Down his fingertips went, trailing over my skin until he could gently grasp my chin and draw me forward into his kiss.

His lips were soft and warm as they met mine, making me close my eyes and focus in on the sensation. The kiss was gentle, but it caused a riot of sparks inside my body that skittered around and lit me up. My fingers in my lap curled into fists, wanting to clench on to him, but knowing it'd be better if I didn't.

The press of his mouth against mine was tame. Restrained.

If I deepened the kiss, I was sure it'd spin wildly out of control. I pictured unbuckling my seatbelt and climbing into his lap, FAA regulations be damned. His hands would settle around my waist and urge me to grind against him while his tongue claimed my mouth.

Blood thundered through my veins, pushed along by my rapidly beating heart, and a dull ache grew between my legs. In my fantasy, his hands edged beneath my shirt and skated upward. My breasts grew heavy with the thought of his fingers inside my bra, touching me how we both wanted, even as the flight attendant was just around the corner and would catch us when she scolded me for being out of my seat.

It was insane to want him this badly, especially when I hardly knew him and needed his help. I'd mixed business with pleasure before, leading to disastrous results.

This was nearly *ten years* of work.

It was too important to fuck up.

But the longer the kiss went on, the faster my resolve began to crumble. He adjusted the angle of his head, inviting me to open my mouth and welcome his tongue inside, yet as soon as I parted my lips, he began his retreat.

He drew back, giving me a glimpse of his hazy eyes and the way his pulse pounded in his neck. It looked as if he'd ended the kiss right on the precipice of him losing control. The rapid rise and fall of his chest announced he'd been as affected as I had been, but he recovered faster. His gaze dropped to my hands, which were still balled into fists, then it returned to my mouth to watch how his innocent kiss continued to sear across my lips.

"That was better." His statement came out even and measured. "Believable."

Of course our kiss was believable. There was enough heat in my body to power Monaco for a week. The question burst from me in a demanding rush. "How long has it been since you last had sex?"

"This is the twenty-ninth day of my challenge."

I pressed my lips together. "That's not what I asked."

A smile spread across his face. "You're right. It's been thirty-seven days."

"Who was she?" The second it was out, I cringed. I sounded jealous as hell, which I wasn't. I *totally* wasn't. Right?

Vance's smile grew into a grin. "Just a friend." His tone was teasing. "Not sure how that's your business, though."

"If this were a real relationship, I'd want to know who you were sleeping with when we met."

The playfulness drained from his expression. "I guess you've got a point. Her name is Kacey Price."

The name was familiar. Where had I heard it before? Oh, God. "The actress?"

He lifted a shoulder. "We met at some event last year, and we've hooked up a few times since. She was in town last month filming something, and we both had some free time, so . . ." He scratched the back of his neck, and I got the sense he was hiding how I'd made him uncomfortable. "It's a casual thing."

"Oh," I said.

"What about you?"

The plane leveled off, but my brain was still hung up on the image of him with Kacey. She wasn't a huge star, but she was still a celebrity, and drop-dead gorgeous to boot. They'd done an excellent job of keeping their hook-up quiet, because they were a beautiful couple and would have looked great splashed across the front of a tabloid.

"What about me, what?" I asked.

"How long has it been since you've had sex?"

Blood rushed to my face, heating my skin. "It's, uh, been a while."

He looked at me like that couldn't be right. "Really? For a girl as *unattractive* as you?" His doubt began to fade. "Wait. How long is 'a while'?"

I ground my teeth, irritated to have to answer his cross-examination, but not enough to back down. "It's been months, Vance."

Six very long, *very lonely* months.

He couldn't think of a single plausible reason. "Why?"

"Because I've been too busy to meet anyone I've been into."

Whatever idea he'd just had, the thought turned him rigid. "Do you . . . not like sex?"

Was he kidding? I loved it but wasn't about to tell him that. "I like sex just fine, but unlike some people," I gave him a pointed look, "I don't need it to survive."

A smug smile curved his lips. "Sounds to me like you haven't had it with the right person yet."

"Yeah," I deadpanned. "That must be it."

I didn't miss who he was implying, but that was so unfair. *I* wasn't the one against us hopping into bed together. If he asked me, I'd say yes in a heartbeat. God, if not for his dumb bet with its stupid rules, I'd—

I sat up straighter in my seat. "You mentioned you and Jillian talked about rules when you made your bet. Tell me about them."

He put his elbow on the armrest opposite me and leaned on it, putting space between us. "Not much to it. I agreed I wouldn't have sex for ninety days."

Excitement fluttered in my belly. He was lying, or at least not giving me the full truth. I saw how his eyes had shifted away, and not to mention, he'd physically retreated. I didn't let him, and leaned in, closing the space.

"Define sex, then."

He pretended to be shocked. "Oh, no. You don't know?" He sighed dramatically. "Okay, Emery, when two people really like each other, sometimes they'll—"

When I placed my hand gently on his leg, the words died in his throat. He stared at my fingers resting on his thigh like he both loved and hated it.

"Sex," my voice rasped, "can be done in a lot of different ways." For emphasis, I slid my hand up a few inches and enjoyed his sharp intake of breath. "Tell me I'm wrong."

His warm hand clasped over mine, but he didn't push me away. His fingers wrapped around my palm like he wanted to prevent me from moving any closer to the center of his legs, but also to hold me in place. To keep up our connection.

"You're not wrong," he said quietly.

Did he know how strong a hold he had on me? Not just where we were touching, either. My whole body was electrified by him, making desire buzz through my system. Hopefully, he couldn't tell, but my needy voice probably didn't help. "Then tell me what kind of sex you can have that won't break your vow."

His mouth opened to say something, but he got lost

finding the right words.

I decided I'd help him out, and although I doubted the flight attendant could hear us, I whispered it anyway. "Masturbation?"

His face went blank. "I fucking hope so, because if not, I lost the bet the very first day." His expression was sheepish, but I found it sexy. "We didn't get that specific. All we discussed was whether or not oral was included in the no-sex ban."

Really? I'd assumed it would be, but his hesitancy made me wonder. My voice was tight. "Is it?"

His unblinking gaze locked on to mine as he took in a slow breath, drawing the moment out. Then, he straightened in his seat and shifted closer. Like he'd been cornered and now he was ready to turn and fight. "She said I could give," his words were wrapped in velvet, "but not receive."

The electricity inside me grew so strong, static played in my brain.

This man radiated sex. Seduction seeped from his pores and dripped from his wicked expression. Vance Hale stared at me with a guarantee in his eyes, a promise that he could deliver enormous pleasure even without the use of his greatest weapon. Or perhaps his mouth *was* his greatest weapon.

Fog filled my head, and I didn't understand why Jillian had said going down on a woman wouldn't violate the no-sex rules. "Why?"

"Why can't I get a blow job, but I'm allowed to use my tongue? Because she knows I love doing that, and she was probably hoping it'd make me more likely to lose the bet."

The image was instantaneous—him on his knees in front of me, my bare thighs resting on his shoulders. Would he close his eyes as his mouth worked me over, teasing me? Or would he keep them open so he could watch every gasp of breath I took?

It was a thousand degrees on the plane, and still I shivered inside my jacket. Despite all the warnings I'd given myself, I threw the same demand he'd issued earlier, only my voice was a whisper. "Show me."

His hand clenched on top of mine, perhaps a reflex at the heat my words caused in him. He squeezed almost to the point of discomfort. "Well, that's a spectacularly bad idea."

Only there was an edge buried in his statement that said he liked my idea very much. He released me, straightened, and adjusted his seatbelt. Or possibly he was disguising the way he had to adjust himself inside his jeans.

With his touch gone, some of the tension between us dispelled, clearing my head. It allowed me to get back on my game. He was another safe to crack, a puzzle to unlock, and I needed a new approach. "You're right," I said. "If you think you can't handle it—that it would be too tempting for you—then we shouldn't."

His icy blue eyes narrowed at my challenge. "I didn't say I couldn't handle it." I expected him to say more, or at least come back with a sharp retort, but instead he scrubbed a hand over his face and sighed. "Emery . . . I'm a third of the way through this thing, and it's only going to get harder the more time we spend together. The bet is ridiculous, and no one's keeping score except me, but . . . it means something to me to finish it."

Guilt sliced down through my center. He was trying to improve himself. Why was I making it harder on him? "I'm sorry," I said quickly. "Forget I said anything."

That probably wasn't likely, but he looked relieved.

It wasn't long after that when the attendant appeared, prepared the cabin for dinner, and then served us. We had linen napkins, fancy silverware, and actual plates—it was like eating at a high-end restaurant. I almost wished Vance had made me sit in the back row where the seats were smaller and wouldn't recline while I was fed a tasteless frozen dinner.

How on Earth was I going to go back to flying commercial? He was, of course, used to the luxury. This was commonplace to a one-percenter like him. He'd never had to sit shoulder to shoulder with the plebs in economy plus and fight to find overhead compartment space.

He finished his salad and set his fork at an angle across his plate, signifying he was done. "If someone helped Jillian fake her death, I don't think it was Lucas Ridley."

"Why is that?" I asked.

After we'd shared sips from the bottle of vodka the night of Jillian's memorial, he'd told me his theory about Lucas running off to the Caribbean with her. It seemed highly unlikely. I knew she'd been taking sailing lessons, but only because she'd called me one afternoon in a terrible mood and said she'd just fired Lucas for being an asshole.

She never mentioned him before or after that phone call.

But I was all for ruling out every suspect, and thankfully Vance seemed to feel the same.

"I spoke with the security manager at the marina," he said. "According to the logs, Lucas didn't use his boat at any time while *The Trident* was out. Plus, he didn't set sail until after the news about Jillian's disappearance had broken." Sadness crept into his voice. "You said she fired him. Maybe Sophia was right. Jillian's death hit him extra hard because they were friends and how things ended between them."

His sadness was mirrored in me, but I refused to let it stay. I didn't want things to be as they seemed, and maybe if I wished hard enough, I could will what I wanted into existence.

"Okay, so it wasn't Lucas," I said. "We'll keep looking, or we'll find a way for me to get back in front of Lambert's safe, or—"

"Both," he said simply.

It was the same thing I imagined him saying to a jeweler when he was unable to choose which outrageously expensive watch he wanted.

"Both," I repeated on a breath, pleased not to have to guide him. He was already onboard with my agenda.

When our plates were cleared, I took the opportunity to visit the restroom. There was plenty of leg room, but he was a gentleman with impeccable manners, so he unbuckled his seatbelt and rose to his feet when I did, giving me more space to pass. I sucked in my breath as I inched my way around him, fighting the urge to rub suggestively against his toned form.

The restroom was at the back of the plane and spanned the entire width, making it as spacious as it was elegant. It had gold taps perched over the sink. Gold *fucking* taps. I stared at myself in the mirror after washing my hands, looking horribly out of place in my t-shirt, sweatpants, and sneakers. I was a girl who'd grown up in the streets of NYC, struggling with her family just to get by. How was I going to fool anyone into believing I belonged in this world?

Pull your shit together, Emery. You can do this.

I paced my way back up the long aisle, past the couch and desk the Hales probably used as a workstation whenever they flew and needed to conduct business, moving until I reached the seat Vance was occupying. Like last time, he stood, but this time I didn't hold back. I set my left hand on his hard chest, using it to steady myself as I attempted to shuffle past. His attention went to that, but also the way I brushed my body against his.

It meant I was free to help myself to his back pocket

with my right hand. While he focused on the way my breasts skimmed against the front of his sweater, he was oblivious to my fingers latching on to his phone. Getting it out of his pocket was done in one quick, clean lift, and to ensure he didn't notice, I let out a soft sigh. Like I was acknowledging the awkward dance between us for me to return to my seat.

His smile confirmed he wasn't aware of anything but me, which was exactly how I wanted it. He didn't see when I slid his phone into the pocket of my sweatpants because the whole lift was done in under three seconds. I took my seat, and he took his, and we made it through dinner and another glass of wine before he attempted to retrieve his phone.

I played dumb as confusion ran through him. I watched him stand and slide a hand into his back pocket, only to discover it empty.

"Is something wrong?"

He turned and looked down at the seat, perhaps wondering if it had fallen out. Then he bent and looked on the floor, while worry filled his voice. "I can't find my phone."

"Oh . . . you mean this phone?"

He paused at my question.

Then his head slowly turned so he could spy me cradling the thin, sleek phone in my hand. The one with a black case that was most definitely his, and a victorious smile burned across my lips.

It only took him a fraction of a second to realize how I'd gotten it. Rather than look annoyed, excitement burst through his expression. "Teach me."

His demand punched a laugh from my chest.

SEVEN

EMERY

After we disembarked the plane at the airport in Nice, we took a short helicopter flight to Monaco and landed on the helipad atop a hotel in Monte Carlo. I'd barely slept on the plane, too excited and anxious about the week, and adrenaline pushed me through the helicopter transfer. But now time was catching up to me, and I stifled a yawn as we rode the elevator in the luxury hotel.

Vance was faring better than I was. It was eleven in the morning here—but felt like five a.m. after a restless night to me. He'd at least caught a few hours of shuteye after he'd given me a primer on Formula One racing and finished going over the itinerary. There were so many events, I wondered if we'd get a moment to breathe between them.

Dark whiskers dusted his usually clean-shaven face, and his eyes weren't as bright as normal, but leave it to him to still look amazing when he was tired.

Last night, I'd declined to show him how I'd lifted his phone. He'd insisted at first, but when he kept pressing, I told him the first one was free. After that, he'd have to show me something in exchange.

He knew exactly what I wanted, and that got him to back down.

The elevator doors were polished to a mirror finish, and I combed a hand through my hair to get it to lay right. The customer relations manager standing beside me noticed and gave me a gentle smile through the reflection in the doors. He was a tall, elegant man with a thick French accent and perfect posture that would make a ballerina weep.

"Here we are," he said after leading us down the hall and unlocking the only door at the end of it. "The *Carré d'Or* Suite."

He said a bunch of other things after that, something about an award-winning designer and the Louis XVI furnishings, but I couldn't process anything once I stepped inside. My gaze was drawn to the floor-to-ceiling picture windows that had sweeping views of the city and the sparkling ocean that lay beyond it.

The manager gave us a quick walkthrough of the penthouse, pointing out features, and I nodded enthusiastically while absorbing absolutely zero of it. On the table in the classically styled sitting room was a bottle of Dom Pérignon chilling in a silver bucket of ice. Beside it waited two champagne flutes, a carafe of juice, and an understated orange bag with the word Hermès printed on it.

"A welcome gift for the madame," the manager commented before moving on.

The tasteful décor was carried through the bedroom and the bathroom that boasted a marble jetted tub, but the real star of the penthouse was the enormous private terrace outside. It was as big as the entire suite. On one side, a dining table sat beneath a large umbrella, and the other side was staged as an outdoor living space with couches and chairs.

"The casino square and gardens are just below." The man turned away from the stunning view to face us. "Would you like to lunch on the terrace now? Or should I make arrangements elsewhere if you prefer?"

"Lunch here would be great." Vance glanced at his watch. "Let's say twelve thirty."

The manager gave a single nod. "Excellent. I'll inform the chef."

I walked to the railing at the edge of the terrace and shielded my eyes from the bright May sunshine, scanning the landscape that wrapped around us. Palm trees dotted the green areas between buildings and streets that wound their way up the cliffside. Down in the bright blue bay, yachts filled every inch of space of the sprawling marina, and plenty more superyachts were anchored offshore in the distance.

It was otherworldly.

So wealthy and extravagant and picture perfect, none of it seemed real.

I hadn't realized the manager had left until Vance appeared beside me. "I'm sorry about the sleeping arrangements. I thought it was just going to be me. I'll take the couch in the sitting room." He pushed up the sleeves on his sweater and rested a hand on the railing beside me. He offered his statement like I needed more explanation. "Our yacht is too much space for one person, so we only bring it when the whole family comes."

"Yeah, no worries." I waved a hand. "We do that with my family's yacht too."

He gave me a lopsided smile. "Shower?" His expression froze. "I meant, would you like to take a shower before lunch? I can take mine after yours."

I thought about making a joke that we could conserve

water and take one together, but I was mature and refrained. As long as he didn't tempt me, I wouldn't tempt him.

But if he did?

Well, then, game on.

Lunch could have been delicious, but I didn't notice. It was taking all my remaining energy to keep my eyes open. I'd mistakenly thought the shower would help me power through, but the moment I sat at the table and stopped moving, exhaustion took over.

We had an appointment later this afternoon, he'd said. We'd meet with a stylist who'd be dressing both of us for the week, and shop together at the designer stores that lined the ultrarich streets of Monte Carlo. When I'd expressed reservations about Vance spending that kind of money on me, he shrugged.

"Being my girlfriend comes with perks, and as I mentioned, there'll be press at these events. Everything you do is unfortunately a reflection of HBHC and my family this week. If you get photographed in a t-shirt and Converses, I'll never hear the end of it from my father, and I don't like talking to him unless I have to."

It was none of my business, but I couldn't help myself. "Why?"

The shift in Vance's mood was visible. "It's . . . complicated." He let out a breath and leaned back, casting an arm over the back of the empty chair beside him. His posture looked relaxed, but I knew better. Tension rested in his shoulders.

"We've both made mistakes in the past, and he wants to apologize, but I don't know if I'm ready."

"To apologize? Or hear his apology?"

He turned to glance at the scenery, and the wind blew, ruffling his soft brown hair. "Both, I guess."

There were numerous options for what Macalister Hale's apology would be about. He'd pushed Vance's stepmother off a balcony and accidentally killed her. He was dating a woman who was half his age and Vance's friend. And as Jillian told it, he'd been a terrible father. Cold and controlling and selfish.

Just like Lambert.

But what mistake had Vance made, I wondered, that he had to apologize for?

"We should both try to nap before our meeting with Petra," he said abruptly. "It'll help us get over the jet lag faster."

He lifted a hand and signaled to the butler that we were finished, ending both our lunch and the conversation. While our plates were cleared and loaded onto a trolley, I followed Vance back inside the sitting area, and my gaze snagged a second time on the Hermes bag. The manager had said it was for me, hadn't he?

I peeked inside.

My 'boyfriend' watched me with casual interest as I pulled the items out and set them on the table beside the bag. Two small cylinders with different bands of color on them turned out to be lipsticks—deep red and a pretty nude. The elegant gray pouch held a silver bangle bracelet. There was a small bottle of perfume as well. I couldn't resist giving it a test and spritzed some on the inside of my wrist.

"How is it?" he asked after watching me take a whiff.

"It's nice." I walked over and held my hand out for him to make his own judgment.

His fingertips were cool when he grasped my wrist, and my breath caught. In our tired state, I didn't think either of us had realized how provocative it'd be for him to inhale the perfume as it wafted from my skin, putting part of me only an inch from his face. It'd take nothing for him to press his lips to the sensitive underside of my wrist, and heat flickered inside me.

Then his gaze drifted over my shoulder, making the flicker burst into flames.

It was because he'd glanced at the bed like he was seriously thinking of carrying me there.

But the butler had finished outside, and the dishes clattered on the trolley as it rolled through the sitting room, shattering the intimate moment. Vance dropped my hand and stepped back, needing to put space between us as quickly as possible.

"Yeah," his tone was detached, "it's nice."

"Can I get you anything else, sir?" the butler asked.

Vance's response came quickly. "No, that will be all. Thank you."

As soon as the door was shut, I couldn't hear the trolley at all as it rolled down the hall. The soundproofing in the suite was top notch. I meandered through the sitting room, gazing at the artwork and the fresh flowers in the vase beside the couch he'd claimed he sleep on.

It looked inviting, but at this point, so did a pile of dirty clothes on the floor. I'd sleep anywhere.

I strolled through the open French doors that led to the bedroom, turned to face him, and sat down on the foot of the bed—the one where there was more than enough room for two people to share. "I can't believe you booked such a romantic place for just yourself."

He followed me but stopped just short of crossing the threshold. Like this was my room and he didn't have permission, which was stupid. He was paying, so I was the guest in his room. And he hadn't had an issue coming into the room earlier, either. The housekeeper had placed our luggage in the dressing room that connected the bedroom to the master bathroom where we'd both taken our showers earlier.

His tone was resigned. "Everywhere in Monaco is romantic. My brother came here on his honeymoon." His expression was weary, but there was something vibrant in his eyes. His tone was teasing. "I know it will be incredibly hard for you, but try not to fall in love with me."

It had been a joke, but his words hung awkwardly in the space between us, and his expression went blank to cover his alarm. There was so much truth in what he'd said. I heard the plea buried inside, and I would do everything I could to honor it.

I had no business being with a man like Vance Hale, plus . . . there was no room in my heart for love. All the space inside it was dark and consumed with the need for vengeance. Some days it was a struggle to think about anything else.

I flopped down dramatically on my back, letting the cloud-like down comforter absorb me. "Don't worry. I'm too busy falling in love with this bed."

I gazed up at the crystal chandelier and the ceiling above, which was wallpapered in a pattern complimentary to the pastel stripes on the wall. The pink floral design was interesting, and—

Wait a minute.

A laugh bubbled up from my chest. "Oh, *now* I see why you booked this room. It's covered in vaginas."

"What?"

I pointed at the suggestive pink flowers with their frilly petals making an elliptical shape. Adding to it was the button-like stigma in the center of each one.

"I don't see it," he said, which had to be a lie.

"You've forgotten what vaginas look like in just twenty-nine days? Come over here." I patted a hand on the empty spot beside me.

He hesitated, perhaps weighing whether it was a good idea, but must have decided it was, because he walked to the bed, sat on the edge, and lay back. I turned my head, fighting to keep my sleepy eyes open, and watched him sink into the comforter as he stared up at the wallpaper.

"Okay," his tone was reticent. "They do kind of look like vaginas."

I giggled. "Told you."

We remained like that, resting beneath the genitalia-themed flowers, in contemplative silence for a long while. Time pressed down on us, making our bodies heavy with sleep, and it took an enormous effort from me to scoot up and roll onto my side so I could comfortably face him.

I said it in a hush. "Can I ask you something?"

He had his hands on his chest, fingers laced together, and his head lolled toward me. I wasn't sure if it was a nod, but I went ahead like it had been.

"It's none of my business, and you don't have to answer, but . . . are you still in love with Jillian?"

This was the last question he expected to hear, and his lips parted to speak, yet all that came out was a breath. Then he blinked and shook his head. "No. I cared about her, but I was never in love. I can't imagine she was in love with me either." Concern rapidly overtook his expression. "Why? What'd she tell you?"

A strange sensation like relief flooded through me, and I disliked it. I shouldn't care if he was still hung up on her.

I tucked a hand under my head as I gazed at him. After his shower, he'd changed into a white polo shirt and a pair of slacks, and he looked so fucking good, I could hardly stand it.

"She didn't say much," I offered. "Just that she was the one to end things, and you guys stayed friends afterward." In my weakened state, my inhibitions began to crumble. "I couldn't stay friends with any of my exes. I don't talk to them anymore."

"That's probably because what you had with your exes was real." Perhaps exhaustion was doing the same to him, pulling his guard down, and his eyes turned magnetic. They sucked me in until I was drowning in them. "Everything in my life has been manufactured," he said softly, "so I've never had a chance at love." He rolled his shoulders toward me, shifting on the bed so we were facing each other. "Fuck, I don't think I've ever even had a real relationship."

He'd grown up with the world at his feet, but also crushed under the weight of enormous expectations. I'd envied Jillian for her wealth but grown to pity her as well. The snarky 'poor, little rich girl' mentality I'd had for her had become real.

She wasn't free, and Vance wasn't either.

And no amount of money could make a person happy when they were trapped living a life for someone else.

He blinked so slowly, I wasn't sure his eyelids were going to open again, but they did. His blue eyes were unfocused. "You and me . . . already feels more real than anything else I've had."

My heart fell out of tempo and tumbled through my body.

We both had a hand resting on the bed, and my gaze trailed over his long fingers, wishing he'd move them. We'd each only need to slide our hand a few inches toward each other to be touching. If he reached out, I'd meet him.

"It can be real," I whispered, "if you want it to be."

But his eyes closed again, and this time I knew they wouldn't reopen. I tried to keep mine open and watch him sleep, but my brain shut down and I couldn't resist the pull of sleep any longer.

A male voice in the distance woke me, and my eyes fluttered open. I was still so tired, and . . . where the hell was I? And what fucking time was it?

Reality came back to me one layer at a time. I was in a hotel in Monaco. It was still bright outside, and sunlight streamed in through the large windows that overlooked the terrace. Vance and I had fallen asleep without even closing the curtains.

Except I was the only one on the bed. I pushed up on my elbows and craned my neck, looking around for him.

He was far away, over by the desk in the sitting room and staring off into nothingness as he held his phone pressed to an ear. It gave me the perfect view of him in profile, and since he didn't notice I was watching, it allowed me to appreciate every inch of him. He could look the part of a cutthroat attorney in a bespoke suit, or an approachable politician in slacks and a button-down shirt with the sleeves rolled back.

But I thought he looked best in the role he wore now—a young, stylish, and confident man who was the symbol of his family and their brand. An embodiment of wealth and class and beauty.

"Yes, hello. I'm calling about Petra." His voice was low, not wanting to disturb me. "I'm running behind and need to push our three o'clock."

Oh, shit. I'd slept so long I was going to make us late.

I sat upright, grabbed the thin blanket covering me, and went to cast it aside, but my movement slowed. The soft throw blanket hadn't been on the bed when I'd fallen asleep—he must have covered me up while I was sleeping.

His kindness was such a simple gesture, yet it made me feel all warm inside.

"Vance, I'm up." I climbed off the bed and stood. "Give me one minute and I'm ready."

He glanced my way as he spoke into his phone. "Actually, never mind. You can let her know we're on our way. Thanks."

"Why didn't you wake me when you got up?" I asked when he pocketed his phone.

He flashed an easy smile. "You didn't sleep on the plane, so I figured you could use a little extra time."

"You didn't have to do that. I don't want to make us late."

A slow smile teased his lips. "Petra won't mind. I pay her and her company enough money not to."

I scurried to the bathroom, ran a brush through my long brown hair, and swiped on some mascara as quickly as possible. Thankfully, the maxi dress I'd changed into after my shower hadn't gotten wrinkled during my nap. I rushed out into the main room, snatched up my purse, and stepped into a pair of sandals.

It was a short walk from our hotel. We met Petra outside a trendy and intimidating boutique, and after introductions, we were ushered to the back of the store. There was a set of sleek leather couches arranged around a low, glass table, and bottles of wine and artisanal water were set on it, along with a rainbow assortment of macarons and other French pastries. It was so we could take in refreshments as we 'shopped.'

Petra was short and fit, and everything about her announced she was a force to be reckoned with, from her custom off-center jeans to her shockingly pink hair. Her cockney British accent was charming at times, but sharp when it needed to be. Her team had at least six people on it not including herself, but it was hard to keep track because they kept rotating in and out of the back room while they presented different looks to the three of us.

Last Friday, I'd filled out a form for her including my measurements, shoe size, and which colors I felt worked best on me. I didn't have to measure—I used the same ones Jillian had taken when she'd designed for me. I'd had to send pictures of myself to Petra, since I rarely posted on social media. She had the itinerary of events, and she'd already chosen a few looks, so it went much quicker than I'd expected.

"Are you okay with this?" Vance asked me at one point.

I gave him a smile. "I'm happy if you're happy. I'll wear whatever you need me to. Seriously. If you want me to wear a chicken suit, just say the word."

I understood my job and our partnership. He was here under obligations to HBHC, and I didn't want to do anything to jeopardize that. Did it bother me that he was spending a fortune on clothes for me? No. He had the money, and I wasn't sleeping with him in exchange for lavish gifts and trips.

Because, shit, I'd sleep with him for free. Maybe I'd even pay him for it.

If you had any money.

Nearly everything I tried on fit me, and while some of the pieces weren't things I'd have picked for myself—like a red midriff baring crop top—Petra didn't dress me like I was suddenly a different person. She expertly found a high-end version of my style, where the clothes were feminine and sexy but not risqué.

When I modeled a white one-shoulder mini-dress with black trim, Vance's gaze worked its way up my bare legs and his smile grew. He liked what he saw very much.

"Gross," he said in a rich voice.

Petra's head snapped toward him, then back to me, like she couldn't believe they were looking at the same thing. Maybe the shock of what he'd said disrupted her filter, or perhaps she was just outspoken. Her tone verged on anger. "Are you kidding me? She looks fabulous."

He laughed. "It's an inside joke. Emery doesn't like when I compliment her, so I do the opposite."

"Oh." Her dismay faded somewhat, but she was still unsettled. "I see." I kind of loved how Petra was willing to go to battle for me, even with the man who was her client. "So, you like this piece?"

"Yeah." His gaze flicked back to me, and his eyes were full of smoke. "I like it a lot."

He was just talking about the dress, right? Because it felt like he meant all of what he was looking at, and my mouth went dry.

By my fourth fitting, Petra had gotten in on it too.

"Awful," Vance said of the gray jumpsuit that seemed tailored to my body and made me feel like a million dollars.

"Yeah," she wrinkled her nose, "truly disgusting."

I laughed. And then abruptly my face crumbled as tears sprang into my eyes. The rush of emotion was so strong, it was all I could do to blink them back.

Vance and Petra were both up out of their seats in a heartbeat, but he beat her to the platform I was standing on in front of the mirrors. His strong hands circled my waist, and he pulled me in until I was flattened against his chest, bringing us nearly nose-to-nose.

"Oh, no!" she cried. "We didn't mean it. You look beautiful, darling."

"Emery." He was full of dread. "I'm sorry, I didn't—"

A stupid, uncontrolled laugh came out of me to try to play it off like I found the whole thing amusing and not utterly mortifying. "No, no. It's okay. It's not that, I just . . . I got caught by surprise."

That did nothing to alleviate his concern. "What happened?"

I dropped my voice low. "Last time I did this was with Jillian. It's so stupid that it's hitting me now, but," I swallowed a breath, "she's gone. Like, *really* gone. I've been telling myself it isn't real, but what if it is? We're never going to see her again."

Our friendship had started as a lie, but it had grown more real than anything else, and now I missed my friend terribly.

His gorgeous eyes widened and flooded with a pain that showed he understood. He didn't turn away from me, but it was clear he was speaking to Petra. "Can you give us a minute?"

"Yes, of course," she said and strode quickly from the room.

"Did I do this?" I whispered. "If I hadn't opened that safe, maybe she wouldn't have—"

His voice was steel. "Stop. You didn't do this." He stared at me as if he could see the weight of all the guilt I was carrying and thought it was unwarranted. "Don't blame yourself for what happened to Jillian. It was not your fault." His hands tightened to keep me from running away from the truth. "But I promise you, we'll do our best to figure it out."

My shoulders lifted as I drew in an enormous, calming

breath. As I evened out, he did the same, and the body I was pressed against began to soften. His hands moved, sliding to the small of my back and then working their way up, inch by slow inch. The air between us grew thick—not with sex—but with neediness.

He needed a connection, just as I did.

Could he see how badly I wanted to create one with him? Not for his help with Lambert's safe . . . but as a friend. Someone to share my secrets and grief with, and possibly my desire too.

Blood rushed through me as he lowered his lips to mine and claimed me in the sweetest, most tender kiss possible. It made my heart stop and my head foggy, and as his mouth moved against mine, the fog swelled until nothing else was visible except us. The pull to him was the same as waves that had crashed against the shoreline and then retreated as they were sucked back into the ocean.

Our first kiss had been measured and controlled. A reading of gauges to evaluate the best course. But this one? It moved with reckless abandon across a turbulent sea. Unguided. Adrift.

Suddenly, a change went through him like wind filling sails, and in this moment, he must have decided who was in command and where we were going. His hold on me firmed up, and one of his hands slid into my hair to cradle the back of my head. He took charge of the kiss, dipping his tongue into my mouth to stroke against me in a way that made my legs go boneless.

He was confident and prepared for that, because as I weakened, he grew stronger. His passionate kiss announced he *had* me. He was here with me, and I was desperate to believe.

Vance was a lighthouse during a storm, a beacon I'd

willingly follow.

Time slowed as his kiss neared its end, and then crashed back upon me when the contact of his lips was gone. My eyelids fluttered open to find him looking at me with bewilderment. He stared at me like a person who'd spent a lifetime at sea and didn't know how to tolerate dry land.

Warmth pooled around my heart. Our kiss had shaken him.

His unfocused eyes cleared and sharpened as reality descended on him. What we'd just done wasn't practice or to convince anyone else we were a couple. He'd kissed me because he'd *wanted* to, and if he felt even a fraction of what I just had, he was in serious trouble of losing his bet.

My pulse sped along, making desire hum through my body, and I stifled a whimper when Vance released me. He stepped back and jammed his hands in his pockets, giving the impression he needed to put them somewhere else, so he wouldn't put them on me.

"Are you okay?" He said it so quietly, it was heartbreaking. "Was that okay?"

"It was more than okay," I whispered back.

He nodded, yet it looked like he didn't know what to do with that information. He climbed down the single step and went to fetch Petra, who after reassurances from me, continued with the styling. But this time, their comments were nothing but glowing praise.

When it became Vance's turn, he disappeared into the fitting room, and Petra went in the back with her team. I got up off the couch and wandered the small, elegant store because my nap earlier had only deferred my exhaustion. If I sat too long, I'd fall asleep.

The place had a minimalist design. The walls displayed clothing on hangars like it was art. Brass table legs were paired with white marble tops and spaced equal distance from each other, allowing shoppers plenty of room to browse. Although there wasn't much to browse. The single stack of pants on the table nearest me only contained one sample of the design in each size.

The door to the front opened, and a man walked in, making me furrow my brow. The boutique had a 'closed' sign hung in the window. The guy, who looked to be around thirty, scanned the place until his gaze landed on me.

French spilled from his mouth as he strolled forward.

"I'm sorry," I said, "I don't speak French."

"Ah, American?"

"Yes."

"You must not work here." His English was excellent, with barely an accent, but it wasn't French either. German? Austrian? He had dark blond hair and a day's worth of scruff covering his dimples when he smiled.

"No," I said. "I don't work here."

He'd strutted in with so much swagger, I immediately sized him up the way I did when looking for marks at Times Square. If I thought Vance oozed cockiness, this guy was an arrogance bomb. He wore black jeans and a simple fitted t-shirt with a brand name printed on it, but one I didn't recognize. His sneakers were probably several thousand dollars, and the clunky silver watch around his wrist was the expensive accessory to complete his ensemble. He was handsome, but his air of smugness was so strong, it overpowered his cologne.

I couldn't tell if this guy had money, or just wanted people to think he did. Monaco was where the filthy rich came to play, but Vance had said it also brought out the wannabes. As the man stared at me expectantly, his smile widened like there was some joke I wasn't getting.

It made me uncomfortable. "I don't know if anyone will be out to help you," I offered. "The store's actually closed right now."

"This is fine." He waved a hand, brushing my comment away. "They will make time for me."

I pressed my lips together and glanced at the doorway that led to the fitting room, silently willing Vance or Petra to hurry up and save me from Mr. Ego.

The man's eyes sparkled with amusement, unable to stand it any longer. "Do you not know who I am?"

It came out before I could think better of it. "Should I?"

My biting reply somehow *delighted* him. "Most people do, so this is refreshing." He evaluated me head to toe and moved closer. "It's nice to meet someone who doesn't." I expected him to thrust out a hand and introduce himself, but all he did was invade my space and continue to stare at me like I was a unicorn.

"So, who are you?" It seemed like he wanted me to ask.

He tilted his head to the side. "Maybe I like it better if you don't know."

Whatever, dude.

Maybe he'd like it even more if I told him to go flirt with someone else. He was obviously some sort of celebrity. Perhaps he was a singer who was big in Europe, or a soccer star. He was tall, athletic, and attractive . . .

There was a charity fashion show later this week on our agenda. "Are you a model?"

He was utterly thrilled by my question and laughed, shifting his weight so he was closer still. His lips parted to deliver his answer, but a male voice across the room interrupted.

"No." Vance's tone was even and controlled, but—was he upset? He looked vaguely unhappy, and it didn't seem to be caused by the fit of his sports jacket. "His name is Niko Leitner," he said. "One of the drivers for Red Bull."

During the primer Vance had given me on the plane yesterday, he'd explained how Mercedes' number one driver had battled all season last year to win the drivers' championship. It'd been a bitter fight between him and another driver, including some questionable crashes and penalties handed down by the stewards. But at the end, Mercedes had lost.

And the man standing beside me was the one who'd won.

EIGHT

VANCE

Kissing Emery made me feel . . . something. I didn't know how to describe it, other than the moment of freefall when you're speeding along and air gets under the hull of a boat. I knew the water was there beneath me and that I'd land safely on it, but that experience of floating just before crashing down was always thrilling.

This wasn't like any kiss I'd ever given before, and it left me disoriented. I wanted more—a hell of a lot more.

You're just tired, that's all this is.

Fuck, I couldn't even convince myself. I'd been with her in Monaco for all of six hours and already kissed her. How the fuck was I going to last a week without having more?

I focused on the task at hand, rather than think about it. The black sports coat fit well enough, and I appreciated how it was lightweight so I wouldn't get too hot under the warm sun. Nearly every event would be outside.

The jacket was paired with jeans and a cream-colored knit shirt. I exited the dressing room to show the women how it looked, only to find Petra missing and Emery talking to—of all people—fucking Niko Leitner.

I didn't want her within a hundred yards of the Austrian Asshole, and certainly not standing right beside him. His reputation on the track was just as bad as it was off it. He was aggressive and selfish in everything. When his brakes overheated, it was the car's fault and not his. If he won a race, he'd deliver the standard line that it had been a team effort, but no one believed it—most of all, him.

Niko had won the drivers' championship last year, but it needed an asterisk beside it. In the final race of the season, he'd interfered with Sem Janssen's line, and when their tires had touched, it had sent his rival into the barrier at two hundred miles an hour. Janssen had thankfully walked away with only a concussion, but Leitner had made the podium, cementing his lead in the points and the championship win.

I understood the drive to win, but even I had my limits. He could have killed Janssen.

Seeing Leitner next to Emery and laughing like they were old friends started a fire inside me, and it grew into an inferno when his focus turned my direction. He gave me a once-over, dismissed me as inconsequential, and returned his attention to her.

Money was power, and if I were my father, I'd use this opportunity to let Leitner know exactly how powerful I was. But I preferred the indirect approach. He wouldn't know me as an adversary if I came at him as a friend.

My tone was warm and pleasant as I strolled toward him. "I've always wanted to meet you," I lied. "Looks like my girlfriend beat me to it." I offered my hand and a disarming smile. "Vance Hale."

The Austrian took it, and his grip was as strong as I expected it to be. "Hale? Like the bank?"

"Yes, like that." I slipped an arm around Emery and was pleased at how she responded. There was no hesitation. She leaned into me and acted like this was natural for us. Her sleepy voice from earlier rang through my head.

It can be real if you want it to be.

Part of me did, but a larger part of me warned that I should be cautious. She'd manipulated the alarm system to get close to me, and then told me in no uncertain terms that she was willing to do whatever needed to be done. I'd gotten the suspicion more than once she wasn't telling me everything. Or that she had an agenda I hadn't been clued in on yet.

But her friendship with Jillian? That seemed real. Her grief and guilt couldn't be fabricated because no one was *that* good of an actor . . . or maybe my lust for her was blinding me. I didn't know what to believe.

Petra materialized from the back. "Niko!" She hurried over to him with a huge smile on her face, grabbed his hands, and dropped a friendly kiss on his cheek. "I thought I wasn't seeing you until tomorrow."

He looked sheepish, but only for a split second. "I came early. Monaco is a special race and I've always loved this track."

If that were true, he had to be one of the only drivers who felt that way. Since the race was run on the winding, twisting streets of Monte Carlo, the cars never got up to full speed, and there were rarely any opportunities to overtake. Janssen told me it wasn't Formula One; it was rush hour traffic.

Petra dropped one of his hands but used the other to pull him toward the back. "Well, then, since you're here, I'll have Phineas pull some ideas together for you."

Because this was my appointment that he'd interrupted. I disliked how he'd put Petra in this awkward position, but she'd handled it well.

"Nice meeting you, Vance," he threw at me over his shoulder. I nodded, glad he was going, but my relief was short-lived. He abruptly pulled to a stop, and his gaze settled on Emery. "You didn't tell me your name."

Her eyebrow lifted along with the corners of her mouth, but I wouldn't exactly call it a smile. She said it with a teasing lilt, but she may have been serious. "Maybe I like it better if you don't know."

Leitner's shoulders straightened as surprise washed through him. He was used to getting whatever he wanted, and her refusal had set him back. But as expected from a professional driver, he adjusted and recovered at lightning speed. He flashed a sinister smile and looked at her like she was a race he wanted to win.

Unease tightened my chest. I'd never been possessive before, but this girl was giving me all kinds of firsts. Emery was my girlfriend, and I didn't want another man looking at her as a conquest.

She was only mine under a fake label, but I was going to have to change that.

After dinner, it was finally late enough for us to have a shot at sleeping through the night, and Emery disappeared into the bathroom to get ready for bed. I sat on the velvet couch in the main room and scrolled through work emails on my phone to keep my mind off the woman next door, or how the couch wasn't big enough for me.

"I'm finished," she said.

I turned to catch a glimpse of her before she crawled into the bed. Her t-shirt was baggy and long, and her shorts weren't, and for a split second I thought she was only wearing the shirt. Her long, bare legs were enticing, and lust flared inside me, hot and urgent. I wanted those legs wrapped around my hips and my hands up under her shirt.

Stop it.

I focused on accomplishing my goal of walking past her without looking as I made my way to the bathroom. I brushed my teeth at the sink that had become mine, since her stuff surrounded the other one. She'd left her overnight bag open, and I could see the silver wheel of pills inside, several days' worth punched out and consumed.

My gaze snapped back to my reflection in the mirror.

I didn't need to know she was on birth control. I'd made the conscious decision not to pack any condoms as a last-ditch effort to stop myself if the opportunity presented itself. I'd never been great at self-control, and she was so fucking tempting—even when she wasn't trying to be.

I was halfway through the bedroom when she spoke, her word breaking the tension in the air and causing me to halt. "Vance."

It was a strange reversal of our meeting, but not equal. When she'd come into my bedroom, I'd been naked except for a sheet, and she'd been fully clothed. Now she was in bed, and I was the one intruding, except I felt just as vulnerable as I did then. Her gaze slipped down over my bare chest and provocatively traced the waistband of my underwear peeking out above my drawstring pants.

I stared at her with breath held in my lungs. She'd washed the makeup from her face, and her hair spilled around her shoulders in soft waves. She looked so small and all alone in that big bed.

She tried to sound casual, but her voice was tight as she gestured to the vacant side. "There's more than enough room for you." When I didn't move, she tilted her head and gave a shy smile. "Don't sleep out there. We've already slept together on this bed."

After the kiss we'd had, sharing a bed would be playing with fire. But it'd be another first for me. The only time I spent a night beside someone else was when I was too tired from fucking to get out of bed.

I liked the idea of being near her, the challenge of resisting what I wanted to do, and not having to spend the night on the couch. "You don't mind?"

She shook her head. "Besides, what would the housekeeper think if she sees the sheets on the couch?"

"She'd probably think we had a fight."

Emery grinned. "So, let's not fight. Come to bed, darling."

I matched her smile. "Well, if you insist."

Emery was gone from the bed when I woke. It was barely six in the morning, but she must not have been able to sleep any longer. I heard the shower running and pictured her beneath the rainfall showerhead. The water sluiced over her bare skin, making her glisten.

As it was a habit in the morning, I pushed a hand beneath my underwear and gripped my cock. It was normal to have a semi, but today I was rock fucking hard, and pleasure zinged up my spine as I squeezed.

I imagined Emery filling her hands with the hotel's rosemary scented soap in the shower and lathering up her breasts. The tiny bubbles she created as she rubbed her tits would slide down over her glossy skin, following the curve of her body to run directly between her legs. The foaming soap would cling to her there, obscuring my view of her perfect slit.

I stroked my fist over myself and closed my eyes. What would she do if I walked in on her right now? Would her sexy mouth fall open in shock and her eyes fill with disapproval? Or would she smile and curl a finger at me, beckoning me to join her?

I jerked my hand faster, finding a rhythm that was quick enough to feel good but not enough to make me come. I thought about all the things I'd do to her. How I'd pin her against the tile and use a hand to explore the same path as the soap bubbles. The way she'd moan as I slipped two fingers inside. How I'd give her a kiss that rivaled the one we'd had yesterday.

My dick jerked at the thought.

How was it that of all my fantasies, kissing her was somehow the hottest?

I hooked my thumbs under the waistband of my briefs and jerked them down, freeing my throbbing dick and giving me more room to work with. I palmed my balls with one hand and jerked off with the other, making the sheet covering me bounce and tent.

My fantasy turned a new direction. How would Emery react if she walked in on me? Would she cross her arms, lean against the doorframe, and gaze at me critically, or would she watch with interest? I imagined peeling back the sheet so she could get a better look. She'd see my tight fist working up and down my hard length and watch the hurried rise and fall of my chest as I struggled to catch my breath.

A groan tried to escape, but I clenched my teeth to hold it in. I pictured her climbing on the bed, seductively crawling over the sheets on all fours to get to me. She ringed her fingers around the base of my cock as the ends of her hair brushed over my thighs.

"It's not allowed," I'd warn.

"Shh," she'd scold back. Her warm breath rolled over my skin as she lowered in, parted her lips, and slid her mouth around me.

"*Fuck*," I uttered both in my head and aloud in the quiet room.

She'd mumble for forgiveness with a mouth full of dick as she made it all the way down. But the heat of her hot, wet mouth sucking on me burned away everything else. No need for an apology. The image made me sweat and my knees weak.

I pumped my hand harder. God, I'd fuck her mouth until I was right at the edge and covered in her saliva, and then I'd roll her onto her back to return the favor. I'd get her good and ready to take all of me. Would she beg me to break my vow?

Or would I beg her to let me?

If I didn't stop, I was going to come, and I slowed with the uncertainty of what to do. Was I serious about letting her catch me jerking off? I wasn't shy, and I'd already told her I did it, but this had the potential to backfire spectacularly. If Emery didn't like what she saw, how would she be comfortable with me? Forget sharing a bed the rest of the week.

If I was going to come, I needed to do it now. I wasn't sure how long she'd been in the shower, so it could end at any minute. I focused my listening to see if I could hear her messing with the bottles and guess how much time I had left—

A soft cry echoed off the tile, just loud enough to be heard.

It didn't sound like she'd been startled or was in pain—this breathy gasp was something *else*. Something that sounded a hell of a lot like pleasure.

Was she getting herself off right now, while I was out here doing the same thing?

"Goddamnit," I groaned. I gave up holding back and stroked furiously. It made a jolt of pleasure burst through me, and as I came, I cupped my fist around the head of my dick to catch the mess I was creating. Each spurt into my hand was followed by a shudder of bliss, which slowed to a tingling stop.

I had both hands clamped between my legs as I lay still and stared up at the vagina-covered ceiling, waiting for my body to finish cooling. I knew I needed to get out of bed, find some tissues, and clean up, but I was lethargic and distracted by a single thought.

Had Emery been thinking about me?

She stayed in the shower longer than it took me to recover, and when she finally emerged from the dressing room, she acted like nothing had happened. She didn't blush or let her gaze dart away from me in embarrassment, so either she didn't think I'd heard her, or she didn't care.

There was no mistaking what I'd heard, though. I'd spent years cultivating my skills and was very familiar with what a woman sounded like when she came.

We took breakfast on the terrace, and then she was escorted to the hotel spa. I had to remote into a meeting at work and then review draft language for a disclosure statement, so I told her to take the day and get whatever she wanted. The only thing on the schedule was a cocktail party this evening hosted by Team Mercedes.

I didn't see her again until late afternoon. She came into the suite wearing one of the outfits Petra had styled. Her hair had been blown out, her nails were painted a shimmering ivory, and her makeup was flawless. This picture-perfect version of her was one my father would begrudgingly approve.

She was undeniably beautiful.

But I preferred the girl who'd appeared in my bedroom with the smoky eye makeup and a provocative dress even more than this carefully packaged one who sat in the chair across from me. She waited quietly for me to finish with work and scrolled on her phone.

I caught her sneaking a glance at me more than once, and my smile was unstoppable.

"Did you have a nice time at the spa?" I asked.

Her lips skewed to the side for a single beat, but then she brightened. "Yes, thank you."

It seemed like time moved twice as fast whenever we left the hotel. We couldn't talk much during the ride on the tender over to where the party was being held because the small boat moved fast and the wind was loud. Once we boarded the impressive yacht where the cocktails were flowing, it was all business. As the face of one of the team's premiere sponsors, I was a VIP, and Emery and I had to float from one conversation to the next so everyone could express their gratitude.

It cost hundreds of millions of dollars to race a single season in Formula One, and HBHC sponsorship helped offset a significant chunk of that. We posed for pictures with the drivers, with the team principal, and other members from the team.

Emery took it all in stride. Could this woman roll with whatever life threw at her? If she disliked working the room, I couldn't tell. She seemed to be at ease at my side, and her smile was dazzling.

"Thanks for coming with me," I said over the engine roar on the boat ride back to our hotel's dock. I'd given her my jacket to keep her warm as we skipped along the waves and were occasionally misted with salty seawater. It was late, and the moon was just a sliver, but there was enough light to see her. She swiped a wayward lock of hair out of her eyes and grinned up at me like I was being silly.

Like she was thrilled I'd brought her along.

We were both eager to get to bed when we got back to the suite, and while I brushed my teeth at the sink, my gaze found her through the bathroom mirror. I watched her swipe a towelette over her eyes, gently removing her makeup, and after this, we'd change and climb into bed together. It was so fucking domestic.

And yet, it didn't freak me out. Why was that?

Maybe it's her.

I'd jokingly warned her not to fall in love, but anxiety found a home inside me. There was no way we could spend a week together pretending to be in love, yet stay impervious to the magic of this place. Monaco was romantic foreplay.

It was tortuous sleeping beside her and staying over on my side of the bed, and it didn't get easier as the days went on. I began to bargain with myself, thinking I could strengthen my self-control if I practiced at it. Start off by facing smaller temptations and work up my way up to the bigger ones.

On Tuesday, we took a tour of the pit lane and garages, and when I grabbed her hand, she laced our fingers together. We each got a chance to fit ourselves in the driver's seat of a Formula One car, and practice changing a tire like the crew did. I forwarded the pictures I took to Sophia, who had someone edit and post them to my Instagram account. I hadn't managed my social media in years and was glad her team was on it.

I grabbed the door handle to the back seat of the Mercedes that would take us to our next event and held it open for

Emery, but when she went to climb inside, I moved to block her. My kiss was sudden and in public, causing her to jolt with surprise, but then her hands were there, cupping my face. She answered my short kiss with a longer one of her own, and it made my heart beat faster.

We had dinner with the director of operations from the French branch of HBHC that evening. A gourmet feast prepared by a three-star Michelin chef and paired with spectacular wine, but the director had been more taken with Emery than with his meal. She charmed and flattered him in a way that seemed authentic. Was this something her charismatic father had taught her? Or was she a natural?

Wednesday morning, she slept in, and it took a considerable effort from me to leave the bed. When I sat up, she rolled over in her sleep, stretching and arching her back to get comfortable. It made her breasts jut out to me and her shirt ride up, revealing a band of bare skin across her toned stomach.

It'd been thirty-three days since I'd made the bet, but it might as well have been thirty-three hundred. My hands itched to touch her. To trail my fingertips over that newly exposed skin and see what kind of reaction I'd get out of her. The craving for her was constant, incessant, and it grew more acute every minute spent in this bed.

So, I stayed and looked, but did not touch for a long while.

The touching came later when I was alone in the shower. It'd taken surprisingly few pumps of my hand to push me over the edge, and I came in a furious rush without making a sound. I knew how good the acoustics were in this shower, didn't I?

The sun was low in the sky when we arrived at the beach and were escorted to our poolside seats for the fashion show. The catwalk for the show was a raised white platform that cut a line across the circular swimming pool of the Plaza Hotel. At one end was the media section, jammed full of photographers. At the other end was the large white backdrop with sponsorship logos laced to the metal frame. Behind it stretched the ocean.

The seats were arranged around the circular pool, and while we waited for the show to start, I pointed out various celebrities in attendance.

"His Royal Highness of Monaco," I said, gesturing to the older gentleman beside the stage.

She smiled and shook her head. "An actual prince. Kind of adds to the fairytale feeling this week is giving me."

If I had any uncertainty about what she meant, she cleared it up by sliding her hand into mine. It was strange how it had such a powerful effect. We'd spent so much time together this week, and yet I woke up each morning eager for more.

I'd had a sexual relationship with Jillian, followed by a friendship, but there'd been no spark. Not even a fraction of what I had with Emery. Maybe Jillian had been right, and sex was sabotaging my relationships. Or maybe I'd just been doing it backward and needed to build a friendship first before jumping into bed.

The fashion show began shortly after, and my smile froze when the first model took the stage.

Emery leaned in to whisper to me. "Is that . . .?"

"Leitner, yeah." I scrutinized the Austrian man who grinned as he strutted down the catwalk in a designer suit. "I forgot that some of the drivers and ladies of F1 walk in the show."

Which meant he'd be at the afterparty.

Unease wrapped itself around me as I remembered the way Leitner had looked at Emery. Normally, I didn't compare myself to other men. There was no need. I was good looking, charming, and filthy rich. My powerful family name opened any door I wanted, and when I flashed my smile, women fucking melted. I'd never met a man who I thought was worthy of challenging me.

But Niko Leitner? Shit, he might be.

I'd been threatened plenty of times in my life before Lambert. There'd been a few sailing races I'd lost over the years, and arguments I'd been bested at while in law school. But I'd never felt jeopardy when it came to a woman. Not with Alice, because she'd made it clear I was just a substitute for my father, and not with Jillian, because neither of us had our hearts invested.

I didn't want to compete with this man. Sure, I had more money than he did, and it was debatable who between us was more attractive, but he lived a sexier lifestyle. Plus, he had one huge advantage on me.

I'd bet my fucking life Leitner wasn't celibate. If anything, he was probably drowning in pussy.

It wasn't all that warm outside, and as the sun began to set, Emery shivered in the cool breeze—but I began to sweat. I heard my father's voice in my head angrily reminding me I was a Hale, and any woman should be thrilled to have me.

But . . . what if I didn't want any woman except the one sitting beside me?

NINE

EMERY

THE FASHION SHOW AFTERPARTY WAS HELD IN A SWANKY LOUNGE, and the cost to reserve a table near the dancefloor was thirty thousand euros a night. I shouldn't have been surprised Vance had booked one. It was for charity and a tax-write off for HBHC, he'd said.

Some of Vance's friends were here tonight. Becca Rosso was an heiress to the Rosso Media fortune, and it sounded like they'd hung out at so many of these events over the years, she was family to him. She brought along with her the lead singer and drummer from the band Joven that had performed at the conclusion of the runway show.

The lounge was bathed in amber light with accents of purple and blue, and wasn't like any of the clubs I was used to back home in the States. The 'tables' were more like booths. Sexy white couches and matching oversized chairs were arranged in cubes around the low, black tables. Several bottles of champagne, vodka, and mixers were chilling as the centerpieces.

I didn't know how Vance was going to top this night, but I'd thought that every day since we'd arrived. As the sun had set, we'd watched the elegant parade of dresses and suits on beautiful people, and now we hung out with movie stars, musicians, and royalty like we were all old friends. None of it felt real.

Well, except for fluttering feeling in my stomach when Vance touched me.

That felt *incredibly* real.

I didn't want this week to end, didn't want to go back to my sad apartment decorated with practice locks and tools, and the reality of what was left to be done. I'd been so focused on what I wanted I'd stopped seeing the forest for the trees, and I was beginning to question if a life dedicated to revenge was worth it. Lambert had robbed me of both my parents. Did I want to let my thirst for revenge rob me of living my life too?

There was another reason I didn't want this week to end, and it was sitting beside me with a flute of champagne in one hand and the other resting comfortably on my knee. Sleeping next to him each night was torturous, and there was nothing I could do to alleviate the ache. I couldn't make the first move, even though I usually had no problem doing so and desperately wanted to. He had to do it because I'd promised not to tempt him.

I was nervous our relationship would evaporate once we were free from the spell of Monaco. So, I shifted closer to him, inhaling the scent of his sexy cologne, and decided to enjoy his company while I still could.

We danced on the dancefloor to the music the celebrity DJ performed, and I was happy to have the excuse to put my hands on Vance. Our table became a revolving door of conversations with the famous and successful. And I drank more champagne than I intended to.

I grabbed my clutch and had to put my lips right by his

ear so he'd hear me over the thumping beats of the music. "I'll be back in a minute."

He nodded and straightened so I could duck past him toward the restroom.

When I finished washing my hands at the sink, I dabbed on some fresh powder and touched up my lipstick, confirming I still looked like I belonged at the table with him. I'd expected to have nothing in common with the one-percenters. They were supposed to be snobs, and while some of them were, I'd been pleasantly surprised by Vance. He was polite and grateful with everyone, regardless of status.

Outside of the restroom, my gaze snagged on the sophisticated gaming chair perched in front of a steering wheel and a wraparound screen. The colorful image danced on screen like it was racing. It was probably the buzz from the champagne, but I walked toward the simulator, interested. The signage around it encouraged people to get in the driver's seat and test their skills on Monaco's demanding track.

No one was waiting to use it, and since the simulator was tucked in a quieter corner of the chamber outside the main lounge, I figured, why not? I dropped my handbag on the side table next to it and put my hand on the back of the seat to steady myself as I climbed in.

"May I offer some advice?"

The unfamiliar male voice made me startle, and I whirled around to face it.

Niko Leitner wore a dark gray suit with no tie, and the top few buttons of his white shirt were undone. Was this one of the suits he'd modeled earlier this evening? It was hard to tell. His gaze wandered over my short, turquois A-line dress, and once he'd finished getting his fill, the corner of his mouth turned up in a suggestive smile.

"Go slow through the Lowes hairpin turn," he said, gesturing to the machine.

I feigned confusion. "I'm sorry, who are you?"

The moment it was out, I regretted it. I'd meant for my joke to irritate him, but—shit—it must have sounded like flirting because his smile widened.

"I'm the man who still doesn't know your name."

I gave him a pointed look. "Do you need to?"

"It'd make it easier for me." His posture was relaxed and his eyes friendly, and maybe for some other woman, this approach would work. But I wasn't interested.

I shifted on my heels, subtly leaning away from him. "How's that?"

"I need to know what name to give to security when I take you and your boyfriend on a private tour of the racing paddock." He set a hand on the back of the seat. It had the appearance of a casual gesture, but it boxed me in between him and the simulator. "Unless," his voice dropped low, "he is too busy to join us?"

Oh, wow.

He had no fear of crashing his car, and no problem hitting on unavailable women. Maybe to him, they didn't exist. All women were available—even the girlfriend of a competitor's sponsor. That was probably the part of me he found most attractive.

I set a hand on my hip. "Thanks for the offer, but we've already toured the paddock."

He tilted his head. My statement caught him off guard, and I saw the moment he determined I must not have understood what he was implying. He'd have to try again.

"Drinks and a tour of the yacht I'm staying on, then. Should we say tomorrow evening after the VIP meet and greet?"

"We're not going to that. HBHC is rolling out a new product, so we'll be at the launch party." Vance had to give a speech and everything.

Niko moved, subtly bringing his body closer, and his voice dripped with seduction. "That doesn't sound very exciting for you. Don't you think you'll have more fun with me?"

I delivered it as plainly as possible. "No."

He looked like I imagined he would if the brakes on his car suddenly stopped working. "No?" His face abruptly changed, and he let out a soft laugh. "Ah, you Americans with your dry humor."

This dude seriously wasn't getting it, meaning it was time to switch tactics.

I smeared a fake smile across my lips, placed both my hands on his shoulders, and leaned in. I had to rise onto my toes to whisper it to him.

"You know what?" I purred. "Maybe I do recognize you. Didn't you win the Constructors' Championship last year?"

I trailed my left hand down his arm. As expected, the muscles beneath my palms hardened. I pulled back just enough to see the pride heat his eyes.

"Yes, I did."

I dragged my other hand down the front of his chest, tracing the line of buttons. "Hmm. I do love a winner," I said. "Tell me. How are you doing this year?"

His reaction was the same as if I'd dumped cold water on him. "It's early in the season. The problem is the car, not me."

Leitner had only finished on the podium once this year and was way behind on the points. I stared up at him with a patronizing expression. "You sure about that? Because most of the stuff I read said you got lucky last year."

His expression soured, and he stepped back, breaking

our contact. "That's bullshit. Who held off Ferrari and got the car across the line on blistered tires last year at Monza? Me. Not Janssen, or my race engineers, or the technical team. *Me.*"

I turned and bent, swiping my clutch up off the side table, and pressed it into his chest. A smile stretched on my lips, but my tone was full of condescension. "If you say so, Leitner."

"Emery?"

My heart thudded and tripped over itself. I'd been so wrapped up in what I'd been doing, I hadn't noticed Vance's approach. I swiveled my head and found him staring at me. My breath caught at how betrayal teemed in his eyes.

I could only imagine what I looked like. I had my purse flat against Niko Leitner's chest, pinned beneath my hand, a smile on my face, and we were standing much too close. It looked intimate between us, but that wasn't the case. I'd only needed to control Niko's focus—

Vance's tone was cold, indifferent. "I was beginning to wonder if something happened to you."

I went ramrod straight, retracting from Niko. "No, sorry. I was on my way back and got . . ." *Ambushed?* "Sidetracked."

Niko grabbed the sides of his suit coat and adjusted how it sat across his shoulders, giving him an excuse to puff up his chest. "I was offering her some advice for the simulator."

There were knives disguised beneath my smile, and I hoped Vance could hear them when I spoke. "Then Niko invited me for drinks on his yacht."

As a driver, he had excellent reflexes and he demonstrated them now. There was barely a moment of concern in his expression. "I invited both of you."

"Right. Unless, as you said, Vance was too busy to join us."

His face didn't change, but the sudden rise of his shoulders gave away that Niko was nervous. He turned his head to the side, looking for an exit and conveniently avoiding looking at the other man.

Vance's posture had stiffened, and the wolf lurking beneath his surface began to emerge. He stared at Niko like he'd destroy him . . . and he would relish every minute while he did it. He put an arm around my waist and pulled me up against him. It was surprising and possessive, sending sparks radiating down my legs.

He issued the words in a voice as strong as steel. "I'm never *too busy* for Emery."

I swallowed hard. Shit, he sounded so believable.

And I wanted it to be true.

"Yes. Well," Niko said, "it sounds like our schedules won't work, so maybe another time. I need to get back to my table." He motioned to the simulator and set his gaze on me. "Good luck with your race . . . *Emery*."

I held my smile with clenched teeth as he walked away. He continued to swagger like his dick was huge—although I'd put good money on it being average at best.

Vance's mood was unreadable, and I fiddled with the purse in my hands.

"Let's get some air," he said finally.

There was a stone side patio attached to the lounge, and I followed him as he marched toward the glass door. When he reached it, he pulled it open and held a hand out, gesturing I go through first.

Such a gentleman. What the hell was he doing with me?

I stepped outside and instantly shivered in the night breeze. One side of the patio overlooked the ocean, and waves rumbled against the rocky beach below. No one else was out here, but music and laughter from a nearby yacht drifted up toward us.

Otherwise, it was quiet, and Vance seemed to be deep in thought as we strolled toward the edge of the patio. I hadn't seen this version of him before. His confidence had flagged considerably. "If Leitner asks you for drinks again, will you say yes?"

Was he kidding? I laughed. "Um, no."

"Why not?"

"Because, unless you forgot, I have a boyfriend. Did you have a little too much to drink tonight?" I teased.

"Maybe." He didn't smile. He was so serious, it was sobering, and he said it like he was delivering bad news. "I . . . like you."

I paused, unsure of what was happening. "Oh." His simple statement made my heart race. I said it softly, like I was shy to put it out there, even when it was the truth and he'd already taken the leap. "I like you, too."

He pressed his lips together as he turned to face me and gripped my shoulders. His strong hand on my bare skin made warmth surge through me. Why did he look so distraught? "I made a vow. You didn't." He grimaced. "I doubt Leitner did either."

I blinked, and then I parted my lips to tell him he was being silly, but his hands moved, sliding gently up and down my arms to help keep me warm. The action disabled my brain.

"I'm asking you to wait," he said.

Oh, man, I couldn't help myself. "You're asking me to . . . *not* sleep with Niko Leitner?" I widened my eyes, pretending this was an impossible task. "What about other people, though? Can I sleep with them?"

"No," he growled, unamused.

Fire flashed over his face at the idea, and I wasn't cold anymore. The goosebumps dotting my skin were entirely his doing. His gaze drifted down to my mouth, studying the way I drew in sips of air.

"You told me this could be real," he said, "if I wanted it to be." His gaze slid back up to mine, and I nearly drowned in how deep his eyes became. "I've decided I want that."

And like he'd probably been trained his whole life to do, he took without permission. His mouth dropped down to seal over mine and claim me as his, regardless of if I wanted it or not.

But, *oh*, how I wanted it.

His kiss was blistering. It seared me from the inside out, and within seconds I was melting into him, greedy for more. How in the world did he do that? Just the meeting of our mouths and his tongue slicking over mine pumped steam through my body. It twisted around me in ropes of desire, binding me like a maiden to the bow of a ship.

"Fifty-seven days," he murmured between kisses. "Will you wait that long for me?"

There was no other answer. "Yes," I breathed.

His mouth traced a line down the curve of my neck, drawing a shiver. "I should warn you though. I don't have the best willpower."

"I don't either," I admitted. Had my shiver made him want to hold me steady? His hands settled on my waist while his lips continued to tease against the side of my throat. God, it felt so good. "Maybe we could work on it together."

He chuckled wickedly. "All right."

Outwardly, nothing between us had changed, but excited energy bounced inside me. Like with Jillian, what had started out as a lie was now becoming real. He'd said the next person he dated would be his choice, who he wanted . . . and that person was me.

My tone was sly as I drew back enough to look at him but stayed in his embrace. "Should we start tomorrow?" I pressed my hand on his chest, covering his rapidly beating heart. "Or right now?"

He didn't understand what I meant but followed my focus down to my hand and then to the chunky silver watch I wore. It was much too big for my wrist and rested halfway up my forearm. His blue eyes sharpened on the heavy face of the watch, and then his gaze snapped up to mine.

"Is that Leitner's watch?"

I shrugged. "He was so busy hitting on me, he must have dropped it."

Vance blinked, and the sinister smile that crawled across his face was so hot, it stole my breath. He was utterly thrilled. "How'd you do it?"

I chuckled, sliding the watch off my wrist. It was so large, I didn't have to undo the latch on the leather band. "It's all about directing the person's focus."

"Show me."

I shook my head. "It's cold out here, and you've probably got a table full of people waiting on you. Plus, I need to get this back to Niko."

"Let me handle that." He snatched the watch out of my hand and put it in the side pocket of his jacket. Then his tone thickened, sounding lush. "Show me what you're good at, Emery," he brushed a lock of hair back out of my eyes so he could study me better, "and I'll do the same."

In the moonlight, his cheeks were more pronounced. He reminded me of the sexy, mysterious man in movies who always turned out to be the bad guy.

"Deal?" he asked.

A voice reminded me that Hales didn't make deals unless

they were benefiting from them, but I was too enamored with him to care.

"Deal."

TEN

EMERY

Vance stood opposite me in the sitting room still wearing the clothes he'd been in all evening. He looked relaxed and comfortable—like he preferred to hang out in his blue suit rather than wear anything else tonight.

It was good. Not only did it make demonstrating easier, but he looked so incredibly handsome like that. Powerful and successful. I took a step closer, invading his space, causing him to evaluate me with suspicion.

"As I come closer," I said, "your awareness of me goes up. But that's okay because I have control over where you're—"

Abruptly, I stumbled forward, my hands flying out to brace myself on his chest and stop me from falling into him. I glared down at the rug I'd just tripped over, and my face heated.

"Sorry," I whispered, my tone full of embarrassment.

I stared up at him with wide eyes, seeing the concern there, but I was fine. When I slid my hands up around his shoulders, his went down to my hips to hold on to me. It allowed us both a moment to catch our breath and adjust to our new proximity. I could smell his enticing cologne and feel the wall of toned muscle hidden beneath his shirt. If I wanted to, it'd be easy to kiss him.

But I reluctantly straightened to extract myself from his hold.

This meant I could close my hand over the top of his watch and slide my pinky finger under the band at the clasp. It was easy to flick it open.

"Anyway," I said, "now that my hand is on you, you might be wondering how I'm going to take your watch off without you noticing. What you don't realize is I've already stolen your wallet."

He froze. "What?"

"Check your inside pocket. Is it still there?"

He looked down at his suit jacket, using one hand to pull it open and the other to reach inside the interior pocket, causing him to pull free from my grasp. And as his wrist left, the watch stayed in my hold.

"How?" He stared in disbelief at his empty pocket.

He was so distracted he didn't notice my hands moving to hide my score in the folds of my dress. When his accusatory gaze snapped to mine, I smiled and let it sit for a single beat before I held up his wallet and gave it a victorious shake.

Vance took it from me, slipped it back in his pocket, and his eyes narrowed in suspicion.

I went in for the kill. "Oh." I feigned innocence. "Would you like your watch back too?"

Vance's focus flew down to his wrist to make sure his expensive timepiece was still there, and was both horrified and amazed to discover it wasn't. He couldn't believe I'd taken two items off him without him knowing—

And how I'd done it so quickly.

"It might be the nicest one I've ever lifted," I added,

holding up the watch to examine it. It had a modern, industrial look to it. Inside the square-shaped face, gunmetal gray Roman numerals and the Cartier logo rested over the exposed cogs inside. The band was a rich black alligator leather.

He glared down at his wrist, mad at it for failing to alert him it was now bare. "Seriously," he demanded, "fucking *how*?"

I passed the elegant watch back to him. "Put this back on and I'll show you."

He took it and kept his gaze fixed on me as he slowly re-did the clasp, watching me like he was sure I'd steal something else if he so much as blinked. It was silly, though.

When his focus was on my face? That was when he was the most vulnerable.

"Ready?" I asked, resetting to stand a few feet away.

He nodded.

"I start with a plausible reason to touch you." I strode toward him. "Let's say I trip on this rug." I repeated the same 'trip and fall' from before, landing suddenly in his arms and with my palms on his chest. The first time, he'd stared at me with worry, but this time his eyes were clouded with suspicion.

Which was warranted.

"I just grabbed your wallet during your scramble to catch me," I announced. "You can't tell it's not in your pocket because my hands are inside your jacket, hiding it. You still feel it where it should be because I'm holding it there right now."

He considered my statement critically, and then accepted it. Interest flared in his eyes as he took hold of my hips like he had last time.

I spoke in a sultry voice. "Because you're such a gentleman, your concern is on me. You're looking at my face, checking to make sure I'm all right. You don't notice the wallet in my hand as I slide it up." My eyes hooded while my hands went up onto his shoulders and I leaned in, bringing our lips closer. "You're probably thinking about kissing me right now—not how I'm passing your wallet from my dominant hand to my other behind your back."

He exhaled, and I got the feeling that for the briefest of moments he'd rather just kiss me than learn how I carried out the rest of my ploy. But then his haziness cleared, and he refocused.

"Sneaky." It was hushed, perhaps not wanting to interrupt my flow.

"Now, the watch." I grabbed his wrist like last time, covering the face of his watch with my palm, leaving my fingers free to manipulate the clasp. "My pinky goes into the loop and undoes it."

I moved slower than I normally would, but kept my gaze locked on his. I didn't need to see what I was doing. I'd practiced this maneuver thousands of times, in a dozen different ways with my father. He'd shown me how to block the mark's view. How to draw their attention back to where you wanted if it began to slip. Ways to use the environment to my advantage.

"I keep my middle finger and thumb pressed against the band," I said. "This holds the watch in place, so you don't feel a weight change or realize it's been unclasped. When I'm ready, I pull your attention somewhere else."

"You tell me my wallet is gone," he said.

A smile teased the corners of my mouth. "Which makes you look down, open your jacket, and check for it." When he performed the same movements as before, I continued the demonstration. "This makes you pull away, which is key. You believe you're in control, which lowers your awareness and lets you do the work for me. I stop holding the band on your wrist and the watch stays in my hand as you leave."

"Shit," he said, impressed.

"And now I'm done. I pocket the stuff while you're distracted and searching for your missing wallet." I brought the black leather billfold down behind his back where he couldn't see, and let my hands hang at my sides, concealing the items in the fabric of my dress. "Well," I added, "I would if this dress had pockets."

My act complete, I lifted my hands and presented the stolen items to him. He acted like he was going to take them out of my hands, but instead he simply held on to them, his fingers overlapping mine.

"You're right. You're very good. That was," he searched for the right word, "impressive."

The way he stared at me . . . I felt it all over my body. A throb began deep between my legs and made my voice tight. "Thank you."

He finally broke the tension between us, pocketed his wallet, and worked to put his watch back on. "How'd you do it with Leitner?"

"A variation of this. He was thinking about my hand moving on his chest, not the one working his watch."

The muscle running along his jaw flexed. He didn't love hearing about how I'd touched the other man. It was shocking how I liked his possessiveness. He didn't own me. *Right?*

"Does it help if I tell you I got him to back away and give me his watch because I insulted him?"

He tilted his head, considering. "Kind of."

"What are you going to do with it?" I nodded toward Vance's side pocket because he was still carrying Niko's watch in there.

"I'll make sure it gets back to him." His smile was cryptic and a little evil, like he was delivering a threat. It was seriously hot. Once he was done fastening his watch band, he tugged at his shirt cuffs beneath the sleeves of his jacket, adjusting the fit. When he set his penetrative gaze on me, it said he was just at ease in the courtroom and boardroom as he was in the bedroom.

His stare was so hungry and sexual, my mouth went dry.

"You showed me what you're good at. Now it's my turn." It came from him crisp and deliberate. "Take off your dress."

Every muscle in me clenched. "What?"

God, the way I was trapped in his gaze—a spotlight I couldn't hide from, not that I wanted to. He lifted an eyebrow in challenge, and although it was a simple action, it rang loudly through my body. He raised his chin and peered down at me like a captain at the helm of a ship and I was one of his crew.

"Got your attention, didn't I?" he asked. "But no matter how much control you give me over that, I don't think I'm getting your clothes off without you noticing."

No, he was so very right. However, my brain was still hung up on his request. "You want me to—"

"Get naked? Yeah." He pushed back the sides of his suit jacket so he could put his hands on his hips. It was the posture of a man who didn't like to be kept waiting. "I've only been fantasizing about it all fucking week."

"You have?"

It became clear to him I was too surprised to move, so he took over. His hands swept around me and traced up my back, searching for the zipper pull of my dress. It put his face beside mine, so he softened his voice and laced the words into my ear. "Every morning when you're in the shower. You make me so goddamn hard, I can't help myself."

I sucked in a breath as his meaning doused me with lava. I matched his soft, seductive tone. "Do you know why I take such long showers?"

His fingertips must have found the small metal tab because he began to drop the zipper, tooth-by-painstaking-tooth. Electricity swirled around us, charging the air.

It was like he somehow knew the answer. His smile was sinful. "Is it because you're getting yourself off?"

I nodded, too foggy with lust to find words. I only saw a flash of his pleased expression before he angled his head and brushed his damp lips over the pulse point in my neck.

"Do you put your hand between your legs?" He was hypnotic, mimicking the steady pace of the zipper as it marched down. "Do you slide your fingers inside your pussy and fuck yourself with them?" His erotic question burned and threatened to consume me. He was all around me and inside my head with his wicked voice. "Do you put your hand over your mouth to stay quiet, so I won't hear you when you make yourself come?"

"Yes," I gasped.

He'd reached the bottom of the zipper at the small of my back and peeled the two sides of my dress over my shoulders. Like I'd done with his watch, he didn't need to see what he was doing when he undressed a woman.

He'd had plenty of practice.

Down the front of my dress went, all the way to my waist. I wasn't wearing a bra, which I was sure he could see in his peripheral vision, but his gaze didn't waver from mine. The phrase *'not yet'* lurked in his gorgeous eyes.

I was a present he wasn't finished unwrapping, and he wasn't going to look until he could appreciate this gift in full.

My breath came and went in shallow, clipped bursts. I wanted his hands on my body so badly, I worried I'd shake apart, but somehow I managed to keep it together. At least, I did long enough for him to give the dress bunched at my hips a final push and send it sailing down my legs.

"I was thinking about you when I did it," I whispered.

He rubbed a hand over his mouth, but it did nothing to muffle his satisfied word. "Fuck."

My dress was pooled around my feet, leaving me clad only in a pair of black panties with a band of lace stretching low across my hipbones. His gaze slowly moved southward, down over the slope of my bare breasts. It wasn't warm in the room, and that, coupled with way he looked at me, made my nipples harden into points.

His steam-filled gaze languished, sinking lower over my nearly nude form until it found the delta of my legs. He liked what he saw so much, I wondered if I had exceeded his expectations.

This time his curse dripped with appreciation. "*Fuck.*"

It was getting harder to stand without excited trembling. Air to draw into my lungs suddenly seemed sparse and impossible to find. Was I going to die if he didn't touch me? It felt like it.

"I don't know if I can do this," he said abruptly, his shoulders snapping back.

It felt like I'd missed a step going down a flight of stairs. "What?"

His expression was pained. "This could be torture."

Yes, but... couldn't he see it already was for me? I grabbed his hand and lifted, setting his warm palm on the center of my chest. "It's all right. You've got this."

Shit. I'd meant it as a joke, but my voice had faltered, and I'd placed his hand over my heart, like I was telling him he had *me*. I didn't want him to read too much into it, or think I was already willing to—

Vance surged forward, crashing his lips into mine. Had the contact of our bodies given him courage to try . . . or had it broken his restraint? Either way, I didn't care right now. His tongue was in my mouth and his palm moved to cup my breast, squeezing the globe of flesh like he needed to learn the weight of it.

I sighed into his urgent kiss and reveled in the way he banded an arm around my back to hold me in place. I'd put my hands inside his suit twice already tonight, but this time I had no motive other than to touch and explore.

He was . . . ravenous.

Shocks of pleasure spiderwebbed up my arms and back when he shifted, tearing his lips away, and bent to capture my nipple in his mouth. My hands balled into fists, and my eyes slammed shut under the power of him.

While I didn't have overly sensitive breasts, I typically enjoyed it when my partner gave them some attention. It was possible I liked both the idea and the visual of what they were doing more than the physical sensation.

But this?

This was *different*. When Vance sucked and licked, swirling the tip of his tongue over my nipple, a bolt of white-hot pleasure coursed through me. I shivered and arched my back, jutting my chest out. And I threaded my fingers through his hair, needing to hold on as his mouth worked me over, roaming from one breast to the other.

He lavished attention on me with his tongue and his teeth and his fingers, making me go boneless and filling my head with steam. I wanted to melt to the floor with him, but instead he straightened and gave me an evaluating look. His hair was disheveled from my fingers and his eyes were wild, and dear God, did I want this wolf to devour me.

He must have had the same thought because instantly he charged forward, forcing me back to prevent myself from being run over by him. The backs of my legs hit the edge of the couch at the same time his hand clasped my shoulder and urged me down.

My heart was racing, and yet it couldn't keep up with him. I'd barely hit the seat cushion before he fell to his knees between my parted legs with a loud thud. His fucking eyes. They stared at me with such intensity, it made me quiver.

And it was stunning how quickly he jerked down one side of his jacket, then the other, and hurled it to the floor. So determined to do what he wanted, he'd flung it away like he was angry it had slowed him down. He moved like he was out of time, or out of his mind . . .

Or possibly both.

It punched a gasp from my lungs when he seized my waist, yanked me right to the edge of the couch, and put a hand on my knee to shove my leg up. It was so he could drape it over the low armrest at our side, further opening my legs to him. He was a gentleman, but he wasn't gentle, and I sank my teeth into my bottom lip to hold in my surprised and delighted laugh.

Which was good because it would have died in my throat anyway. Vance hooked two fingers into the side of my panties, jerked them out of his way, and swooped down to press his mouth to the most intimate part of me. It was the exact spot where he'd created a throbbing ache.

"Oh, fuck," I groaned, turning my head to the side and arching my back at the sudden and acute pleasure.

His warm lips parted to allow his tongue to come out and play. The sensation of it brushing over my clit—*holy shit*. Sparks skittered across my skin. His seductive kiss was aggressive, and it was almost violent the way he fucked me with his mouth. All the urgency he'd had leading up to this moment was still there. It didn't diminish—in fact it seemed to intensify.

I heaved air in and out and clawed at the cushions beneath me. Vance's forearms were under my legs, and he had both hands curled around my thighs, my underwear still pulled out of his way by his fingers. He knelt on the floor in front of me, completely dressed in his expensive clothes, and there was something incredibly appealing about it. Like what he was doing was solely about my pleasure.

Not his.

I'd never had a partner who'd focused singularly on me. One who didn't value their enjoyment over mine. I would have thought Vance would be a selfish lover because he hadn't had to work for anything in his life, but . . . maybe I was wrong.

As the tip of Vance's tongue ran up and down through my bare slit, he peered at me with a hooded, desire-filled gaze. Was it possible he was enjoying this nearly as much as I was? He seemed to be.

Wait, no. That couldn't be true, because it physically felt so fucking *amazing*, and his pleasure was by proxy. How could it compare to mine?

I moved my hips, either encouraging him or simply because I couldn't control myself. I writhed beneath his incessant mouth, and he pulled desperate moans from my lips. It felt like we'd moved too fast but also frustratingly too slow.

Every second since we'd met . . . that had been foreplay.

Now, I was eager for him to make good on his promise.

My legs shook. Sweat dampened the hair at the back of my neck. Blood roared in my ears, and my heart pounded as he increased the pressure of his tongue's strokes. His lips closed over my clit and sucked gently. Tension corded my muscles as I felt the pull toward an orgasm.

But he drew away and sat back on his legs, which took his incredible mouth away from me, and I sighed at the loss. He also let go of my panties, making the damp lace snap back into place and cover me.

It was momentary, thankfully. His warm, strong hands smoothed over my legs, caressing my sensitized skin as his fingers inched up to the waistband of my underwear.

His voice was thick with wickedness. "I don't think you need these anymore. Do you?"

I swallowed hard and shook my head furiously, making him chuckle at my response. He trailed his fingertips along the edge of the lace before grasping it with both hands and began tugging. It urged me to raise my legs and put my knees together, making it easier for him to draw the panties up and off.

They fell silently to the floor as he cast them aside. He slid his hands between my knees, peeled them apart, and stared down at my nakedness. Blood heated my cheeks. He'd already seen me, but now I was completely nude. I didn't mind how the lights were on, and I wasn't shy about my body, but the carnal expression painting his face was so powerful, I flushed in response.

"Look at this pretty pussy." He said it like he was talking to himself. "All wet and *bare* for me. So fucking sexy." He dragged the pad of his thumb over my swollen clit, and I jolted from his touch. The pleasure he created was gripping and sharp. His gaze flicked to mine, and a smug smile teased his lips. "Looks like my money was well spent at the spa."

"Oh, my God."

When he'd sent me to the spa, he'd told me to get whatever services I wanted, so I had. The first ever Brazilian wax I'd had would likely be my last one too. I imagined the luxury spa had top-notch staff and technique, but it certainly hadn't been pain-free as advertised, plus I'd had to have all my lady bits on display to a complete stranger.

Today was the first day my skin wasn't hot or tender from the wax. I liked the results but wasn't sure it was worth the effort. Vance, on the other hand, looked thrilled. He swiped his thumb over me again, enjoying his unhindered view and how I flinched from the sensation.

"Did you get it done just to tease me?" he asked. "Because when I saw the charge on the invoice, I almost made you show me the results."

I'd thought it was a little poetic at the time, how he'd pay for it and not get to see the results, but I was kidding myself. I'd hoped for this moment. "I've never been waxed before. Do you like it?"

Oh, his grin was delicious. "I do." He pretended to examine it thoroughly. "The quality of work seems to be excellent."

He turned his palm up to the ceiling and ran the backs of his two middle fingers over the smooth skin at the cleft between my legs. Back and forth he sawed them, up to my clit and down to my entrance, over and over again. It felt so impossibly good.

"Do you like it?" he asked.

Desire was building inside me, making it difficult to focus. "Yeah. I like how it feels," I panted, "especially when you're touching me."

He took in a deep breath, and satisfaction flooded his face. "Like this?" He rocked his fingers once more over the nub of flesh that sent electric bliss surging through me. "Or do you like *this* better?"

On his downward stroke, he pushed his middle fingers

inside me.

"Oh, fuck," I cried.

My toes tightened into points at his intrusion. The stretch around him wasn't uncomfortable, but it was a lot, and I threw a hand up behind my head in a futile attempt to grab a handful of couch cushion. His other hand had been resting on my knee, but it skated up the curve of my body, not stopping until he had hold of one of my breasts.

A loud, deep moan tore from the back of my throat when he pulsed his fingers inside me. I watched his hand thrust and his fingers grow slick, and I had to shut my eyes because it was so goddamn hot, I worried it would burn my retinas and cause permanent damage.

But even in the darkness, Vance was there. His palm massaged my breast and pinched my nipple. His thick fingers stroked and drove into me, hitting the perfect spot to push me over the edge.

"I want to fuck you so bad," he whispered, "you have no idea."

But I did. *God, how I did.*

He continued to pump his fingers, and I imagined that was the same tempo he'd fuck me at. He kept his steady pace. "Do you want me to?"

My brain was overwhelmed with lust, so it was impossible to tell if he was serious or not, but there was no other answer. "Yes."

"You want me to slide my cock right here, Emery? You want me to fuck you on this couch and come all over this perfect pussy of yours?"

"*Yes.*" It was a whine. A plea.

His taunting tone was so sinful, it was almost cruel. "But what about my vow?"

Fuck your vow, I wanted to say. I hadn't made one.

Except . . . I had. I'd told him we could work on resisting temptation together. I struggled to sound strong. "Just because I want it doesn't mean it's going to happen." I peered at him over my rapidly moving chest to deliver my warning. "Don't tease me, and I won't tease you."

He considered my statement thoughtfully and must have taken it to heart because he gave an acknowledging nod, leaned down, and resumed using his tongue on me. He painted bliss with every flutter, making me gasp and contract with jolts of pleasure.

I was a quivering mess as I watched him work. His pink tongue caressed and massaged in lush strokes. The relentless thrust of his fingers had enough force it caused the couch to creak beneath me, and waves of goosebumps to dot my skin.

He'd turned the tables on me in the sense he was the master safecracker now. He tried different techniques, investigating the right combination to crack me open, and it didn't take him long to find it.

"Shit," I whispered. "Oh, my God."

He'd lined up all the notches, and my cry was the same as the click of the fence dropping into place, signifying he'd done it. I pictured Vance at the front of a safe giving the wheel its final turn to draw the lock bolt back, pulling open the door to let my pleasure storm through.

Ecstasy thundered through my body. It crackled like heat across my skin and left a delicious tingling sensation behind. And as I came, Vance watched me with victory burning in his eyes, noting every wave of satisfaction he'd caused.

All the quick orgasms I'd given myself this week while I was alone in the shower had just been a temporary fix. A way to placate the worst of my craving and lust for him. The sexual tension between us had remained, building toward this release, and now that it was here it poured from me in a loud, pleasure-filled moan.

I lay back on the couch, drained and blissed out, and everything was fuzzy as he rose onto his knees to plant a surprisingly gentle kiss on my lips.

"You're right," I murmured. "You're good. That was," I swallowed a breath, "impressive."

His soft laugh gave me an aftershock of pleasure. "Thank you."

Our kiss was slow and deep, like he wanted to give me plenty of time to recover. His hands slid around me and pulled me to sit upright so he could fit me around him. It was nice being in his arms. My body began to cool, but his was still hot, and I could feel the effect my orgasm had caused in him.

His considerable erection pressed between my legs.

But he didn't move. He didn't reach down to undo his slacks and try to alleviate the ache he was surely feeling. He didn't rub his body against my naked one or make room so I could fit my hand between us and touch him. Was this all the temptation he could handle for one night?

When the kiss ended, he pulled back and let his fingertip trail down the hollow of my spine, causing me to shiver. What was that look in his eyes? It deepened until it was darkly sexual, like a wolf who'd finished eating his kill but discovered he was not yet satisfied.

"Do you think I'm done?" His eyebrow lifted at the same time as the corner of his mouth. "Because, Emery, we are just getting started."

ELEVEN

VANCE

For the second time since arriving in Monaco, I slept next to Emery with my clothes on.

She was still naked, but disappointingly hidden under the covers. Her brown hair was splashed across her pillow, and as she slept, my gaze drifted over her pretty face. She hadn't taken her makeup off last night, so her dark eyeshadow was messy and left a faint smudge on the white pillowcase beneath her head.

One could argue that was my fault. After I'd gone down on her on the couch, I'd guided her into our bedroom and showed her a second time how much I enjoyed using my mouth and fingers to make her come. Thinking about the way she'd squirmed and twisted the bedsheets in her hands while my head was nestled between her thighs would have made me hard—if I wasn't already.

Jesus, I needed relief.

After her second orgasm, she'd put her hand on my fly, tried to get in my pants, and I'd nearly given in. I wouldn't survive if she had really touched me. Instead, I pulled her hand away and laced our fingers together, distracting her with a mind-numbing kiss.

She'd asked it when I'd brushed the shell of her ear with my lips. "You don't want me to—?"

"Not tonight," I admitted.

Because I didn't want to break my vow, or beg for sex, but also—it seemed easier to resist losing control when all my focus was set on her. If we were going to spend the next fifty-six days *not* having sex, it was probably best to pace ourselves with the other stuff.

So, I'd collapsed on the bed beside her and drifted off to sleep with a painful hard-on, trying not to think about how the vagina-themed wallpaper was mocking me or that a gorgeous woman was just out of reach. Now it was morning, and Emery looked so sweet and peaceful as she slept, I squashed my selfish thought of disturbing her to take a peek beneath the covers.

The hardwood floor was cold under my feet as I got out of bed and padded into the dressing area. As we got closer to the race on Sunday, our schedule would be more hectic, and I needed to stay focused. There was the new app HBHC was rolling out for Europe, and although I wasn't in sales or promotion, my last name dictated I attend the launch and say some nice words about the team who'd developed it.

As I stripped out of my wrinkled clothes, my mind wandered to the girl I'd left in the room next door. *My girlfriend.* The first real one I'd ever had. Last night at the lounge, I'd come looking for her, and when I discovered her with Leitner, something like panic short-circuited my brain.

Royce and I had grown up under our father's oppressive rule. He'd told us everything we had came from him, and my brother and I had learned not to get attached to anything. Macalister Hale owned everything, and it could be taken away from you at his whim.

Yes, he'd changed since his time away, but my paranoia had lain dormant for years, and it came back with a ferocious roar when I spied Emery's hands on Leitner. She'd smiled at him in a way I wanted her to save for me. Fuck, I couldn't lose her . . . especially when I hadn't even had her yet.

It was too soon and too fast to be in a relationship, but all the calculation I'd learned from being a Hale apparently evaporated around her. I didn't know if I could trust her, plus I had the terrible suspicion she wasn't telling me everything.

You aren't either, an irritated voice reminded me.

Because I hadn't told Emery about Lambert's threat. In my defense, I hadn't told anyone, nor had I done anything to address it. Like a lot of things I didn't want to deal with, I set it aside to be handled later.

I jerked off in the shower while thinking about all the things I planned to do to her. My vow meant I'd have to get creative, but I didn't hate the idea. As she'd said, there were plenty of different ways to have sex, and I was intrigued to find all of them.

I came in a hot rush, one hand bracing myself on the tiled wall of the shower, and the other clamped tightly around my dick. It'd been difficult to strangle back my groan, but I'd been mostly successful, and then drew in a deep breath to even myself out. It was fucking unreal how fast I'd gotten off.

I finished my shower, banded a towel around my waist, and took a few steps toward my sink when the door swung open, and Emery appeared. She hadn't knocked, but that was probably my doing. I'd purposefully left the bathroom door open an inviting few inches.

She wore one of the hotel's white bathrobes, and it teased me mercilessly because she barely had it cinched around her waist. The deep V of exposed skin down the front of her displayed an amazing amount of cleavage.

Her gaze started at my bare chest, still dotted with water droplets, and moved down over my abs before ending where the terrycloth began. Disappointment pinched her eyebrows together, and warmth swelled inside me. She wasn't happy about missing her opportunity to see me in the shower.

"I was coming to see if you wanted company," she said.

I smiled and jammed a hand in my damp hair, shaking out the water. It gave her a nice view of my bicep tone, which I used every opportunity to flaunt. I worked out with a trainer three times a week, and my hard work had paid off. I looked damn good.

"Not today," I said with regret. "We've got a lot on our schedule."

Which was true, and it was good I'd finished myself off so quickly. If she'd joined me in the shower, we'd be in there a while, and that was guaranteed to make us late to our first event. I stalked toward her, grabbed the knot at the belt around her robe, and pulled her up against me.

"Maybe some other time," I uttered before lowering my mouth to hers.

I always enjoyed coming to the Monaco Grand Prix, but Emery made it a million times better. We ate a long lunch at a rooftop restaurant which overlooked one of the race turns while practice commenced below. We watched the cars slide around the corner, navigating the tight turn of the street that was boxed in by the barriers, and listened to the high-pitched whine of their engines ricochet off the surrounding buildings.

Janssen said it was like driving in a cage, and I could understand why. Tall chain-link fencing rose above the barrier wall to ensure no debris flew off the track and damaged the buildings lining the streets. I'd seen video from inside the car during the race, and it was terrifying.

I'd been to this race enough times, I knew what to expect, so getting to witness it through Emery's eyes was both satisfying and entertaining. She was more impressed with the living flower arrangement on our table than the sophisticated engineering on display as the Mercedes car sped across the pavement so fast, it looked like it was gliding.

"I returned Leitner's watch this morning," I told her after one of the cars zoomed past. "Well, I had someone from concierge handle it."

"Oh." She blinked, and her gaze drifted off. Was that a frown?

I chuckled. It *was* a frown because she was disappointed. "Don't worry. I had them return it with a friendly note."

I'd grabbed a pen and the hotel stationary from the desk, scribbled out a message, and slipped it in the envelope before turning the watch and the letter over to the customer relations manager. Asking him to deliver it to Niko Leitner was no easy task, but he assured me it would be done. If nothing else, he could get it to someone from Red Bull's team and they'd take it from there.

"What'd you say?" she asked.

"That he should be more careful because he'd dropped his watch while he was talking to you. He might have thought it had been stolen, but *I* would never try to take something he cares about."

She picked up her glass of wine, considered my statement, and a pleased smile warmed her lips. "Do you think he'll get the subtext?"

"I do."

After practice concluded, we went back to our room and changed for the launch party, and I was irritated when Royce called to check in. I had limited time alone with Emery, and my brother's call used nearly all of it. By the time it was over, she was already dressed, and I had to rush to catch up.

As much as she tried to hide it, I could tell Emery was unfamiliar and uncomfortable with the lifestyle I had. When it came to buying things, my only concern was the quality, never the price, and that always surprised her when I bought something.

I knew she was enjoying this week because she'd told me so, but during the ride home from the launch party she made the comment she expected the Mercedes to turn into a pumpkin at any moment.

Like Cinderella, because none of this felt real to her. I hoped that wasn't true. What we had felt real to me.

After my 'great work, team' speech, we'd spent the evening being far more affectionate in public than my father would have tolerated if he were here. Thankfully, he wasn't.

That night, after we climbed into bed, rather than fool around, she wanted to talk. She asked about my time in college and law school. If I'd passed my bar exam on the first try, which I had. We talked about sailing and how she'd become a safe technician apprentice right after high school.

There were topics that neither of us wanted to touch. We didn't discuss Jillian or Wayne Lambert, or talk about our parents. It was like she wanted the conversation to be happy and simple, and I was pleased—it was exactly how I wanted it, too. Plus, we couldn't do anything about the Lambert situation right now, anyway.

As it got later and we were both tired, it seemed to have lowered her inhibitions enough to talk about it.

"So, about last night . . ."

"Yeah?" I asked.

She pressed her lips together, like she wasn't sure where she was going with it. "You didn't come."

"You noticed that, huh?"

She wasn't distracted by my attempt at a joke. "Why not?"

"Because if you'd touched me, I would have given up right then on my vow and asked if we could do more." I gave her a sheepish look. "I might have begged." I mashed the pillow under my head, and my tone turned serious. "I was thinking, if I'm going to have a shot at getting across the finish line, maybe it'd be better if we, like, pace ourselves."

"Meaning, what? You don't want me to touch you?"

"Just for a little while," I said quickly. "I'm sure I'll regret it immediately. You're so hot, I kind of need to build up a tolerance to you."

She laughed and peered at me as if she thought I was kidding, but perhaps she recognized the sincerity in my expression, because she sobered. There was a gravity to her words. "Okay. We can do that."

Friday was the final day of practice for the drivers, and as VIPs, we got to spend it with the team in pit row. We sat on folding chairs with the rest of the crew, watching the monitors and listening to the radio as the two Mercedes drivers negotiated the turns and evaluated their cars.

Tomorrow was qualifying, and it was the most important one of the season. Since overtaking was nearly impossible at this grand prix, the only way to move up was if a competitor made a mistake, so starting position on the grid was everything.

When practice was over, we went to the yacht show, followed by a cocktail reception with the drivers. Leitner was there, but he steered clear of both Emery and me. The watch was back on his wrist, so our message had been received.

That night when we returned to our hotel room, she let me help her out of her dress, but then admitted she'd had a lot to drink—way more than she had intended. So rather than spending the evening exploring her body, I pulled a bottle of water from the beverage station, scooped ice into a glass, and told her to drink the whole thing.

"Two years ago, I spent race day hungover, and let me tell you—it fucking sucked."

"I'm sorry," she said feebly. "I didn't realize how much I'd had until it was too late."

I gave her an easy smile. "Don't worry about it. The alcohol is always flowing at these things." Usually because it made the money flow. Donors were more willing to write checks, or sponsors considered extending contracts. "Do you need anything else?"

She shook her head, fighting her embarrassment, but it was unnecessary. She wasn't used to the weeklong, nonstop cocktail parties that was typical for Monaco. If anything, I was impressed she'd made it this long without issue, and I told her so.

Emery drank the rest of her water and got settled while I

finished getting ready for bed, and when I came back into the room, the only light came from my bedside lamp. It cast a soft glow, and I felt strangely warm as she watched me round the bed and walk to the side that had become mine.

She wasn't gazing at me with desire, but some other kind of look I struggled to understand. Was it longing? I got under the covers and turned off the lamp, plunging the room into darkness, and a terrifying and thrilling idea descended on me.

I'd warned her not to, but Emery seemed like the type of woman who did as she pleased. Was she . . . starting to fall for me?

Emotions clashed inside my head. Part of me was excited at the possibility, but another part was cautious. I wasn't the most trusting guy and did not want another transactional relationship. I'd be a fool not to consider all scenarios. What if I was only seeing what she wanted me to?

When we'd talked last night, she'd steered the conversation away from her past even better than I'd done to her. She had a reason, though, didn't she? She'd been arrested and had a record, and it was clear she was ashamed of it. She'd offered that information honestly.

What was my excuse?

I froze when the bed shifted. Every night we'd stayed on our own sides, but now Emery ventured out across the mattress, closing the space between us. Her soft hand grasped mine and dragged it up, making room for her beneath my arm. I swallowed hard as she hesitantly tucked herself in, laying her head on my bicep and a hand on my bare chest.

Her breathing was hurried and uneven. She'd done this not knowing how I'd react and was nervous she'd overstepped. She whispered it like I might somehow be asleep already and didn't want to wake me. "Is this okay?"

With her hand on my chest, could she feel how quickly my heart was beating? I didn't mind if a girl wanted to cuddle after sex, but I'd never done it before, or in place of it. I wasn't used to connecting this way, and before tonight, I would have said 'no, thanks' to it.

But... I liked it so much, I tightened my arm subtly, pulling her even closer.

"Yeah." I said it more for myself than for her. "It's okay."

I had my hand on my dick and was mid-stroke in the shower when the bathroom door creaked open. Everything slowed to a stop as the hazy figure appeared in the doorway. I couldn't make her out exactly because I hadn't put my contacts in yet, but also because the shower door was fogged. I swiped a hand on the glass to clear away the steam, and found her standing only a few feet away, wearing the same bathrobe as she'd been the other morning.

She stared at me with an even mixture of determination and trepidation. Like last night, she wasn't sure if this was a risk she should take—but she was going to try anyway. She unbelted the robe, pushed it off her shoulders, and let it drop in a heap to the floor.

Fuck me. How was it she looked even better than the last time I'd seen her naked?

Her stare was intense, and mine back at her was probably the same, and we engaged in a wordless conversation.

She could have asked if I wanted her to join me earlier because she'd been awake when I gotten out of bed ten minutes ago. We'd had a quick conversation where she'd said she was good and didn't feel hungover, so I'd kissed her before leaving to grab my shower. Maybe she'd needed the extra time to work up the courage because she was silently asking me if I wanted company now.

I straightened and pushed open the door.

It gave her the first look at me completely naked, and even though my less than perfect eyesight meant I couldn't make out every detail of her expression, I saw the path of her gaze as it worked down my body. She liked what she saw, and her throat bobbed with a swallow as she reached my favorite part. The longer she stared at me without moving, the hotter I became.

But she'd asked to join me, and she couldn't do that if she remained in the center of the room. My voice was tight with something that felt a hell of a lot like need. "Did my amazing dick distract you? Get in here."

My statement jolted Emery into action, and she came forward, stepping into the well of the shower and pulling the door closed behind her.

The space was big, with jets and a handheld nozzle in addition to the square rainfall showerhead that loomed over us. The tile was various shades of tans and ivories and some with an iridescent sheen, and Emery studied it like she'd never seen it before, even though she'd taken a shower every day since we'd arrived.

I didn't like this unsure version of her. Her confidence was sexy, and I wanted to remind her of that. I walked through the falling rain until I was on the other side, letting the water continued to stream down the curves and notches of my body.

"Did you come in here to give me a show?" I asked.

Her gaze snapped to me, and heat pooled in her eyes. Ah,

there she was.

And she was so fucking gorgeous, I couldn't help myself. I closed my hand around the tip of my cock and pushed the head of it through my tight fist.

Her voice was throaty and filled with more steam than the shower. "No, I came to watch the show, Vance."

I squeezed against the pulse of satisfaction her words gave me. "I don't see why we can't do both."

Her chest rose as she drew in an enormous breath, but her tone was strong and provocative. "You want to watch me touch myself?"

I was an attorney, which meant I liked specific and clear communication. "I want you to show me how you played with your pussy when you were thinking about me."

She licked her lips and pressed them together, giving me the suspicion she'd done it to quiet whatever surprised, excited sound she wanted to make.

I pumped my fist down the length of me, causing my wet skin to shift and slide through my fingers. "I'm already showing you how hard you make me. What I have to do whenever I think about all the things I want to do to you."

When she backed away, my heart stopped, but then it lurched forward as I realized what she was doing. Emery put one foot behind her and then another until she was leaning back against the glistening tiles. Her gaze was pinned to me as she raised a knee and placed her toes on the edge of the bench running along the adjacent wall.

It opened her up so I could see everything, and she didn't hesitate to slide a hand down over her toned stomach, all the way until her fingertips covered her clit. I halted mid-stroke once more, not wanting anything to distract me from witnessing this erotic sight.

Her eyelids went heavy as her fingers began to stir, rubbing a small circle, but her gaze didn't waver from me. It was like she was entranced. Her focus bounced between my face and my hand that grasped my dick, and then she was wordlessly demanding I hold up my end of the deal.

I'd promised her a show, after all.

It always felt good when I jerked off, but this? It was *way* better. I loved how her lips parted as I began to fuck my fist and watched her slowly mouth the word *fuck* as I glided my hand over my erection. Her breasts undulated with her hurried breaths, making her tight, dark nipples rise and fall.

"I want your tits in my mouth," I said. It wasn't against the rules, and I'd done it before, but I'd had my clothes on then. I'd asked her not to touch me and for us to pace ourselves. It seemed incredibly risky to touch her, not to mention . . . I wouldn't be able to keep watching.

Her fingers moved faster, and she sagged against the wall under the weight of her pleasure. "And I want your dick in my mouth."

"Shit," I groaned. "I want that too. So. Fucking. Much."

"Yeah?" She was breathless. "Tell me what you'd do to me if you could."

Perhaps to encourage, she used her free hand to cup one of her breasts, and my mouth watered. Her sexy taunting was torturous fun, and two could play that game.

My smile was sinister. "I'd give you the best fuck of your life. The kind of sex that once you have it, you don't want to live without it." She raised an unimpressed eyebrow, but I wasn't finished. "You want to know how I'd do it? For me to give you the play-by-play in exact detail?"

She tried to look disinterested but failed miserably, so I didn't wait for her answer.

"I'd come over there and put my hand between your thighs. I won't move it or rub your pussy. I'll just leave it there, so that when I suck on your nipples, you'll squirm against the side of my hand. You'll rock and grind and try to get me to touch your needy little clit—but I won't. Because I'm enjoying how you're fucking my hand too much."

She blinked rapidly against the onslaught of my words. Were her legs already shaking?

"And then," my voice grew thicker with lust, "when you can't stand it anymore, I'll slide a finger inside you."

Her hand came down off the breast to join her other fingers already pressed between her legs. It was so she could push one of her index fingers deep inside, all the way to the last knuckle. "Like this?"

Heat shot across my skin, tightening the muscles in my legs, and I groaned. "Fuck, yeah. Just like that."

She pumped the finger in and out at a sluggish pace, and with her other hand, she spun slow circles on her clit. It probably wasn't going to get her off, but it teased and primed her. I was doing the same myself. Long, deliberate strokes with a pleasurable amount of tension in my fingers.

Her question nearly got lost amongst the sound of the shower. "And then what?"

My gaze drilled down between her parted thighs, watching intently. "When you're all wet and starting to moan, then I'll use two fingers."

It was unreal how much I loved it when she closed her eyes, tilted her head back, and unleashed a throaty moan. She buried a second finger inside her pussy, and I sent a loud sound of satisfaction ricocheting off the tile walls. Watching her was fire, but getting to direct her? That turned me into a scorching inferno.

"I'll take you as close to the edge as I can get you," I said, "and since I'm guessing you can come standing up, I'll get on my knees, and I won't finish licking your sweet pussy until you're coming on my face."

She gasped and her eyes burst open, reeling around until she found me. I couldn't tell if it was the vulgarity of my statement or the pleasure flowing through her that had her so shocked.

"You can do all of that now," she whispered.

She was so eager to have me carry it out, her comment was more like a demand, but it was one I couldn't meet. I'd want to escalate, and I worried I wouldn't be satisfied until I had all of her. It left me with no choice but to pretend I hadn't heard her.

"After you come and while your legs are still trembling, I'll spin you around and push you up against the wall. I want you so goddamn bad, I'm not even nice about it. But you don't mind, Emery. You like how my fingers dig into your hip. You like the way I put my hand on the back of your neck and keep your cheek pressed to the tile." My voice was dark, filling up every inch of space surrounding us. "Don't you?"

"Yes," she said between two labored breaths.

Her focus drifted down to watch me, like maybe she was too turned on to maintain eye contact. Her hands moved faster, matching the quicker tempo of my own. It was sweltering, and I wouldn't have been surprised if water sizzled on our skin if either of us stepped under the showerhead.

"I'll tease you by sliding my dick over your pussy, back and forth." I repeated the phrase at a measured pace, wanting to paint the image in her mind. "Back . . . and *forth*. Fuck, it feels so good, doesn't it?"

I didn't make it clear if I was talking about the fantasy

or what we were doing right now, but she nodded vigorously. "God, yes."

"You beg me to put it in you, and when I do," I paused for effect, "when I slide all of *this* dick inside you, you'll have to hold back a scream."

As I watched her, the image seared into my memory forever. She was slumped back against the wall, leaning on it for support, with one of her feet perched precariously on the edge of the seat. She'd never stood under the water, so she was dry for the most part, but the mist of the shower had dampened her skin, giving her a dewy look. Her eyes studied me, and her lips were parted so she could swallow large gulps of air as her hands worked in tantum to bring her pleasure.

It was hard to stay focused because she looked so amazing, and I was using both hands on myself now, so it was feeling really, *really* good. Need throbbed through me, pounding for release.

"I fuck you so hard," I said, "it sounds like our bodies are slapping together. You have to put your hands on the wall to hold your position because you don't want to change the angle. You love it. Where you can feel every goddamn inch of me thrusting into you."

Emery whimpered like what she was doing to herself felt so good, it might be *too* good.

My vision began to tunnel, and I knew I couldn't hold off much longer. "I can tell you're getting close because your tight pussy is clenching on me. So, I reach around and put my fingers on your clit. I rub, and rub . . . and *rub* until you—"

A huge gasp punched from her lungs, signaling there was no need to continue talking. I could focus completely on how the orgasm rang through her body. The way it made her shoulders flinch and her bent knee turn inward to squeeze against the ecstasy. How her eyes slammed shut and her chin tucked down into her chest, her face twisting with pleasure. The way her hands stopped moving but she left them between her legs, cupping herself.

It was the hottest fucking thing I'd ever seen.

And it pulled the trigger on my own climax. Pinpricks of fire traveled up the backs of my legs and surged forward. I heaved my fist over my dick at a furious pace, focusing more on the head so I could maintain the speed I needed.

None of this had been planned, and I didn't have time to ask permission as I stumbled forward, throwing my free hand up on the wall beside her head so I could lean on my extended arm. Instinct took over. It didn't make sense to me to do it anywhere else. I wanted to share this intimacy with her and mark her as mine, even if it was temporary.

Her orgasm was beginning to subside, and when I loomed over her, she reached up to curl a hand around the back of my neck. It was so she could lock our gazes together. She wanted me focused on her as it happened.

Please. There wasn't a chance in hell I'd think about anything other than her.

I came with a groan that was so deep, it vibrated in my chest before escaping from my throat. Wave after wave of pleasure burst out, making me paint ropes of my cum across her stomach. She didn't drop her gaze, so I could see how her gorgeous eyes melted in response.

Emery didn't just approve of what I'd done—she'd liked it.

My fist slowed, squeezing the last few drops from my sensitive tip, causing me to shudder a final time. I sucked in a slow breath and blinked the post-orgasm fog from my eyes. It allowed me to think clearly and realize . . . If it was going to be like this with her every time we were together?

It wouldn't be a challenge to make it the remaining fifty-four days.

And I'd say she'd get to be my prize at the end, but the kind of sex we'd just had was deeply satisfying. Not to mention, anticipation could heighten your desire and make it even better when you finally got what you wanted. I was sure the same was true of her.

"That was so fucking hot." My gaze skated across the curves of her magnificent body to watch the result of my orgasm drip down her legs. "And you look so good like that, Emery. Naked and covered in my cum. Do you like it?"

She didn't answer, and my gaze flew back to hers in alarm. But there was nothing to worry about because she pulled my face down to hers, pressed her urgent lips to mine in a blistering kiss, and we stumbled together under the beads of falling water from the shower.

TWELVE

VANCE

The most exciting part of the Grand Prix weekend happened late in the afternoon during qualifying. One of the McLaren drivers overheated his brakes and went careening into the barrier, leaving the track littered with carbon fiber, a wheel, and most of his front wing. He'd been okay, but there was no way his team could repair the damage in time to make the starting grid on Sunday.

Janssen secured the pole position, and Leitner qualified all the way down in fourteenth.

"What a disappointing day for the defending champion," one of the broadcasters commented over the speaker playing nearby. "Team Red Bull can't be pleased with that result."

I flashed a smug smile to Emery, who mirrored it right back.

Qualifying took up most of the day, and we finished it off with a late dinner. Our time together in Monte Carlo would be ending soon, and the closer we got to our flight home, the faster time seemed to move.

On our walk to the hospitality suite above the finish line

where we'd watch the race, I realized I only had one morning left where I'd wake up beside her, and the thought caused me to scowl. I liked the noises she made when she stretched, and how she stole the covers from me, only to claim she was too hot when she woke.

She'd flung the covers off this morning, which was a total invitation if I ever saw one, so I'd put my hand down her sleep shorts and made her come so quickly, I wondered if I'd have time to pull a second orgasm out of her using my mouth. Instead, she'd gotten up, tugged me toward the shower, losing her clothes along the way, and asked what I'd do to her if I could.

I'd told her I'd make her get on her knees so I could fuck her mouth, and while I was describing how I imagined it, she dropped to the tile floor in front of me. The visual of it was so perfect, it'd only taken a few rough pumps of my hand before I came on her tits. After, she'd let me help wash it off.

It was packed on the side streets with fans heading to their viewing spots. Some were wearing clothing in support of their favorite driver or team, but most were dressed more like Emery and I were. Upscale and refined, while staying on top of the trends. Petra had done an outstanding job making my girlfriend look great.

The harbor was lined with yachts, and people milled about onboard, enjoying the perfect prerace weather.

We were escorted by the hospitality staff up to the covered balcony where we'd spend the day, and while we waited for the test laps to begin, I snapped a picture of Emery. She stood at the edge of the balcony, one hand on the railing, and her VIP lanyard flapping gently in the breeze. Our host offered to take one of us together, so I fit myself in beside Emery and wrapped an arm around her waist.

It been so long since I'd held a genuine smile on my face, but this one came easily.

I took my phone back and evaluated the picture, only to discover the guy had taken several. He'd caught one where we were both mid-laugh and she was looking up at me. It made my heart go out of rhythm. Not just from the enamored way she seemed to gaze up at me, but at how natural and real we looked together.

Like a couple utterly smitten with each other.

I forced the thought from my head and forwarded the pictures on to my social media team, letting them choose which image to post and write whatever caption they thought was appropriate.

Some years, the Monaco Grand Prix was full of action, or crashes, or a come-from-behind victory, but this year's concluded without much drama. Driver error and car trouble for some of his competitors helped Leitner finish in eighth place, which allowed him to score some points—but he was nowhere near a podium finish. The checkered flag went to Janssen, who'd executed a nearly flawless run, and I was thrilled for him and the entire Mercedes team.

We stayed in the balcony to watch the award ceremony and the three drivers douse each other with champagne, before beginning our walk back to the hotel. We were nearly there when she talked me into visiting the casino. We gambled and chatted with other race fans from all over the world, and I didn't mind how unlucky we were at roulette, because I was having too much fun with her.

I leaned in close and lowered my voice so no one else would hear. "How long do you think it'd take you to break into the vault here?"

She laughed like my question was hilarious. "Right now?

It'd be impossible."

"Not *Ocean's Eleven* style. I mean, like if they asked you to do it."

"Still impossible. I don't have my tools and I don't know anything about what kind of vault it is." She picked up the remaining stack of chips we had. "When's your birthday?"

"January eighteenth."

She placed the chips on the red eighteen. "It's not like what you see in movies. What I do is technical, like surgery. I'm trying to manipulate the open without damaging the safe, so the customer can continue using it after I've finished the job."

She was contemplative for a moment, watching the people around us also place their bets.

"Plus, I need to know everything I possibly can about the model I'll be working on, so I know which attack to start with. Some of them, it's easier to drill into the back panel. That way I can bypass the lock and countermeasures completely, and once I'm through, I'll use a rod to punch open the quick-release."

"Is that what you did with Lambert's?"

She shook her head. "I can't get to the back of it because he had it installed in the floor. The only option was to go in through the front. I had to drill a three-millimeter hole above the glass panel and use a borescope to see the wheel pack. After that, it was easy. All I had to do was rotate the dial, line up the notches, and watch the fence fall into place."

"You drilled a hole in his safe? Don't you think he might notice?"

"Three millimeters is tiny, and easy to cover. I bet the paint was dry by the time Jillian left the room."

The dealer spun the roulette wheel, and all eyes focused in on the white ball as it circled the outer rim, running opposite of the spinning wheel. Its circuit slowed, and it dropped down onto the game board, bouncing a few spots before finally settling in.

"Red sixteen," the dealer announced, repeating it in French.

A couple at the other side of the table cheered.

Emery faked disgust as she glared at me. "Ugh, you're so unlucky."

"I don't know, I feel pretty lucky." I gave her an exaggerated, sappy smile. "I met you, didn't I?"

She laughed. "You know luck had *nothing* to do with it, Vance."

Emery and I hadn't seen each other since we'd landed in Boston six days ago. We said goodbye in the airport hangar, I watched her ride away in the Rolls I'd had Elliot book for her, and I went home to sleep like the dead for the next twelve hours.

We'd spent our final night in Monaco at the Grand Prix Gala, which was another charity function and gave the ultra-wealthy and famous an excuse to wear black-tie. I'd put on a tuxedo, and Emery had worn an ocean blue dress with lace on the top and a flowing, shimmering skirt.

I made her leave it on when we got back to our hotel room after because I loved getting to put my hand up a girl's skirt. I had the layers of the front of it bunched over my forearm as I stood behind her and fucked her with two fingers. I enjoyed how I could pull my hand away at any time, her shirt would drop, and no one would know what we'd been doing a second ago. I didn't take my fingers away from her, though. Not until I'd made her come and she'd leaned back into me, quivering from her orgasm.

But now we were home, and it forced us to return to our regular lives.

She'd left for New York on Tuesday morning for a conference and had squeezed in a quick job on Saturday before heading back. I'd had a ton of work to catch up on, but we'd texted every night, checking in to see how the other's day had been.

It was Friday afternoon when my father marched into my office without so much as a knock on my door. He was no longer a chief executive, but he was the primary shareholder and president of HBHC, and his office sat ten floors above mine. It meant I wasn't allowed to act pissed by this behavior.

"Family dinner is this Sunday at six," he announced. "I expect you and your girlfriend to attend."

"What?" I rolled back in my chair and stared at him.

Displeasure sliced through his expression because my father *hated* repeating himself. What he didn't realize was he could cut down on that if he'd just stop blindsiding people.

"Consider this my invitation for her to join us."

I narrowed my gaze. "You sure you don't mean Sophia's invitation?"

"No, I did not misspeak." His expression was unreadable stone. "I would like to meet this woman who you seem so taken with."

Damnit. On top of the media pictures from the gala, my social media team had leaned into the romance angle and posted the picture of Emery and me laughing. The one where we looked like we were in love. Had my father bought it? He usually was so perceptive.

Oh, shit. What if he was?

Did he see something I refused to consider?

"You've already met her," I said, knowing this was a battle I was going to lose.

Unacceptable, his dark look said. Macalister Hale was world famous for his intensity and how he could make a person feel small, and I wished I was immune—but my gaze shifted away.

I cleared my throat to hide my discomfort. "I don't know if Sunday works with her schedule."

He delivered his order the same way he'd been doing my whole life. It was absolute. "Make it work."

The discussion was over, so there was no reason for him to stay in my office, especially not when we both had work to do. He turned and exited in an identical manner to how he'd arrived—without pleasantries or respect.

Time and mistakes had reshaped my father over the last few years, but this man? He was the old version. Cold and authoritarian. It was like he hadn't changed at all.

When my father had ruled over our house, we'd had weekly family dinners in the formal dining room, and he'd run them as a corporate meeting. Alice would summarize the projects she was working on and tasks still needing attention, and he would approve or reject any proposals she made before he'd turn his attention to his sons.

Royce had taken the brunt of it, not just because he was older, but how he'd resisted our father's command. I'd always gone with the flow and told myself I didn't care. It was pointless to fight because it was win at all costs in our family—so, who was supposed to win when we went up against each other?

No one did, as far as I was concerned.

I sat on the couch in my bedroom, scrolling absentmindedly through the news on my phone while digesting none of the information. Emery would be here soon, and while I was excited to see her again, I dreaded the evening. No amount of prep work could prepare her for what was in store.

My father could be ruthless if he found a person lacking. Jillian had been fucking terrified the first time I'd brought her to family dinner, and she said it never got any easier. And this was the nice version of my father—she'd been handpicked for me by him.

Before his downfall, he'd had aspirations of sitting on the board of the Federal Reserve, and since Wayne Lambert golfed with the president twice a month, my father was sure uniting our families would help both his goal and my political career.

I still remembered the family dinner where he'd told me to seduce Jillian.

It didn't matter she wasn't single at the time, or how she'd had a one-night stand with Royce—my freaking brother—a few years prior. My father and Alice had discussed it, he'd said, and made this decision for me. I'd tried to hide my look of betrayal as I turned to my stepmother. We'd been having an affair for months at that point, and even though she'd said sex with me meant nothing, I hadn't truly believed her until that moment.

So, I'd caried out my father's orders with flawless precision, and to prove to Alice that sleeping with her meant nothing to me as well, I'd let the whole family catch me with Jillian in the back of a limo, balls deep inside her.

It was stupid and childish—not to mention—*dangerous.*

I hadn't realized how unstable Alice had become, and it was likely my stunt had helped push her over the edge. Her first attempt on Marist's life was yet another item to add to the long list of things I felt guilty about.

After prison, my father moved out and turned the estate over to Royce. When my brother became the head of the household, he'd resumed the family dinner tradition, although it was infrequent. There was a marked change in the tone of the dinners as well. There was no agenda or proposals, and Marist forbid cell phones at the table, forcing everyone to have actual interactions and conversations.

I wouldn't admit it to anyone, but I . . . didn't hate attending.

It was kind of nice to know what everyone had going on in their lives, pretend for a few hours our family wasn't broken, and that I wasn't a big part of the reason for that.

But the way my father had been at the office left me feeling anxious. If he had returned to his former self, it was likely he'd go on the attack toward Emery, and I wasn't going to allow that. It was past time I learned from Royce and started to push back.

Had he known I was thinking about him? A text message rolled onto my phone's screen.

Royce: Can you come into the library?

I didn't bother responding because it was faster to simply walk down the hall and turn in to the room that shelved some of my family's most prized possessions. The walls were lined with books, many of them rare printings. Marist's mythology-themed chess set usually sat on the desk so she could play my father whenever he came to visit, and Royce or Sophia would watch from the reading chair. But tonight, the chess board had been moved to the side table under the window.

It was because my father sat behind the desk, a leather portfolio pinned beneath his hand resting on the desktop.

Royce was by the window, looking out at the grounds and the sprawling hedge maze that was a source of pride for our family. My grandmother had started it, and my father had doubled its size, making the tall hedge maze more complex and challenging.

Royce had his back to me, but he heard my entrance. "Shut the door."

Unease gripped me like a vise and made a cold sweat bloom across my skin. Royce had been trying to get me to talk to our father for months. *"He can't forgive you if you don't apologize,"* he'd lectured me.

He was absolutely right, but still, I struggled. So much time had passed since Alice had cruelly thrown the affair in our father's face that it had built up and added another layer to my guilt. I didn't visit my father when he was sent away because he'd asked me not to. He'd claimed he didn't want me to see him like that, but I knew better.

He couldn't tolerate seeing me after what I'd done.

When he got out two years later, he was a different person, and I didn't know how to navigate the situation with him. I'd wanted to apologize but didn't have a clue how to go about it. Still, I'd tried once. The day of Sophia's accident, I'd brought fresh clothes to the hospital for him as a peace offering. I'd planned to use it as my opening, but everything went . . . sideways.

He'd *hugged* me.

It was the first time he'd done it since my mom had died, and I froze. It was like capsizing in the middle of a storm, and being so disoriented, you think you're swimming for the surface, only to discover the sandy ocean floor at your fingertips.

I did not deserve his love. I was so ashamed of what I'd done, and my avoidance in dealing with it increased that shame ten-fold. The task of apologizing seemed insurmountable.

I pulled the library door closed and filled my lungs with air. Royce had ambushed me with this, and while I was angry with him, I had to focus and steer the conversation away from anything I wasn't prepared to talk about. The best way to do that was to stay in control.

"If this is about my approval on marrying Sophia," I leveled a gaze at our father, "you have it."

His reaction was subtle, but I caught it. He hadn't expected this and was pleased, but then skepticism took over. He didn't trust my statement and wondered why I was telling him what he wanted to hear.

His tone was guarded. "Is that so?"

"You had it the day you asked for it, but we were interrupted. I haven't been able to find a moment in private since to tell you."

He still didn't believe me. "We were alone in your office when we spoke on Friday."

"You mean when you appeared without warning and stayed all of thirty seconds?"

A scowl darkened his face, but it seemed self-directed. "I may have been brusque with you because I was dealing with another issue." He pushed away the frown, and something like hope lit his pale eyes. "I have your approval, then?"

"Yes. I like Sophia, and you two are good together." I was being genuine. Their relationship was strange, but it worked. I straightened, took a page out of his book to use my body language to signify the conversation was over, and turned toward the door. "If you'll excuse me, I—"

"We have another matter to discuss." His voice was firm but not sharp, telling me this 'matter' was going to be difficult, and I swore in my head. "It concerns the woman you're seeing."

I froze.

Royce had remained in the background, but at some point he'd turned to face us, and he lifted a hand to rub a crease from his forehead. "Dad wanted to do this at dinner, but I talked him out of it." He dropped his hand and gave me a pointed look. "So, you're welcome."

My anger over Royce's ambush evaporated in a second. He'd pulled me into the library to prevent my father from ambushing Emery, and I was grateful.

I did my best to prepare my defenses. If my father was going to try to take her away from me, he was about to have a war on his hands. "What about her?"

"Are you aware she has a criminal record?"

I nearly let out a sigh of relief.

Two things that hadn't changed about my father were his paranoia and his thoroughness. He had an army of investigators on his personal payroll, and everyone who entered our family's circle was properly vetted. A detailed background check was likely enclosed in the leather portfolio where he rested his hand.

"Yes," I said. "She told me."

Something was . . . off.

Usually, he reveled in exposing people's flaws and secrets, but today, he hesitated. It was almost as if he didn't want to be asking me these questions.

"And you're aware of her connection to Wayne Lambert?"

My bones turned to ice, locking me in place. Emery had told me no one knew she'd broken into Lambert's safe except

Jillian, and then me. How the fuck had my father's investigators figured it out?

Maybe they hadn't. Was it possible this was some kind of bluff? Or did he mean a connection I didn't know about?

My voice wasn't as strong as I wanted it to be. "She was friends with Jillian, if that's what you mean."

"It's not." He opened the portfolio and glanced down, although I was sure he'd read the report thoroughly and already knew all the information it contained. "Her father went to prison for breaking into Lambert's house."

Oh, fuck.

THIRTEEN

VANCE

My sharp intake of breath was all the confirmation my father needed.

"So, she didn't tell you that," he stated quietly. He wore reluctance, but it was a terrible fit on his broad shoulders. "I understand she changed her name after her father's death. That's why you must have missed it."

No, I'd missed it because I didn't do a background check at all. I'd foolishly taken Emery at her word, and, shit, she hadn't even told me her real name? After everything we'd shared? The hurt of it stung like she'd injected toxin straight into my heart.

This betrayal... it was white-hot, searing me and melting my tongue so I couldn't even speak.

"She's a pretty girl," my father offered. "But presented with this evidence, I've come to the conclusion she's using you to further some agenda, and it would be hard to convince me otherwise."

It was so unfair, and exactly what I deserved, that the first real relationship I'd gotten to choose would end up being full of deceit. I'd fallen for it, and she hadn't just made me feel like a fool—she'd made me look weak in front of my family.

Fire bubbled in my stomach like a cauldron. "Maybe I'm using her, too."

His eyebrow arrowed up. "For what?"

I wished I hadn't said anything. I wasn't about to tell him how Lambert had threatened me, and I especially didn't want to explain what Lambert planned to use for blackmail. I had no choice but to lie.

I said it in a casual, careless tone. "Sex."

I expected him to bristle, but he was too smart and perceptive. He was excellent at reading people and their lies. "I don't believe you. You care about this girl, Vance."

Up until one minute ago, I did. My feelings toward her now were a gray, overcast sky, with a storm looming on the horizon. Despite that, I couldn't just shut my emotions off.

He'd had this information on Friday, he'd planned this dinner, and my need to protect her couldn't dissolve fast enough.

My voice was dark. "You were going to, what? Humiliate her with all this in front of everyone?"

"That was my initial plan, yes. When I see a threat, I choose to confront it."

Was he kidding? "What *threat*?"

"The threat she poses to you, Vance. I do not want to see you get hurt, and there's no way this doesn't end badly."

I shot a dubious glance over to Royce, checking to see his reaction. The idea that our father was worried about me getting my heart broken was so utterly ridiculous, I expected my brother to call him out on it.

Our father hadn't cared about anyone else's feelings before—*especially* not his eldest son's. The shit he'd put Royce through, the things he'd done to Marist . . . He'd nearly succeeded in crushing both their hearts.

My brother didn't look outraged, though. Fuck, if anything, it looked like he felt the same way as our father.

I swallowed harshly, gnashing my teeth, and my tone was frosty. "While I appreciate the concern, it's not needed. I'll be fine."

Under my family's scrutiny, my suit suddenly became too tight. I needed to get the fuck out of this room and start planning what I was going to say to Emery when she arrived. Regardless of how I felt, this new information didn't change the fact I still needed her help getting inside Lambert's safe.

I adjusted the suit coat on my shoulders. "I'll speak with her and clear this up."

"Take this," my father closed the portfolio and pushed it toward me, "and make sure the story she gives you matches the truth."

I begrudgingly moved to the desk and snatched up the leather-bound folder. I didn't like how it felt in my hands, her whole life and its secrets in my grasp. I didn't want to find out this way.

"Thanks for bringing it to my attention." I reached for the door and lobbed the statement at them over my shoulder. "I'll see you at dinner."

Neither of them said a word as I strode from the room.

I didn't get a chance to organize my thoughts because Elliot appeared in the hall with Emery in tow. Her whole expression brightened when she saw me, but it was a knife in my chest. She had to be acting. This reaction—like our relationship—wasn't real.

"Thanks, Elliot." I nodded to him, signaling he no longer needed to escort her to my room. I turned my focus to her as he left, and tried to ignore her sexy smile, or how I wanted to peel the tight dress off her body.

"Hey, there," she said. "Sorry, I'm a little early. I wanted to see you." She sensed something was wrong when I didn't match her smile. "Is everything okay?"

"We can talk about it in my room."

Her whole demeanor shifted, and anxiety spiked in her eyes. She followed me unquestioningly through the doorway, walking a few steps into the sitting area of my bedroom, and remained silent as I closed the door.

She held tension in her shoulders and took in a shallow breath, unable to stand it any longer. "What's wrong?"

"Why do you want to get inside Lambert's safe?"

Her chin drew back, like my question had thrown her. "Because I want to know what Jillian saw. Maybe it could help us find—"

"That's it?" Irritation colored my voice. "There's *no* other reason?"

Her lips parted to say something, but nothing came out. Whatever it was, she was conflicted about revealing it. Finally, she spoke, but the words were feeble. "Okay, I have another reason, but it's . . . complicated."

"Complicated enough it sent your father to prison, I'm guessing?"

Her gaze dropped to the floor in shame. "Yes."

For a single nanosecond, I wanted to undo what I'd said. To remind her my father had gone to prison, too, so I carried that secondhand shame as she did. But her lesson in the hotel room in Monaco came flooding back to me. She'd 'tripped' on the rug and played the victim to control what I saw. To distract.

I wasn't going to fall for the same act today.

She sank down, sitting on the edge of the couch, and

curled her fingers around the front hem of her skirt like she either needed to hold it in place, or wasn't sure what to do with her hands. Emery had the posture of a woman who was ready to confess her sins, and I walked to the chair that faced her, took a seat, and gave her a look that said I would listen.

"I told you," she said softly, "my dad knew how to get things from people, or *for* people. One of them was Wayne Lambert."

"Your father worked for him?"

"Officially? No." Her expression was a mixture of sadness and anger. "What he asked my dad to do was sometimes illegal, so there couldn't be any affiliation between them. My dad became Lambert's solution when he needed something and everything else had failed."

It was more of a statement than a question from me. "He was his fixer?"

She nodded. "Anything Lambert wanted, no matter the risk, my dad got it done. He thought if he ever ran into trouble, Lambert would be there for him." She leveled her gaze at me, and I saw every lick of fire burning inside her. I heard the disgust that filled her mouth. "But he wasn't. When my dad got diagnosed with cancer, Barlowe was starting clinical trials of a new drug. One that was designed to slow or stop the growth of tumor cells in the lungs, and it showed a lot of promise. It wouldn't have saved my dad's life, but it probably would have bought him more time."

Her eyes began to glisten with unshed tears. I sensed what she was going to say next, and I hated it.

"Lambert refused to put him in the trial. My dad was stage four, he said, so it wouldn't help him. All it would do was make Lambert's precious trial results look bad."

"Fuck," I uttered quietly, not wanting to interrupt.

"My dad was completely betrayed, plus he was running

out of time. I think he wanted to secure a future for my mom and me, and the only way he knew how was if he got something he could use against Lambert. He hadn't kept any records, but he knew Lambert did, and he knew *exactly* where they would be."

Should it have bothered me that she was talking about blackmail? Because it didn't. Lambert was obviously no stranger to it.

Emery glanced at the ceiling and wiped a finger under her eye, brushing away a tear before it could roll down her cheek. She was holding herself together by sheer force and sustained anger.

"My dad was pretty good at cracking safes, but he never got the chance with Lambert's. The housekeeper came home early, heard an intruder upstairs, and called the cops. He hadn't even started drilling by the time they arrived."

My fingers tightened around the portfolio in my hands. "Lambert didn't say it was a misunderstanding and have the charges dropped?"

"Are you kidding me? My dad had tried to steal from him. Lambert wanted him prosecuted to the fullest extent of the law."

My brow furrowed. "He wasn't worried about what your dad was going to say?"

Her smile was cruel, devoid of any warmth. "Like anyone would believe him. He was a criminal who'd broken into Lambert's house, and Lambert claimed he'd never seen my father before. Plus, my dad had no evidence." She said it like the thought had been eating at her for a long time. "I don't know why he trusted Lambert so completely."

It was quiet for a moment, before she drew in a cleansing breath and was ready to press forward.

"Lambert bought my dad's silence, promising him he'd look out for his family, but that was a lie. The only reason I even knew about the agreement was because my mom freaked out when the money stopped coming." She raised her chin in an effort to look strong. "It was three months after my dad died. Just long enough to make sure we didn't have anything to come forward with."

The bitterness rolled off her in waves, keeping me pressed into my seat, and when her gaze bore down on me, it turned me into a statue.

"When my dad got convicted, it was a death sentence." Her chin quivered, but her voice stayed detached and even. "The doctors gave him a year to live, but he only made it eight months. He died in that prison infirmary alone, rather than surrounded by people who loved him. If he'd been free, we would have made the most of the time he had left, but no. Wayne Lambert stole that from us." Injustice swelled inside her, spilling from her lips. "He stole that from *me*."

"Yes," I agreed, "he did."

I'd spent so much of my life trying not to feel or care, but it was utterly impossible now. I hurt for her and the family who had lost precious time together. I would have given anything for more time with my mother before her death.

Emery swallowed thickly, perhaps trying to wash down some of her emotion. "My mom fell apart," she said. "Even when things were good, she'd had a hard time staying sober, so once my dad was gone, she spiraled. I tried to get her help, but I didn't have any money, and more importantly, she didn't *want* help."

I had no idea what kind of expression was frozen on my face, but maybe it was too much for her, because she pulled her gaze away and stared vacantly at my bed.

She delivered it in a matter-of-fact tone, like a broadcaster reporting sad news. "She drank herself to death when I was eighteen, and maybe she would have done it no matter what happened to my dad. I shouldn't put her death on Lambert," she sucked in a breath as her vengeance came back to life, "but I fucking do."

Jesus.

"Emery." Her name slipped from me as I tried to convey what I was feeling, but words were inadequate. I had no idea what to say.

Her attention drifted back to me so slowly, it was painful. Everything was tense, everything ached. All the power she'd had up until this moment was fueled by wrath and anguish, but when her eyes landed on me, the power abandoned her. She appeared so vulnerable and devastatingly real, I refused to accept this as anything other than the truth.

"I was going to tell you," she said quietly, "but, Vance, I've spent nearly ten years working toward this. If Lambert finds out, I'll never get another chance. I couldn't trust anyone. I had to be careful."

"I understand that," I answered automatically. Even though I'd given her no reason not to, she didn't trust me yet with everything, and that was fair. Cape Hill was full of liars and cheats. Plus, I hadn't confessed to her why I wanted to get inside Lambert's safe either. My reason was defensive and selfish, but hers was much stronger.

I wanted this revenge for her.

Abruptly, I sat up straighter in my chair. "Wait a minute. You already did it—you cracked into Lambert's safe."

It was like I'd punched her in the stomach. "That didn't go as I'd planned."

"What do you mean?"

"Once I got it open, I thought Jillian would ask me to stay, or at least tell me what she found inside. We were friends, and I'd hoped she'd trust me. Instead, she disappeared without saying a word."

Skepticism filled my head like a whisper of smoke. It was obvious she'd used Jillian to get close to Lambert. Had she orchestrated their relationship the same way she'd done to me? Was she really even friends with Jillian, or had it all been an act? "Tell me again how you two became friends."

Her expression was resigned. "I didn't technically lie about that. I was there at the house as part of a Sovereign job, and when one of the workers hit on her, I came to the rescue. She asked me if I wanted to grab lunch afterward as a thank you."

I tilted my head, studying her critically. "Elaborate on why you used the word 'technically.'"

"Because the guy was a plant. My friend Eddie doesn't work for Sovereign. I was the one who got him in, so he could do me a favor." When I scowled, distress washed over her face. "She started as a job, but I didn't have to fake the friendship. She was so nice, and fun, and I really liked her—even when I didn't want to."

"Did you feel conflicted about what you planned to do to your new friend's father?"

She nodded aggressively. "It got easier when I saw the way he treated her, and how she actively wanted out. And if that's what happened, that Jillian is out there somewhere right now, free from her father's grasp, then I'm fucking thrilled. Believe me." Her shoulders deflated a single degree. "I just wish she'd given me a warning or . . . something."

I set the portfolio down on the coffee table separating us, keeping a hand on top of the folder while fighting a losing battle not to channel my father. "I want to trust you," I said, "and I want you to trust me."

She peered down at the portfolio with guarded eyes. "What's that?"

"Everything my father's team of investigators collected on you."

Panic swam across her face, but I had to ignore it.

"I haven't looked at this yet," I said, "but his investigators are thorough. If there's anything you don't want me to know, chances are it's in here already. So, this is your opportunity to," I searched for the right phrase, "warn me."

Did she understand what I meant? If she wouldn't come clean to me now—if she hoped any other explosive secrets she had could stay hidden—I had no shot at trusting her.

She considered her answer carefully. "I changed my last name, legally, about eight years ago."

"Why?"

"A lot of reasons. To stay off Lambert's radar. My record. My dad's record. I mean, that shit doesn't magically disappear, but a name change helps bury search results." She crossed her arms over her chest, but it didn't look confrontational. If anything, she'd done it to try to protect herself. "I took my mom's maiden name after she passed away."

"Anything else?"

She wasn't happy I was about to dig into her life, but rather than argue or get up and leave, she sat back against the couch like she was getting comfortable. "Nothing I can think of."

Since her posture and attitude challenged me, it left me with no choice but to flip open the folder with a quiet thud. I felt her gaze needling into me as I pulled out the stack of papers and evaluated the collection of printouts and photos.

On top was the normal stuff. There was a copy of her driver's license and passport. Her credit score, previous addresses, and work history. She'd continued her education post high school at a community college but hadn't earned a degree. While she had some social media accounts, she wasn't active on any of them.

Her criminal report only listed the single count of petty larceny. Although she'd been charged as an adult, I suspected the fact she was sixteen at the time had helped her with the plea bargain. She'd paid a fine and done community service, which prevented her from serving any jail time.

There was a background summary report on her parents, focused primarily on her father, that I skimmed quickly. At the bottom of the stack, there were a few brief news articles about how she'd won the Vegas Vault safecracking contest the last two years. I paused, lingering over the picture of her holding up the award plaque, grinning as she stood under the contest's banner.

What had my father, who always loved a winner, thought about that?

I racked the papers and tucked them back into the portfolio, feeling an even mixture of relief and sadness. She'd been truthful, and there didn't appear to be any other bombshells in her past. But I felt for the woman who'd had so much struggle in her life, and I was stunned at how well she hid it.

Like the universe could throw anything at her and she'd survive it.

Her tone was biting, probably overcompensating to hide the truth in her question. "Did I pass your test?"

I didn't answer her. Instead, I pulled out my phone and began to type.

Her annoyance and concern grew, making her launch

forward, back to the edge of her seat. "What are you doing?"

"Sending my father an email, asking him to delete any files he has about you." I tapped the 'send' button, set my phone down on the table, and pushed the portfolio toward her. "This is yours. There's a paper shredder in the office downstairs if you'd like to use it when we're done here."

Emery's mouth dropped open, and she blinked, too stunned to move otherwise.

"Yes," I added. "You passed the test. Now let's see if I can pass yours."

"Um . . . what?"

I shifted in my chair. Shit, I was already uncomfortable, and I hadn't even started talking yet. I cleared my throat, which might have been a subconscious stall tactic.

"Trust is a two-way street," I said finally. "You told me why you want to get inside Wayne's safe, so I'm going to tell you why I need that to happen, too." I hooked a finger under the collar of my shirt to loosen the constricting knot of my tie. "A seat on HBHC's board of directors might become available soon, and he wants it. He expects me to help him with that, and if I don't, he's made it clear I'll regret it."

Her eyes went wide. "He's blackmailing you?" When I nodded, her voice turned gentle. "With what?"

"I suspect he has compromising photos or video of my late stepmother."

"Like, a sex tape?"

My pulse sped up a notch. "Yes."

Confusion made her gaze fall from mine. "Not to be heartless, but why would that matter to you? Didn't she—"

"Because I'm on the video too."

My confession dropped like an anchor, stopping us both in place. Her surprised expression froze, hiding whatever she really thought about this revelation. It made her unreadable, which I couldn't tell if that was better than seeing disgust.

"Oh, shit," she whispered. "You and your stepmom..."

"Yes."

Emery looked utterly lost on what to say next. "Well," she couldn't find any other words, "shit."

The need to explain myself was strong and urgent. "It's complicated, but the short version is I was young, Emery. Young, and very fucking stupid." I swallowed a breath. "I'm not proud of what we did, and especially that we both did it to hurt my father."

"Does he know?"

It was hard, but I wanted to get through it and have no more secrets between us. "It was the last thing Alice said to him before he..." I frowned. "Before her accident."

She pressed her lips together and leaned back, hopefully just to give herself time to consider what I'd said, and not in an effort to put distance between us. I'd told her this to bring her closer, to prove I trusted her.

"Only a few other people know because they were there when Alice announced it. You," I set my gaze on her, giving it my full intensity, "are the only person I've ever told. If this video gets out, it'll ruin my chances at a political career, not to mention what it'll do to my family emotionally. We've started to repair some things, and this would probably undo all of that."

She nodded. "I get it. I'm glad your dad was able to move past it."

I lifted an eyebrow. "Yeah, I don't know if I'd go that far."

"He hasn't forgiven you?"

I wiped a hand over my mouth. "I haven't asked him to. Like I said, it's complicated. We've both made a lot of mistakes, and I'm still not ready to have the conversation, even though we probably should have had it years ago." I grumbled it under my breath. "At least, that's what Royce keeps telling me."

Silence fell between us, and it was uncomfortable, but at least it wasn't tense. Once again, she wasn't sure what to say, and that was my fault. I glanced down at my watch to check the time, only to discover we were running out of it. Macalister Hale did not tolerate tardiness.

"We've shared our secrets," I said. "So, did I pass your test? Do you trust me?"

She peered over at me as if she was making her final evaluation, and it made me uncomfortably hot. But she didn't let me sweat for too long.

"Yes."

"Good. After dinner, we can talk about how we get you back in front of Wayne's safe." I stood from my chair and extended a hand to help her up off the couch. I hadn't realized how much I wanted to touch her until she accepted it and allowed me to pull her against me. "One more thing." My voice was weighed down by its seriousness. "You know I'm committed now, so if whatever this is between us is an act, you don't need to continue."

She blinked her pretty eyes in startled surprise, and . . . was that hurt that threaded through them? "You think it's an act?"

A thrill shot through me, easing the tightness in my chest. "No, not anymore." My hands slid around her, one coming to a rest on the small of her back while the other worked its way up to cup the back of her head. "But I had to be sure."

"It's real, Vance." It came from her lips as a whisper, just before I covered her mouth with mine.

FOURTEEN

EMERY

Confessing everything had set me and Vance free, and honesty spilled from his mouth as we rode in the back seat of his family's Range Rover, heading to a charity auction that benefited the Museum of Fine Art.

"I want to fuck you so bad, you've given me a permanent erection."

Should it have bothered me the driver up front could hear everything we said? Because it didn't. There was nothing subtle about Vance when it came to sex, especially his dick. How had he described it when I'd gotten my first look in the shower? Oh, right.

Amazing.

He wasn't lying about that, or the erection he was currently sporting, tenting the fly of his slacks.

A smile teased my lips, and I leaned into him, setting my hand on his thigh. "Tell me what you'd do to me if you could."

It'd become my catchphrase, and as he did, blood rushed to heat my face. God, his mouth was *filthy*. It was in stark contrast to the perfect gentleman he could be with his impeccable manners, and I fucking loved it. In the last two weeks he'd told me all the ways he wanted to have me when his vow was done.

He was basically two-thirds of the way now. Only thirty-three days to go, and we were both counting them down. We were so freaking horny, it was laughable.

That night after our clearing of the air and an awkward dinner with his family, he'd taken me back to his room, and while I'd talked about Lambert's safe, he bent me over the back of his couch, lifted the hem of my skirt to my waist, and buried his face between my legs. I'd come while we brainstormed ideas of how to get me unnoticed into the Lambert estate, and it was the most fun I'd ever had while planning.

I nuzzled the side of his neck, nipping his skin just enough to get his attention. "Do you want a hand job?"

"Fuck, yeah," he groaned, dragging my hand up over his fly, before disappointingly easing it away. "But we don't have time."

It was because the car was now in line to drop us off, and he needed to get himself under control before we stepped out on the red carpet.

It'd been surreal in Monaco when we'd done this at the Grand Prix Gala, and this time wasn't any easier. I clung to Vance's side as we exited the car and walked down the sidewalk that was blanketed in red and paneled in sponsor logos. It was June now, and the sun hadn't set yet, but the cameras flashed like shuddering strobe lights, disorienting me.

He was unfazed. Accustomed. He smiled and guided me to pose with him like this was a normal, everyday occurrence. I rolled with it, pretending I was just like him. Emery Mendenhall wasn't frightened by the red carpet or the reporters who shouted at her like they had a right to know every detail of her life.

It was better once we got inside the museum. They served cocktails in the event area space, which was a grand room with a back wall of glass separating it from the courtyard. There were tall trees there, which helped to bring the outside in to the space.

I didn't recognize most of the people who approached Vance and struck up a conversation but acted like I did and that I belonged. I smiled, nodded, and laughed when appropriate. It wasn't unpleasant, but it was draining to be 'on' the entire evening.

Two older gentlemen had cornered us at one point, trying to feel Vance out and see if they could get him to join their racing crew.

"I wish my son could do it," one of them said, "but he hasn't shown much interest, and I'd have to teach him."

The other man nodded. "If you don't have time, I think I heard George Ridley's boy gives lessons. He was giving them to Lambert's daughter, before she . . ."

His words petered out because he must have realized who was part of the conversation, but the other man was oblivious.

"Is that what they were doing?" The guy shrugged. "Looked more like swimming lessons to me."

Vance tilted his head. "Swimming lessons?"

"Yeah, they had a swimmer in the water flag up, and a couple buoys out. I figured she was training for an open water event, but they picked a weird spot because the boat was way out there."

My pulse jumped, and I was sure it was the same for Vance, but he did an excellent job of looking only casually interested. "Oh, yeah? Where was this?"

"Over by the stumps on the north side, maybe a mile or so out?"

"There's not a beach anywhere near there," Vance said.

The guy nodded. "That's why it stuck out to me."

Vance turned to throw a glance my direction. "Yeah, that is strange."

The thoughts churning in his head were the same as mine. What were Jillian and Lucas doing out there? Was she practicing?

Breath halted in my lungs, and I instinctively gripped Vance so tightly, his attention dropped to my hand on his arm, then up to me in alarm. It was because Wayne Lambert was making his way toward us.

I'd never been face-to-face with him. Before, I'd only had pictures of the man who'd taken so much from me. He hadn't been home the few times I'd been to the Lambert estate, and I'd purposefully stayed in the shadows at the memorial reception. It probably wasn't necessary. We'd never met, and I wasn't even a footnote in his life.

It gave me dark satisfaction to know Vance and I were going to change that.

Lambert didn't bother to look at me because his focus was only on his target—Vance. As far as he was concerned, I didn't exist at my boyfriend's side.

Vance's greeting was so bright, it was undeniably fake. "Wayne."

The two gentlemen we'd just been talking to collected their drinks from the high-top table and scurried away, making plenty of room for Lambert and his overblown ego.

"Vance." Lambert's greeting matched Vance's fake one. "I was hoping we—"

"Let me introduce you to my girlfriend. This is Emery Mendenhall."

I wasn't the least bit surprised when Lambert looked

annoyed. In his mind, he had better things to do, but he wouldn't be rude, so he gave me a cursory glance and a smile.

"Emery," Vance said, "this is Wayne Lambert."

"It's nice to meet you," I lied as I thrust out my hand.

"Yes, likewise." His handshake was cold and aggressive and thankfully over quickly. His attention swung back to the person he'd come to see. "I was hoping we could speak privately for a moment?"

"About what?" Vance's tone was dismissive. "How you're blackmailing me to land a seat on HBHC's board?"

I had to stop a surprised sound from escaping my throat.

Lambert's reaction was much bigger. He took a subtle step back, lifting his hands in the air as if surrendering, and his loud, grating laugh was total overcompensation. His gaze darted side to side, checking to see if anyone had overheard what Vance had just said.

The cocktail party was crowded, and no one seemed to notice, making Lambert's eyes glitter above his evil smile. "That's an awfully strong word to use, don't you think?"

"It feels appropriate," Vance said.

The older man looked at me, gauging my lack of reaction, and I understood now why Vance had done it. He'd sent a message to Lambert to let him know the discussion could happen in front of me.

He must have decided if Vance was okay with it, he was, too. Lambert looked every bit the smug prick I imagined him to be as he spoke. "Damon Lynch announced he'll be retiring from the board at the end of July, so I imagine the search for his replacement is starting soon. Where are we on that?"

"I have a few things in motion," Vance said. "But I suggest you offer to host Damon's retirement party. That's a way to curry favor with the current board."

Lambert didn't like the suggestion. "Macalister put him on the board. He should be the one to do it."

Vance's laugh was hollow. "Never in a million years. See, he likes dating Sophia, and I think he'd prefer to keep doing it." He wrapped a hand around his drink, swirling the amber liquid inside. "It's been a while since you've hosted at your house. I'm sure Serena would love a chance to show off the remodel of your kitchen."

"If I did this, I'd be worried it'd come off as self-serving."

Vance's tone was incredulous. "Are you thinking you'll get the seat on merit alone? There have to be at least a dozen other people just as qualified as you. You want the seat, you gotta play the game." He took a sip of his drink. "And who cares if it looks self-serving? The only votes that matter are the eight guys you just bailed out of having to host a retirement party for a man none of them respect anymore, but etiquette dictates someone has to."

I watched with bated breath as Lambert considered it. This was the 'in' Vance and I had come up with. While all of Cape Hill partied on Lambert's dime, he'd be too distracted to notice when we slipped away and ventured upstairs.

"I'll discuss it with my wife," Lambert said. "She might not be ready to take on something of this scale so soon after Jillian."

"That's certainly understandable." There was a hesitation in Vance, like he was calculating a course adjustment on the fly. "Something to consider is having it at your home gives the board an opportunity to really see who you are and how well your family has coped during . . . the unimaginable."

Lambert stiffened. "What are you saying? I should play the sympathy card?"

He slowly lifted one shoulder. "I'm the type of guy who

would play every card he's been dealt."

Because it was win at all costs to him.

Rather than look disgusted, Lambert scrubbed his fingers under his chin and thought about it. "That's a valid point." His shoulders lifted right along with his mood, like he hadn't just been talking about his daughter's death. "Lots to consider. I'll give you a call next week and we can discuss it some more, plus your progress."

Vance did nothing to disguise his sarcasm. "Great. Looking forward to it."

Lambert didn't say goodbye to either of us, he simply moved off and disappeared into the crowd. I blew out a breath, feeling so much lighter I worried my feet might leave the ground.

"Do you think he'll go for it?" I asked.

"Oh, yeah. He wants that seat more than anything. I mean, he barely paused when I brought up Jillian."

"True," I said quietly. "Fucker."

"You should know, I'm proud of you." When I gave him a confused look, he smiled. "I thought you were going to take his watch when you shook hands."

I laughed softly. "It was tempting, but no."

He knew I had my sights set on something much, much bigger.

The following Saturday, I met Vance at the marina, and he took me sailing on his boat, *Favorite*. I didn't ask about the name because I could guess—he owned multiple boats, but this was the one he took out the most. It was large and elegant, but not too big for him to man himself.

Once we'd left the harbor, he shut off the engine and did whatever was needed to make us move using the power of the wind. There were large steering wheels on either side near the back of the boat, and I sat on a bench seat in front of one of them, watching him as he cranked a handle to raise one of the sails.

Goddamn, he was so good looking, it wasn't even fair. The wind played with his hair, making the ends light up a golden brown under the hot summer sun. His thin, white linen shirt was unbuttoned and open, revealing his sculpted chest, notched abs, and trim waist that led my eyes down to his navy board shorts.

We both had sunglasses on, but I also had a wide-brimmed straw beach hat to keep the sun from blinding me. It glinted off the rippling waves of the ocean, trying to get at me.

It was quieter now that the engine was off, and once he'd finished with the sails, he padded on his bare feet back to me and stood at the wheel, making another adjustment. The water was calm and there weren't any other boats around, and it felt like we were all alone in the world.

He offered it casually, like it wasn't a big deal. "Lambert has decided he's going to throw the party."

I'd started unbuttoning the shirt over my bikini top, but my fingers slowed. "Good. So, now we have to figure out how I get upstairs undetected."

"How long do you think it will take you to get the safe open?"

"If he hasn't changed the combination? Ten seconds. If he has, then maybe five minutes to put my scope in and line up the wheels."

I slipped my shirt off, folded it up, and tucked it into the bag I'd brought with me, then retrieved my sunscreen. Vance's sunglasses were pointed at my gray bikini top for a long moment as he watched me, and I grinned. It was nice to know he was just as attracted to me as I was to him.

I held up the bottle of lotion, waving it at him. "Do you mind doing my back?"

He checked the instruments, set the autopilot, and pulled the sunscreen from my grasp.

Even with the wind, the sun was hot, and a bead of sweat rolled down his delicious chest as he sat beside me on the bench, uncapped the sunscreen, and squeezed a dollop into his palm. The lotion was cool and pleasant as he spread it across my shoulder blades and down the length of my back, working it gently into my skin.

"You know," his voice was seductive, "this would be easier if these straps weren't in my way."

I swallowed a breath. "Then undo them."

He made a sound of approval, and a muscle deep between my legs clenched in response.

Gentle tugs undid the knot at the center of my back, releasing the tension of the bikini. He didn't bother to undo the one behind my neck. The second the fabric went slack, his hands smoothed around my sides and slid up to cup my breasts.

I was never going to get tired of having his hands on my body, but I both loved and hated his vow. It was amazing to have a partner who focused completely on me, but he still hadn't lifted his rule that said I wasn't allowed to touch him. My hands were desperate to explore and return some of the pleasure he gave me.

I sighed and leaned back against his chest, gazing out at the blue water that stretched all around us, enjoying the coconut scent of the sunscreen and the slippery way Vance's hands moved over my sensitive skin. He lowered his lips to the side of my neck, kissing the pulse point below my ear and causing a shiver of pleasure.

Fuck, a girl could get used to this.

I wouldn't allow myself to think about the future with him, about what happened after we'd accomplished our goal and exposed whatever dirty secrets Lambert had locked away. Vance's celibacy vow was set to end two weeks before the retirement party, which meant he'd have everything he wanted from me by then.

A tiny voice in the back of my mind warned me to be cautious. He was a man who got whatever he wanted, so part of the appeal of our relationship might be the delayed gratification. I hoped what we had wouldn't change after he got it because I worried it was too late for me.

I liked Vance Hale a *lot*.

Enough that my feelings strayed dangerously close to the territory of love.

"Okay," I said breathlessly, sitting up and easing his hands away. "I think I'm good. You were very thorough." I twisted my arms behind my back, finding the strings, and worked to tie a knot.

He reached for me, grasping my chin with his thumb and forefinger, and used that to turn me into his kiss. His lips moved slow and deliberate, tasting me in a rhythm that matched the gentle water lapping at the hull of his boat.

"Tease," he whispered playfully.

With that kiss, he was the bigger tease. I longed for him far more now than when his hands had skimmed over my breasts, ghosting over my skin. Every time I tried to crack the combination to what was inside him, his kiss would blank out my mind and I'd have to start over.

He got up off the bench, handed me the lotion, and went down the steps into the galley, returning with two bottles of beer and the lunch his chef had prepared for us. He sat on the bench seat across from me, and as we ate, we sailed up the coast, keeping an eye on the shore for . . . something. Any kind of clue as to what Jillian and Lucas had been doing out here.

I played with the zipper of the insulated koozie wrapped around my beer bottle. "Can I ask you something? It's about your dad."

Vance's clear eyes turned stormy. "What is it?"

"I'm wondering why you haven't apologized."

His mood rapidly declined, and he took a long sip of his beer, rather than answer me.

"Hey, look," I said. "It's probably none of my business, and I know you said it's complicated, but just hear me out for a second." I filled my voice with gravity. "You only get so much time with people before they're gone. There's nothing you can do to change that or buy it back."

His posture stiffened. "I'm aware."

He was defensive, but I wasn't going to let it deter me. "I'd do anything to have more time with my dad. I'm sure it's the same with you for your mom." His expression shifted, softening, confirming I was right. "What I'm getting at is nothing is certain. He could be gone tomorrow, and then you'll never get the chance to make it right. You'll spend the rest of your life wishing you'd had more time."

Vance's chest lifted as he took in an enormous breath, but he couldn't seem to find words.

"Or maybe something happens to you," I continued. "You told me he wants to forgive you. Do you want to take that opportunity from him?"

"Emery, it's not that simple."

"It could be." I leaned forward, bringing us closer. "You just have to try."

"Are you finished?"

I had no idea if he meant with the conversation or my lunch, but I pretended it was the latter. I nodded and stood, reaching for our plates that rested on the table between us, but he abruptly shot to his feet. His hand went out, latching on my wrist and causing me to halt.

"I'm sorry." He stared at where he had hold of me, and his voice was more uneven than I'd ever heard it. "I let so much time go by, and now it's . . . hard."

There was so much he wasn't saying, but I understood. All the shame and resentment had twisted inside him, creating something new and terrible, and he didn't know how to deal with it.

"I know, but it's not too late," I said.

His face lifted and searched mine like he wanted proof that what I'd said was true. I didn't have proof, only hope and a gut feeling, but maybe that was enough.

Behind him, the rocky shore drifted by, and something glinted, stealing my focus. I squinted, trying to zero in on the flash that had been there one moment and then was gone.

"What is that?"

I pointed over his shoulder to the rocks just as the tiny light winked at us again. He turned, peering off at the rocks but not seeing anything.

"There!" I said when the thing glinted again. "Did you see it?"

"Yeah."

It only took him a minute to change direction, and as we began to motor toward the shore, I stood at the side of the ship, holding my hat in place. The flashing had no discernible pattern to it, so it didn't seem to be an actual light.

"It's a reflector," Vance said when we got closer.

Sure enough, I could make out the small silver disc attached to one of the taller rocks that jutted out of the water.

He shut off the engine when we were one hundred and fifty yards from shore and worked to drop anchor. "I'm going to check it out."

"Can I come too, or do I need to stay with the boat?"

He undid the latches, folding down the swim platform at the back, revealing steps and a folded ladder. "No, you can come. She'll be fine."

She, meaning *Favorite*. I took off my shorts, hat, and sunglasses, and glanced at the reflector again. Beyond it, the water lapped at the shoreline and the rocky hill that wasn't quite tall or steep enough to call a cliff. The silver disc had been placed here to mark something . . . but what?

When we were both ready, Vance jumped in the water first. He treaded in the waves, running a hand over his hair, and slinging back water as he stared up, waiting for me to join him.

I was hot from the sun, and I was sure he'd say the water was warm, but it still took my breath when I jumped in. But I rubbed the briny saltwater from my eyes and followed him as he swam toward the stump of rock.

It got shallow surprisingly fast, and although the shoreline was littered with rocks, the ocean bottom was smooth and sandy. The water was only knee deep as we plodded our way up to the stump and examined the reflector.

"It's in decent shape," he said. "I'd be surprised if it's a year old."

"Is it glued on?"

"Looks like it." He lifted his gaze, scanning the area, and

then his head tilted. "Is that a path?"

From the boat, the rocky hillside dipped down and looked bowl-shaped, but now we could see that wasn't the case. It was two separate slopes, one in front of the other. It would be generous to call the sandy area in front of it a beach, but a small path led away from it, disappearing behind the slope and into the woods up the hillside.

I dodged a clump of seaweed and wrung the seawater out of my hair as we moved up onto the shore, muddy sand squishing through our toes. We didn't talk about following the path. Maybe we both sensed we were on to something. Hyperawareness rolled through me. This spot was so secluded, it made sense now why it'd been marked.

Tree branches and overgrown grass closed around the path which was so narrow we could only walk single file. Sunlight dappled through the leaves overhead. Sand gave way to sticks, rocks, and exposed tree roots, and I ground my teeth. I was tender footed and wouldn't be able to go much farther. I was about to tell him that when Vance pulled to a stop, causing me to run into him.

"What is it?" I asked.

He turned to the side, allowing me to see. There was an ancient-looking chain link fence with a large gash in it and the ends bent away from us like people had been pushing their way through it for years.

On the other side of the fence, there was a road.

He pushed one side of it away from him and stooped to go through the narrow opening, but I grabbed his shoulder. "Wait, do you want to get tetanus? You don't even have a shirt on."

It was enough to give him pause, and he stood back up, releasing the fence. When it snapped back in place, something on the forest floor moved with it. I motioned toward it. "What's that?"

He bent, brushed the dead leaves out of the way, and retrieved the thin, black tactical flashlight whose wrist strap must have gotten snagged on the jagged edges of the metal links. I put a hand on his arm, leaning in to look at it as he rotated the flashlight in his hands.

There was yellow printing on the handle, but it was faded and worn off in some places.

"Any idea what that says?" I asked.

His tone was odd. "Seas the day."

I peered closer at the writing. "Wow, good guess."

"It's not a guess. I have the same one on board *Favorite* right now. This was the senior gift we gave to the underclassman." He pointed to the series of letters at the end. "Cape Hill Prep Sailing Club."

My gaze snapped up to meet his. "Do you think it's hers?"

"It's not Lucas's. He dropped and broke his the same day he got it. I remember because we all gave him shit about it." Vance's gaze turned toward the road beyond the fence, and then down to the flashlight in his hands.

Was the same idea forming in his head? Maybe the truth was Jillian had willingly stepped off the deck of *The Trident*, abandoning her father's ship to the sea. But instead of drowning, she'd begun the swim she'd been training for.

It came from me in a rush. "What if she swam here, went through the fence, and someone picked her up?"

"My money's on Lucas or Tiffany." He clicked the button on the back of the flashlight, discovered it still worked, and then clicked it off. "Fuck, it had to be a long-ass swim to make sure the tide took *The Trident* out to sea and not back to the cape."

"But you think she made it."

He settled his gaze upon me, and I saw the same conclusion I had reflected in his eyes. That Jillian was like us, and she'd do whatever it took to get what she wanted.

"Absolutely," he said.

FIFTEEN

EMERY

Sovereign Systems was an elite protection company, but the home office was a total shitshow. Desks were surrounded by mismatched partition walls they'd cobbled together over the years, and all the office equipment was ancient. A lot of days I was glad I had to travel so much because sitting at my workstation was depressing.

I set my purse and my laptop bag on the seat of my chair and stared in confusion at the large, flat box that took up most of my desk. It must have been delivered while I was out, finishing a job over in the North End. A hotel had discovered an old safe in the basement, and I'd manipulated the open quickly, but all that was inside were some master keys for locks that no longer existed.

The brown cardboard box was in rough shape, and a customs form was pasted on one side. I hadn't ordered anything recently, and definitely not anything international, but my company's name was printed on the label with the attention listed as Emery Mendenhall. The return address was a shipping company in Aruba. I grabbed a pair of scissors out of my pencil cup and sliced through the packing tape.

I peeled back the flaps and the tissue paper, and my confusion grew. Fabric? I lifted the swath of green out, stunned at the heavy weight of it, and it tumbled open, revealing it was a dress. I pulled it out of the box and held it up to see it completely. The garment was strapless with layered folds placed over the bustline and fitted down through the waist before opening into a skirt that looked longer in the back than the front and had a thick hem. It draped beautifully as if the curves of the full skirt had been expertly hung.

Was this from Vance, sent via Petra?

It was gorgeous, and I couldn't resist flattening it against me to see if it would fit, even as I sensed it would.

Of course, this was the moment my older, male boss rapped his knuckles on the metal frame of my cubicle and walked in.

"Pretty dress," he said.

I shoved it back in the box as quickly as possible, pretending he hadn't just seen me fawning all over it. "Hey. What's up?"

"I forwarded you an email chain from last week. You don't need to do anything, but Stan said you liked to know whenever a client changes or upgrades a safe."

"Yeah. I poke around on the forums and get familiar with the model if I'm not already."

We safe technicians had a tight-knit online community, and we all shared information to help each other with faster, damage-free opens. There were several times over the years I'd been stumped and someone else had a tip that helped me push through.

There were really only two kinds of safes. Ones to shield the contents from fire, and ones to prevent burglary. Naturally, fire safes were easier to open, so I didn't concern myself too much with clients who had them. But the security safes? I had a database in my head of who owned what and tried to keep up to date with attack methods in case someone got locked out.

"It's a Lagerfield," he said.

"Whoa. That's serious." A strange sensation coasted down my spine, and dread settled in my stomach. I somehow already knew, I but asked it anyway, keeping my voice nonchalant. "Which client?"

"Cape Hill address." My boss tugged at his earlobe as he tried to recall, then found the answer. "Lambert."

Fuck.

My voice was tight. "Okay, thanks."

As soon as he disappeared from my cube, I closed the box and set it aside, making room for my laptop. I needed to see the email. Was there any chance the safe wasn't being installed until after the party?

No, there wasn't. The delivery was scheduled for Saturday—

In two freaking days.

I stood up from my chair so quickly, it rolled back and thudded quietly against the wall. I snatched up my purse, told Justin in the next cube over I was stepping out for a bit, and hurried for the elevator.

I thumbed a text message out to Vance, hoping he wasn't in a meeting.

Me: Please call me ASAP.

Thankfully, my phone rang as soon as I stepped outside the building, and I hurried along the sidewalk, walking with no destination other than to keep moving.

"What's wrong?" he asked, and if I wasn't freaking out, I would have been touched by the concern in his voice.

"Lambert's getting a new safe installed this weekend," I

blurted. "We're totally screwed."

He took a breath, probably still processing, but his tone was soothing. "Okay. It's going to be okay. We'll figure it out."

I couldn't tell if he was saying this simply to calm me down, or if he was just more rational than I was. All I could see was this enormous setback. I'd already been dealt one when Jillian vanished, and I wasn't sure I could overcome another so soon. All I'd worked for had been so close, and it was impossibly cruel to have another opportunity disappear.

"I don't think," Vance said, "you can get in his house in the next thirty-six hours."

"No," I bit out.

"Then," he said it with confidence, "we stick to the plan."

I pulled up short, making the guy walking behind me issue a disgruntled sound as he narrowly avoided a collision. I ignored his dirty look as he walked past.

"You don't understand. I knew how I was getting in the Browning safe. This one, I'm starting over. I don't know which attack method is going to work. And do you know how loud drilling can be? How long it can take?" My mind raced, spiraling downward. "How many drills I'm going to burn up before I even get inside?"

"Take a breath, Emery."

It didn't matter how softly he said it, that only made me more upset. "You take a breath! It could take me days to get it open, and how the fuck am I going to get all my equipment inside? I think people will notice when I show up with a duffle bag."

I despised how I was losing control of my emotions, but everything was breaking down.

Everything . . . except Vance. "Do you know anything about the new safe?"

"Yeah." Bitterness leeched from my words. "It's a fucking Lagerfield."

He paused, maybe expecting me to elaborate. "And that's bad?"

"For us? Yeah, that's bad. In addition to being notoriously hard to drill, it has countermeasures to protect against that. There's a chance if I drill in the wrong place and crack the plate, I'll activate the relocker system. Then everyone is locked out completely, and if Lambert wants his shit, he'll have to destroy the safe and hope the contents survive."

"That's not going to happen." He sounded certain, and it was the reassurance I desperately needed. I pictured him secluded in his fancy office, wearing a suit and a look of determination. "I know how bad you want this, and I'm telling you, we can do it. The party is a month away, so we have time." He was intent on solving the problem. "Let's not worry about anything else right now and start with the safe. What do you need to get inside?"

I tried to compartmentalize my fear and focus. "It'd be easier if I knew exactly what I was going up against. Like, something to practice on. But, Vance," I swallowed a breath, "a Lagerfield is over a hundred thousand dollars."

"Okay." There was no hesitation, because money was no object, and it was win at all costs. "How many do you want me to buy?"

The next morning, I had an email sitting in my inbox, informing me that a Lagerfield had been ordered for the Hale estate. After I'd calmed down during our phone call, I'd asked Vance about the dress, but he didn't know anything about it.

It was tailored to me and there was no label inside, confirming my suspicion.

This dress was from Jillian, a message she was alive.

I'd spent every available minute researching attack strategies while waiting for the safe to be delivered. When I posed the hypothetical question, my group of fellow master safecrackers arrived at the opinion I should manipulate the lock, but this scared the shit out of me. I was more comfortable with my drill and my borescope than going meticulously number by number on the dial to find the low spots.

I promised myself I wouldn't make any decisions until I was face-to-face with the beast.

A week later, it was delivered and installed in the room Vance referred to as the office, although he said it was only staged that way. No work was done in there—the room hadn't been used in years.

The Hale home office mimicked a two-story tall library. There was a spiral staircase on one side that led to the balcony with a reading area in front of the shelves full of books. On the other side stretched an enormous fireplace that had to be original to the house. It was decorated with an ornate, wood carved mantel that was absolutely gorgeous.

Calling the Lagerfield a beast was somewhat misleading. It wasn't a vault. Usually, safes were placed out of the way or concealed entirely, but this one was set out from the wall, near the center of the room.

Vance stared at it skeptically. "It's smaller than I expected."

It wasn't as tall or deep as the space saving refrigerator in my apartment in Port Cove, but it was close. The door was dark silver and had a faceted texture to it, making it look like art. The four-spoke handle on the left had a perfect symmetry with the black dial on the right. I opened the door, peeking inside at the different drawers and the spot at the bottom to store larger items.

"It's beautiful," I said.

And intimidating. Not just with how difficult it'd be to penetrate, but I didn't want to accidentally destroy it and waste so much of Vance's money.

"It is," he agreed. "But he's going to hide it in the floor?"

"No. The install paperwork said it was to be placed upright in the same room as the safe they removed. He might hide it behind something, though."

I finished my examination, and my heart sank.

"What's wrong?" he asked.

"I'm going to have to manipulate the open."

"Meaning?"

I put my hand on the dial, turning it slowly to feel the tension. "It's a process where I use touch and sound to figure out the combination." I watched the numbers as they ticked by. "The good news is it won't damage the safe. Lambert will never know we opened it, and I'll only need to bring one piece of equipment—an amplifier."

He tilted his head. "Okay. And the bad news?"

"It's a long, three-step process . . . and I don't know if I can do it."

"You can." He said it like it was just that simple. He closed the door, turned the handle, and spun the dial to lock it. "Show me."

For the first time in a long while, I looked at a safe without certainty I could get it open. Once I'd gotten good at cracking them and started taking on bigger jobs, I'd developed a bit of an ego. Every safe was a puzzle I knew I'd solve; it was only a matter of how long it'd take me and the best method to get it open.

"You reset the combination already?" I asked. "Because you'd be amazed how many people use the manufacturer's default."

His smile was sly. "Yeah, I reset it."

"Grab a seat, then. This will take a while."

I went to the tool bag I'd brought with me, unzipped it, and retrieved the black box that housed my amplifier and headphones. There were two tall chairs set in front of the fireplace, and he turned one of them around to face the safe before sitting in it.

"The first step," I said, "is to determine the contact points. That's the notch at the front of the drive cam that the lever falls into." His blank look told me he didn't get it. "It's like a master gate that once every wheel has lined up and the fence drops, I turn the handle on the door. This makes the lever move into the notch and pull the bolt back. So, I start by listening for the contact point clicks from the lever."

I got out the amplifier, which was a small, thick, black disc that held an extremely sensitive microphone, and the battery pack which was the same size as a stack of notecards. He said nothing as I used duct tape to place the microphone right beside the dial, slipped the wired headphones over my ears, and flipped the switch on the battery pack.

"One click tells me where the notch starts," I said, "and another tells me where it ends."

I began turning the wheel slowly, listening to the sound of each number as it went past. There were one hundred numbers on the dial, and they all sounded identical. I took a deep breath, closed my eyes, and reminded myself that patience was the greatest tool of all.

Click ... click ... click.

My eyes popped open, and I looked at the number I'd stopped on. There was a black grease pencil in my bag that I dug out, scribbled the number on the front of the safe, and tucked the pencil behind my ear. Then I kept turning the dial until the next click that sounded off. It was jotted down beside the first number.

I removed my headphones and motioned to my notes. "The contact area is between twenty-one and thirty. That's the first step. Now I can use this to determine how many wheels we're dealing with. Each wheel is another number in the combination, so let's hope for a low number."

He sat in his chair, looking as elegant and refined as the rest of the room, and it felt weirdly like I was a peasant performing a show for royalty. He seemed fascinated, and I was happy to entertain him.

"I park the wheels on the number opposite the contact area. On this dial, that's seventy-one." I spun the numbers until I hit the one I wanted and took my hand off. "I'm going to let it rest for a second, so when I start again, the cam will reengage from here." I slipped my headphones back on. "I rotate the dial, and every time I pass seventy-one, I'll hear a click as I pick up another wheel. I go until there are no more clicks."

He was an excellent audience member. Vance didn't move a muscle or do a thing to distract me as I turned the black knob, listening intently.

Two.

Three.

Four.

My stomach turned. Every number added meant exponentially more combinations I'd have to try. Four wheels generated fifteen options. Five was one hundred twenty.

Anything above that would be *impossible* to complete in the time I'd have.

Please don't let there be more than five.

I completed the fifth rotation, only to hear . . . nothing. I blew out a long breath, pushing off my headphones. "Four wheels."

"Yes." Vance's pleased smile made my heart beat quicker.

But I sobered when I focused back on the safe and wiped away my scribbles. I drew two horizontal lines across the door, which wasn't easy given the textured front. I marked zero at the left side and ninety-nine on the right and broke it up by tens to create my graph.

"That was the easy part," I said. "Now I have to graph the left and right contact points." I spun the dial to the right a few times to clear it before landing at the beginning. "I start at zero and go around the dial, marking places of interest. Maybe I hear a click, or I feel tension in the dial. Once that's done, I park the dial at three, and go around again. I park it at the sixth position, and repeat. I keep going in increments of three until I have it all mapped out."

His smile drained away. "What?"

"Yeah, forget what you see in movies. It's not a quick thing."

I put the headphones on, did my best to tune everything out, and got to work. This was a puzzle that wanted to be solved, I told myself. It was my job to set it free.

I turned the dial, charting the high points on the top half of my graph and the low points below. It was painstaking process, but by going in increments of three, I used the lock against itself. What seemed like twenty-four on the first round was revealed to actually be twenty-five the more times I started from a different position.

It took me more than an hour to map the numbers out,

and I didn't feel that confident about the four I'd settled on, but I was willing to cut myself some slack. It was my first attempt, and I hadn't done a manipulation like this in a very long time. I would get better with practice.

I wrote down the four numbers with dashes between them. "I don't know the order, so I'll have to try different combinations until I hit the right sequence. But you can save us time and tell me if any of these aren't the right number."

Vance stared at my scribbled notes with an unreadable expression. Had he done it to disguise his fear? He didn't say anything.

My heart fell to the floor. "Oh, shit. Are *any* of them right?"

He stood from his chair and put a hand out in a reassuring gesture. "Yes, sorry. I'm just impressed. Three of them are right, and the one that isn't? It's very close."

"It's twelve that's wrong, isn't it?" I studied my graph critically. "Eleven?"

He rubbed a hand on the back of his neck and nodded. "Eleven."

"I was fifty-fifty on that one."

He strolled toward me, plucked the grease pencil from behind my ear, and wrote the correct sequence of the combination beneath my graph. His numbers were printed nice and neat and far better than mine, and that made sense. He'd probably had classes in cursive and handwriting to go along with his etiquette training.

I turned off and put away my amp before dialing in the combination. When I turned the handle, there was no sound of the bolt sliding back, but that was due to the excellent craftsmanship. The door swung open.

"With practice, I'll get better," I said, peering in at the empty safe. "But I don't know if I'll get faster. There wasn't any time pressure tonight, and I wasn't worried about getting caught. So, that's going to affect me, and it'll make me second-guess everything."

His voice was not unlike a coach to his star player the night before the big game. "The party will go on for hours, so you'll have time. And until then, you'll practice, and I'll try to replicate the environment as much as possible."

"Going in without my drills, with no backup plan . . ." My gaze sought his, making sure he'd see how anxious I was. "It's terrifying to me."

He took a deep, steady breath. "I know, but we won't need a backup plan. I'm telling you, Emery. You've got this."

I wasn't able to practice every night. On the Fourth of July, Vance had a fundraiser event we needed to make an appearance at, and then later that week I had to stay overnight for a job in Atlanta. Otherwise, if I wasn't at work, I was at the Hale house practicing.

I was getting better. And I was getting faster too.

On my ninth day, I manipulated the open in fifty-one minutes. Vance had been sitting in his usual spot—the tufted chair in front of the fireplace—while he watched and timed me. He bolted up out of his seat, grinning as he announced my new record.

I'd switched to a regular pencil and paper graph to save time. That way, I wouldn't need to draw or erase evidence of my work on the safe. I also began wearing latex gloves, so I could get used to the feel of the dial, without leaving fingerprints behind.

But tonight, I was tired, and my knees hurt from kneeling in front of the safe, and it allowed negative thoughts to creep in. No matter how good I got, it wasn't going to matter. The stakes on the night where I had to do this for real were impossibly high. I'd be on my own and in the dark—literally. In case anyone wandered by Lambert's bedroom, it needed to look unoccupied.

Before I'd started tonight, Vance had turned off the lights, and I'd clicked on my headlamp, but now my mood matched the darkness surrounding me. Even though he was barely lit by the screen of his phone, he must have noticed.

"What's wrong?"

I turned toward him but stared at his feet to keep from blinding him with my headlamp. "I'm off tonight. Like, nothing feels right and I'm all up in my head." It wasn't the full truth, and he deserved to know. "I'm scared I'm going to get overwhelmed by the pressure."

He rose from his seat and spoke his warning in a soft voice. "I'm turning on the lights."

When they flooded the room, I blinked, turned off my lamp, and pulled the headband down, sinking back to sit on my feet. My posture probably reflected my defeated attitude.

"Stand up."

His tone was so sharp, it made me jolt, and a weird tendril of desire curled around me. I didn't like being told what to do, so . . . why did I follow his order without hesitation?

He was pleased when I climbed to my feet, and his eyes sharpened with calculation.

"You want me to add some pressure?" The corner of his mouth hinted at a wicked smile. "Take off your clothes."

I glanced at the doorway to the left, and then the one

on my right since there were two exits. Neither door was closed. He'd said no one came in here, but his brother and sister-in-law were home, not to mention the staff. "Someone might walk in."

"Yes, that's the idea. I want you naked right fucking now, Emery. You can get dressed again once you've got my safe open."

He'd poured flames on my body, and it burned up all the exhaustion and boredom I'd had moments ago. While I highly doubted anyone would catch us, this sexy game had a hint of danger, and more importantly—stakes.

I didn't just approve; I was eager to play.

His pleased expression was back as I gripped the hem of my t-shirt and lifted it up over my head. His gaze zeroed in on my fingers as they worked to undo the button at the top of my jeans. And his eyes hooded with lust when my bra dropped to the rug.

Once I was naked except for the white latex gloves, he returned to his chair and sank down into it. He placed an elbow on the armrest and crooked a finger over his lips like a judge evaluating an audition. I was hot underneath his powerful stare, and uncomfortably turned on.

And I felt the worst of his *pressure* deep between my thighs.

"One more thing," Vance said as I knelt in front of the safe. "In forty-five minutes, I'll text Elliot and have him bring you a glass of water."

Holy shit.

SIXTEEN

EMERY

Vance wasn't kidding. His sexy and sinister expression said he was absolutely serious.

It was amazing what a little motivation could do. Suddenly, the tension was back in the dial. Suspicious clicks were easier to discern. My pencil hurried to plot out the different points, and even though I was naked and the air conditioning was strong, sweat blossomed on my skin.

An invisible clock loomed over my head, counting down and pushing urgency through everything I did. This timed puzzle had another layer too. I had to battle against the distraction of his relentless gaze on me. It hovered over my breasts, trailed down my waist, and caressed my thighs. It made me want to shiver, and I had to redo a rotation, worried I'd missed the click I was looking for around the number eighty-nine.

I marked a spike around fifty on my paper, dropped the pencil, and put my hand back on the dial, trying to steady myself. I couldn't rush or I'd miss valuable information, but . . .

"Time?" I asked.

"Nineteen minutes left until I send my text."

Fuck. I had less time than that to determine the four numbers, because I'd need time to try the different sequences.

Slow down, a voice in my head warned. *Breathe.*

Eighty-nine was definitely one of them, and I was starting to feel confident about the others—

In addition to my noise canceling headphones, I'd had my eyes closed to block everything out, so I hadn't seen or heard him move. Vance knelt on the floor behind me, his knees on either side of my legs. His t-shirt covered chest pressed against my back as his hands grasped my waist.

It was a whole new level of distraction when his mouth trailed a line of kisses along the top of my bare shoulder. He pushed the curtain of my hair out of his way, moving up the curve of my neck.

"I can't concentrate," I whined.

"That's the point," he whispered, knowing to be quiet because of the microphone.

It got infinitely harder when he eased a hand between my legs and used his fingertips to strum my clit.

"Shit, don't do that." Only my breathless voice told him to keep going.

"Focus," he commanded. His fingers massaged, and I weakened under their featherlight touch. Oh, God, it felt so good. I swallowed hard and stared at the dial, trying to ignore the man at my back who seemed to know exactly where to touch and kiss to derail me completely.

"So fucking wet for me," he murmured. "Spread your knees."

It was so hard to tune him out, and doing what he said seemed the best way to conserve my time. He backed away from me as I widened my knees, and then I didn't need to imagine the ticking clock because he set his phone face-up on the floor, showing the timer running onscreen.

On some level, I'd heard him shuffling around behind me, but I hadn't realized he'd lain down with his back on the rug, until he began to scoot beneath me.

I flattened a hand on the safe door to stop my jolt of surprise. "What are you doing?"

Shit, his voice was sexy and playful. "Helping."

I stared down in disbelief as he positioned his head between my knees. "How is this helping?"

"You don't want anyone to catch me eating your pussy, do you?"

There was no time to process what he'd just said. His strong hands clasped around my thighs and pulled me back onto his face. His lips parted, and his tongue licked a line from my entrance up to my clit, and my entire body shuddered with pleasure. It made my fingers curl inward, and I scratched my nails across the textured front of the Lagerfield.

His mouth was bliss.

I had to fight the urge to lean forward and rest my forehead against the safe door. Time was running out on the clock, plus if I was too loud, it might draw someone in here. They'd walk in to see me naked except for a pair of headphones and thin latex gloves while I straddled Vance's face.

As he always did, he seemed to be enjoying using his mouth as much as I enjoyed experiencing it. His hands slid forward and up on my thighs, so he could use his fingers to peel me open to his lush tongue.

My breath came and went in shallow bursts, and my vision hazed from the pleasure, but I fought to focus in on the clicks coming through my headphones. His tongue lashed at me, fluttering and cartwheeling, but I didn't dare look down. I was sure he was watching me, and if I looked into his eyes right now, I'd abandon my task and grip a handful of his hair to position his mouth at the exact spot to send me over the edge.

"Fuck," I breathed.

I was so close. Not just to being ready to try the sequences, but to losing control. It was a race against the clock and my orgasm. I ticked the dial, focusing in on the telltale heavy click I'd come to learn was what I was looking for.

My hand shook as I listed out the four numbers on the piece of paper taped to the door. I dialed the sequence as written, pulled the handle, and when it didn't budge, I zeroed it out and tried my second sequence.

When Vance saw what I was doing, he kicked into overdrive. His lips closed around my clit and sucked, sending sparks of heat shooting down my legs. I groaned, half with pleasure and half with desperation.

"Goddamnit," I whispered when my next three attempts didn't work.

I spun the dial as fast as I could, holding back the sensations he caused. The fifth attempt failed. As did the sixth. Blood rushed loudly through my ears, and my heartrate climbed toward the ceiling.

The seventh attempt wasn't right.

The eighth wasn't either.

"Motherfucker," I bit out under my breath.

When the tenth attempt failed, I started to second guess myself. Which number was I least confident about? If all fifteen combinations didn't work, would I have time to start over with a new set? What if I had the right combination sequence and had blown past it due to my shaky hand?

My anxiety spiraled around me like rope, twisting tighter with each turn of the dial. The eleventh sequence wasn't right. I sucked in a breath and held it, spinning the wheel as steady as I could, given my whole body was shaking.

The timer from Vance's phone went off, ringing its startling electronic trill at the same moment I twisted the handle, and the door cracked open.

Yes.

Victory poured through me, and I grasped the spokes of the wheel in both hands, falling forward to rest my forehead on the backs of my palms.

One of his hands came off me and slapped around on the rug until he found his phone and shut off the incessant timer. And since I'd done it, he seemed determined to give me a reward. His tongue flurried over my skin, with just the right amount of pressure, and in just the right place, and . . . and . . .

"Oh, God, I'm coming," I sobbed with relief.

It was one of those orgasms where it made every muscle contract, and as it gripped me, wave after wave rolled through. Heat blasted up my spine, sending fireworks out along every nerve ending. I squeezed so hard on the wheel, I expected it to break off in my hands.

I was left tinglingly numb as my climax receded, and the tension in my muscles began to fade. The air in the room was thin, and I struggled to drag some of it into my lungs, using the last of my waning strength not to sag into Vance and smother him to death.

Thankfully, he retreated, giving me room to drop down and shift so I was sitting to one side.

"You are," I said between hurried breaths, "way too good at that."

He moved so he was beside me on the floor, giving me a perfect view of his dazzling smile. "And you," he dropped a kiss on my shoulder, "are pretty damn good at that." His head tilted toward the safe.

I pulled my gloves off and tossed them aside. "I had help."

Electricity glimmered in his eyes. "You did it *despite* my help."

He leaned in, and I met him halfway, causing our mouths to collide in a kiss that contained enough heat to power a small city. My victory made me feel invincible, and I cupped his face in my hands, climbing into his lap.

I'd had an orgasm, but I wasn't satisfied—not until he'd had one, too.

When I pushed a hand between our bodies and palmed him through his pants, a soft groan came from him. The muscles along his sharp jawline flexed as he locked his teeth, but he didn't discourage by urging my hand away, and he didn't tell me to stop.

Not even when I sat back and used both hands to undo the button and drop his zipper.

I touched his erection through the soft, thin fabric of his underwear, and he dropped down onto his back, giving me more room. It was a clear signal he was okay with this.

"Finally built up that tolerance to me?" I teased with both my words and a fingertip tracing the outline of him.

He didn't use words to reply. Instead, he hooked his thumbs in his underwear and pushed the waistband down until it was stretched across his thighs, leaving him totally available. Then, he lifted his head and peered at me with a silent challenge.

He wanted me to touch him.

Finally.

I closed my fist around his dick, and an aftershock of pleasure spiked through me when he blew out a long, satisfied breath. He was so hard and throbbed in my hand as I gave him a slow, tight stroke. I loved the way his chest rapidly rose and fell. How his hands at his sides tightened into fists. The low groan he gave when I moved faster.

It was a little like being back in high school, the way I worried about someone coming in and catching us fooling around. I liked the added element of danger, even when it wasn't a big deal now. We were both adults, and yes, I was naked, but we weren't having sex. A handjob was relatively tame.

I barely got a second hand on him before he launched upright. He seized my shoulders and pulled me down, turning me onto my back. It was an awkward tangle of limbs, and he was constricted by the pants around his knees, but when I was beneath him and he settled between my legs, all the air whooshed out of my body.

We were only a heartbeat away from sex.

His kiss was urgent, and he rubbed against me, letting me feel the full length of his cock against my clit. Holy fuck, I couldn't stop myself from responding. My hips moved to line us up.

"Can we forget about my 'no sex' policy?" he whispered in between mind numbing kisses.

Yes, my body chanted, but I ignored that. "What?"

His mouth brushed over my cheek as his lips made their way to my ear. "I don't care about it anymore. All I care about it you." He delivered a tender kiss just below my ear and pushed up on his arms so he could look at me. His eyes were full of need, but also longing. "I mean it, Emery. You're all I can think about."

I lifted a hand and pressed my palm over his heart. "It's the same for me."

"I don't want to wait any longer. I just want to be with you, in every way possible. Don't you want that?"

God, how I did. "Of course, but you're so close to finishing.

Only three days left."

"That's a lifetime."

Maybe he was joking or maybe he was serious. It was impossible to tell. He returned to my lips, delivered a kiss that was full of seduction, and his hips moved, making him slide subtly between my legs. The sensation of his bare skin against mine sent goosebumps flooding down my calves. All I'd have to do was move an inch and give him the word he was desperate for.

It simmered inside me, wanting to come out.

The temptation of him was so overwhelming, I nearly broke under it.

But he'd told me how important this vow was and that he wanted to complete it, and I'd promised to help him if his willpower faltered. How could I let him give up when he was so close to the finish line? I didn't want him to look back on our first time with regret.

Plus, he'd been there for me every night, chasing my doubt away when I worried I couldn't conquer my goal. I needed to do the same for him.

"You're not giving up," I said, easing him back so there was space between our bodies. "In three days, you can have me," I wrapped my hand around him and filled my voice with gravity, "*any* way you want."

He jerked in my fist and his eyes filled with steam. I clamped both hands around him, squeezing a grunt of satisfaction from him.

My voice rasped with sex as I spoke. "Let me tell you what I'd do to you if I could."

I'd never talked dirty before, but it poured from me with ease. I told him how I wanted to use my mouth on him. Tease him with my tongue. Wrap my lips around his big dick and take him deep. And as I detailed my fantasy to him, I stroked my hands steadily along his length.

His mouth hung open and he gazed at me like I was too sexy to be real, but I thought the same of him. His expression was carnal, and I saw the ravenous wolf I'd gotten hints of before. My tempo was quick, but not as quick as he would have liked, because his hips began to move. It made him slide back and forth between my tight fingers, like he was fucking my hands.

"Is that how fast you want me to go," I asked, "when I fuck you with my mouth?"

He groaned in approval. I had my hands clasped low above my stomach, letting him rock over me, and heat fogged everything outside of him. But my hands were dry, and I wanted it to feel as good for him as possible, so I lifted one hand to my mouth. His eyes darkened as he watched me lick my palm.

I did one, then the other, making it easier for him to glide through my hands and imagine the dampness of my mouth.

"God, I can't wait to do it," I purred. "I can't wait for you to come in my mouth and feel every pulse when you do it."

It was like I'd punched the words from him. "Oh, *fuck*."

He was already close, but suddenly, he was very, *very* close, and I loved the idea that my fantasy was helping push him over the edge. We moved as a team, working together to get him there, and I watched in amazement as his eyes slammed shut and the muscles in the arms around me corded with tension.

His hips slowed to a jerky stop as he came, and wave after wave of warm, thick cum flicked onto my stomach and breasts. There was something primal about it I enjoyed. Physical proof that I'd given him satisfaction, and symbolic proof I was his.

Vance pushed out a long, shuddering breath before rising

onto his knees, and gripped himself to wring out the final drops of his orgasm. He stared down at me, surveying the work we'd done, and—God—his smile blasted heat into every inch of me.

I lay still on the rug while he stood, pulled up his pants, and zipped up. The room was quiet other than his muted footfalls as he strolled to the desk and tugged several tissues from the box there.

He asked it in a soft voice, like it was more for himself than me. "What are you doing to me?"

How was I supposed to answer that? Surely the effect he had over me was more powerful. I should be the one asking him that.

He came over and knelt beside me, using the tissues to clean me up, and when it was done, he curled up on his side. He tucked a hand under his head and stared into my eyes like they had the answers he desired.

I rolled onto my side toward him, bringing us closer, but it made a lock of hair fall over my face. He reached out, tracing a fingertip over my forehead to brush the hair back, and tucked it behind my ear. If he were trying to manipulate opening my heart, this tender gesture would have been a suspicious click, letting him know he was on the right path to discovering the combination.

"Thank you," he said quietly.

I gave him a lopsided smile. "For jerking you off?"

His short laugh was warm, but sincerity moved in, taking over his expression. "I meant thank you for not letting me give up."

"Of course."

This time, the click in my heart was much louder, and I had to swallow a breath to disguise it.

SEVENTEEN

VANCE

The final three days were torture. I was dying to be with Emery, and I'd meant what I said. I didn't just want her physically, but in every way. I spent each day at the office counting down the time until I was home, and she'd arrive for practice. I'd watch her work, and when it was done, we'd simply spend time together.

We'd talk, or watch something in the home theatre downstairs, or we'd fool around like virgin teenagers—which was way more fun than I ever remembered it being. Plus, I loved watching her practice with the safe. Whenever she heard a certain sound in her headphones, her eyebrows would tug together, creating a cute little crease between them.

Fuck, she was sexy.

Gorgeous and funny and dangerously smart. I liked how confident she was when it came to her field of work. She wasn't just competent, she was an expert. If she had an ego, it was earned, and that was fucking hot.

I began my final morning of my vow like I always did—I jerked off while thinking about her and my plans once the leash was off. I went to the office, sat in my meetings, and researched the statutes for compliance with the rest of my team to prepare for an upcoming policy change. All the while, time ticked away in my head, building anticipation for when I'd get to see her again.

I had plans for tonight and was anxious to get to them.

A helpful distraction rolled into my inbox at three-thirty. It was an email from the investigator I'd contracted with out of Miami. The dress Emery had received had come from Aruba, so I'd had the guy start there. Attached was a summary and a few pictures for confirmation.

Jillian was alive.

I gazed at the pictures of her and Lucas together. There was one were they shopped together at a grocery store, and I imagined them deciding what they were going to cook for dinner that night. A picture of her walking down a sidewalk while she carried a plastic bag of produce, the buildings behind her bright and colorful.

Something stirred inside me when I double-clicked the last picture, making it fill my laptop screen. The image had captured Lucas barefoot on the deck of his boat with an enormous smile on his face. He had the bag of produce in one hand, probably the same one Jillian had been carrying in the last picture, and used his other hand to help her step aboard. She held her flip-flops by the straps, and like him, wore a huge grin.

Had the image been snapped the moment they were both laughing, or was this now their permanent state of being once they got away from Cape Hill? They looked so goddamn happy. They'd kept their relationship a secret, fooling everyone—including Sophia—but I wasn't mad at them.

It was impossible to be anything but happy for my friends.

The investigator's report said they were living on Lucas's

boat in Oranjestad and had the dock fees paid through the end of the month. The investigator confirmed he would check back with me then and see if I wanted to keep track of their movements.

I forwarded the email on to Emery, knowing she'd want to see and would probably feel the same way I did. Jillian spent so much of her life living for someone else. Hadn't she earned the right to be free?

I was weirdly nervous when I picked Emery up for dinner that night. Perhaps nervous was too strong of a word, but there was a tightness in my chest and an uneven feeling in my stomach. I'd spent the last two months talking myself up to her.

What if I couldn't live up to the hype?

The nerves dissolved when she opened her apartment door and gave me an easy smile. Her black dress was short, and her eye makeup was smoky, and she looked so good, for a split second I wondered if I could convince her to operate on Greenwich Mean Time. It was already tomorrow in that time zone.

Instead, I took the overnight bag from her hands and gestured to the waiting Range Rover that would drive us to the restaurant.

We hadn't really been out on a date since we'd returned from Monaco. She'd gone with me to events, and we'd had dinner together at the house several times, but this was different. I wasn't usually a show-off, and I didn't like to flaunt my wealth, but that died when we walked into the place and nearly every male head turned her direction.

Mine, I wanted to fire back at them.

Their stares of envy bubbled in my bloodstream. They thought she was beautiful, and they were right, but they didn't know the half of it. She was the whole fucking package, and I was proud she'd chosen to be with me.

When this thing with Lambert was over, I was going to make more of an effort to romance her, and if I got to show her off while doing it—well, that was the icing on the cake.

We ate dinner and drank wine, and talked about politics, of all things. When the conversation strayed toward the photos I'd forwarded to her, we both avoided saying Jillian's name. It was extremely unlikely anyone was listening to us, but some of my father's paranoia had rubbed off on me, and I didn't want to accidentally undo any of Jillian's hard work to escape.

Like me, Emery was happy for our friend.

After dinner, we rode back to my house, and I put her overnight bag in my bedroom while she went to the office and got set up for practice. By the time I made my way down there, the lights were off, her amp was hooked up, and her headlamp was on. I took a moment to appreciate her like that, lit only by the glow of her flashlight as it reflected off the metal door of the safe.

She knelt in front of it, wearing her sexy dress, and her unsexy headphones, lamp, and white gloves. But all that did nothing to detract from her. I assumed watching her was like watching a painter create art, only her canvas was a paper graph taped to the front of the safe door.

I used the light from my phone to guide my way to the chair I watched from and did my best to stay quiet. I didn't want to distract her, and yeah, it'd probably be better if I wasn't in the room, but . . . I liked being near her. So, I attempted to be a statue, so she'd forget I was there.

I was surprised how long it took her to catch on to what I'd done tonight. She marked a dot on her paper, only to erase it after another pass around the dial, and glared at her graph like it was written in a foreign language.

Abruptly, she pulled off her headphones, straightened her posture, and began to dial in the combination. She turned it to the right until she hit sixty-nine, spun to the left to get to zero, and then repeated with the same two numbers. When the wheel on the door was turned, the safe swung open.

She flashed me an amused smile and yanked off her gloves with a snap of the latex. "Nice."

I tossed a hand up in a 'why not' gesture. "Let's go for a walk."

Once she had everything put away, I took her hand, led her through the house, and out the back onto the balcony. It was late and the sun had set hours ago, but it was also mid-July, which meant other than the humidity, it was nice outside.

Her heels clicked across the stone tiles as I pulled her toward the stairs that led down to the gardens. The landscape lights were on, casting a warm glow on the trees surrounding the perimeter of the lawn.

"Where are we going?" she asked, genuinely curious.

"You'll see."

We came down the stairs and took the path to the left that curved around the roses I'd been told my grandmother planted, heading for the thick wall of meticulously maintained evergreens. The hedges were nearly eight feet tall, and the maze was full of dead ends and switchbacks. To a regular person trying to solve it, it was likely confusing during the day. With the subdued light at night, it had to be daunting.

We stepped off the stone paver path and onto the pebbled one, making our feet crunch softly as we walked through the entrance. Emery's eyes went wide as she gazed around, taking in the hedges and the narrow tunnel they created.

"This is amazing," she said.

Like Monaco, I got to see it through new eyes as I watched

her experience the maze.

"Do you want me to show you how to get to the center, or do you want to try—"

"Don't tell me." She was already a few steps ahead and considering which side of the first branch to take. "I want to try."

I chuckled. "I figured."

She guessed wrong, but I kept my mouth shut. When she turned the corner and reached a dead end, she peered at the statue replica of the Venus de Milo for a moment, and I half expected her to ask it for directions. Instead, she turned around and breezed right past me, determined to get back to the fork and try the path she hadn't chosen.

We meandered through the maze, not in any rush, but she moved with an excited quickness. She was a lot like me in that she viewed life as a series of games, and she was competitive too. I was glad she always played to win.

She began to drag her feet at turns, drawing lines in the pebbled path in an attempt to mark her progress. It was a smart idea, but it wasn't much help as we got closer to the center. There were two long walls strategically placed that created loops, leading back to where she'd started.

But Emery was so clever, I suspected she'd drawn a map inside her head, and she knew exactly where to try next. She turned to her left, rounded the corner, and gasped when she spied the tiered water fountain at the center of the large, open space.

When I'd put Emery's overnight bag in my room earlier, I'd texted Elliot the go-ahead, and now I surveyed his execution of my instructions. I'd told him I planned to stargaze with Emery at the center of the maze, and he'd taken my directions and improved upon them. Was it possible he'd done this more for her than for me? Elliot was always quick to smile when she was around. She'd charmed him completely.

He'd probably enlisted the help of one of the groundskeepers to get the thick mattress off the double lounger on the patio and bring it in here. The bed rested on the pebbled ground off to the side of the fountain. It was lit by the landscape lighting, but several flameless candles surrounded it, flickering in the night.

Her gaze moved from the fountain to the picnic basket beside the mattress and the two overturned champagne flutes resting on top of its lid, waiting to be used. The space was incredibly romantic, and maybe a bit overboard, but Emery's breathless reaction caused satisfaction to roll through me.

"I thought we could watch the stars." My statement came out in an uneven voice, and I cleared my throat, trying to shake loose the nerves that had come out of nowhere. This would be our first time together, but not my first time *ever*.

So, why the hell did it feel that way?

"The Perseids meteor shower started tonight," I added.

She nodded and stared at the bed, and whatever nerves I had, the same ones seemed to be getting to her too. But that made it easier, because now I could push my anxiety away and focus on making her comfortable.

I strolled to the picnic basket, grabbed the stems of the glass flutes between the fingers of one hand, and lifted the lid to reveal the bottle of Dom Pérignon that was perched in a bucket of ice. Beside it was a box of chocolate covered strawberries.

Really, Elliot?

Did he think I was going to propose? The champagne had been the only thing I'd asked for.

"What's up?" she asked. "You're making a weird face."

"Nothing." I grabbed the bottle by the neck, pulled it out,

and closed the lid. "Want a drink?"

She eyed the dripping bottle. "Champagne, huh? Are we celebrating the loss of your second virginity?"

I laughed and set the glasses down so I could work on peeling off the foil and cage around the cork. "Maybe."

She sat down on the edge of the mattress and undid the ankle straps of her shoes, and once I had the cork popped and the glasses poured, I joined her.

"To midnight," she said as a toast, clinking the edge of her flute against mine with a soft *ting*.

We took our sips and set the glasses down, then stretched out side by side on the bed, staring up at the sky dotted with stars. I used the app on my phone to turn off the landscape lights, plunging us into darkness except for the wavering candles.

The house loomed nearby, and I was glad Royce and Marist had redecorated and moved into the master bedroom once my father had left. It would be unlikely anyone would see us out here in the near dark, but his old room had a perfect view of the maze, and the bubbling fountain at its center.

I wanted Emery and this night all to myself.

She didn't know constellations, and I was pretty rusty myself since all the sailing navigation I did relied entirely on instruments. Instead, we made up our own pictures in the stars, and she groaned when I kept pointing out the ones I found that looked like penises.

Emery was the first of us to see a shooting star, and when she gloated about it, I told her it wasn't a competition—although it totally was. She said she didn't believe in making wishes, but I suspected she had made one and didn't want to say for fear of it not coming true. Her wish had probably been about Lambert's safe, but I selfishly hoped not.

I wanted it to be about me.

As time ticked by, we both grew more anxious. We'd spent months waiting for this, building it up, and now that it was almost here, the pressure tried to surpass our desire. But I wouldn't let it. I propped myself up on an elbow, brushed my fingertips over her cheek, and lowered my mouth to hers.

She warmed to my kiss instantly, and something like a sigh of relief slipped out of her. As if she had been waiting on pins and needles for me, and now that we were connected, she could finally breath again. Thoughts swam in my head, competing with each other. I'd planned the evening, scripting how I wanted it to go. But now a million different ideas descended on me, all clamoring for attention, and I had no fucking clue which one to do first.

Emery did.

She rolled me onto my back and straddled my hips, and when she ground herself against me, my hands went naturally to her waist to encourage her to do it again. Our clothes were still on, but the way she rubbed against me, simulating what we planned to do . . . it made me insane with lust.

Our mouths stayed connected as my fingers walked up her back and searched for the zipper to her dress. I wanted her naked. I needed her tits in my hands, my teeth teasing her nipples. My tongue filled her mouth as I peeled the back of her dress open, but she had to break the kiss to sit upright on me. I watched as she grabbed the bottom hem and lift it in one big swoop, pulling her dress off. It was tossed aside, and then her black bra was undone and thrown on top of the pile.

Blood thundered in my veins, rushing to my dick as her breasts were freed. I reached out to cup them in my hands, but that wasn't what Emery wanted. She put her palms against mine, laced our fingers together, and pushed our hands down until they were pinned on either side of my head.

Hot.

I preferred to be the one in charge, but I certainly wasn't going to complain about her aggression. She could manhandle or have her way with me anytime she liked, as far as I was concerned. Her mouth crushed over mine and her tongue plunged in my mouth, pumping more heat into my body.

Our kiss was rough and urgent. When it ended, she climbed off to kneel beside me and shimmied out of her black panties, like she was in a rush to get naked. She glared at my shirt, irritated it existed, and then uttered the phrase I'd said to her so many times before.

"Take off your clothes."

If I wasn't dying for her, I would have shot back a smartass remark and teased her about being patient. But I *was* dying for her, so my fingers raced over the buttons of my shirt to undo them. She seized on my belt, and then the button and zipper beneath.

I didn't hide my excitement in my voice. "You're so fucking eager."

She hesitated and glanced at me sideways. "You're saying you're not?"

It drew a short laugh from me as I sat up, yanked my arms out of my sleeves, and threw my shirt on top of her dress. I ticked my head toward my lap and my erection that was splitting my fly open. "I think it's pretty obvious how eager I am."

I went to take my watch off, only to discover it missing, and my momentary confusion faded when I discovered it clasped to her wrist.

"Oh, sorry." A sheepish smile flashed across her lips. "I needed to borrow your watch."

When had she taken it off me? Probably when she'd

pressed my hands above my head and kissed me. She'd stolen my watch and my focus, and I was beginning to wonder if she'd stolen something much bigger, something I'd never given away before.

She was determined to get me as naked as she was, so when she grabbed the sides of my pants and pulled, I lifted my hips. She jerked the fabric, heavy from my undone belt, down my thighs, which made the contents of my pocket spill out onto the mattress beside her. My wallet, my phone, and a black foil packet that her gaze zeroed in on.

I watched the bob of her throat as she swallowed, and she picked up the condom by the wrapper's edge. She wasn't nervous, though; this was something different. She was considering something.

"If . . . uh," she started, "you wanted to forget about the condom, I'm okay with that." She took in a breath. "I'm on the pill, and neither of us has been with anyone else in a while. But if you want to use it, I'm totally okay with that too."

I paused.

My father had lectured me and Royce repeatedly that unprotected sex was the fastest way to disappoint him and screw up our lives. A lot of women only saw dollar signs when they looked at a Hale man, and he'd already made up his mind that Emery was using me.

But she wasn't.

I trusted her, and . . . dear God, did I want this. The idea of being with her with nothing between us was too tempting to resist. I plunked the packet from her fingers, tossed it away, and threaded my fingers through her silky hair, drawing her back to me.

Our kiss was hungry and intense. My heart sped along as it tried to keep up with the fire building between us, the one that dampened my temples and the back of my neck with sweat. I kicked off the pants and underwear around my knees and tried to get her to climb back on top of me, but she had other plans.

Her mouth left mine and dropped a line of kisses down the front of my throat. She carved a path across my bare chest, the strands of her hair dragging over my skin as she continued to move south. My lungs forgot how to fucking work as her mouth descended over my stomach and narrowly avoided where I most wanted her to go.

We'd had foreplay. *Months* of it. I wasn't sure I wanted any more until her fist closed around me and she pumped from the head all the way down to the base. The need in my body was so strong, it verged on painful, and I wasn't sure how much longer I could wait.

But she'd taken my watch, and so I endured her exquisite torture without knowing when it was going to end. Each slow stroke of her hand pressed me closer to the brink of losing control. I'd push her hand out of the way, roll her onto her back, and drive into her. I'd fuck her all the ways I'd spent the last six weeks describing in vivid detail, and we'd both love every second of it.

Emery was bent over me on her knees, her face close enough to my dick that I could feel her warm breath touching me. This merciless teasing was the worst of all, and I clenched my fists to keep from putting them on her head and pushing down. The muscles in my legs corded, twisting with tension.

She flung the curtain of her hair back out of her way so I could see better, and then dropped her forearm across my stomach. It was so she could see my watch she'd borrowed and the second hand on it as it ticked closer to the new day.

I was aware waiting until midnight was dumb. The bet

was immature, the deadline subjective, and the rules ridiculous. Yet it still felt like an achievement as time crept toward midnight and my victory. I tried to better myself, to resist temptation, and look what I'd gained. I had this beautiful woman not only as a lover, but as my partner.

"Ten," she whispered and planted a kiss on my stomach. "Nine." Her lips brushed lower across my skin. "Eight."

On her countdown went, with kisses dropped in between the numbers, her path circling from the top of one thigh to the other. I clenched my jaw, holding back a groan of anticipation.

"Two." Her word was a ghost, barely louder than the water gently falling in the fountain. Her lips brushed across the sensitive underside of my tip, and before the pleasurable sensation could storm up my body, she uttered the final word. "One."

The wet, velvet heat of her mouth was searing as it closed around me, and my brain emptied of thought. Down she went, pushing her lips as close to the base as she could, and my vision tunneled.

"Oh, fuck," I moaned. "*Fuck.*"

I couldn't find any other words to express how amazing it felt. It took all of five seconds for me to determine it was the best goddamn blowjob of my life, and if I wasn't careful, it would be over much too quickly. And I'd be damned if I'd come like this and ruin the fun before we really got started.

So, I let her slide her mouth up and down me and swirl her devious tongue until my legs shook and my hips ached to thrust. She marched me right up to the edge before I grasped her shoulder and urged her back.

Her head lifted and her eyes were wide. She was stunned by the interruption, probably because she hadn't been down there very long, but that was entirely her fault. What was it she'd said to me the other night?

"You are," I tried to catch my breath, "way too good at that."

I sat up and grabbed her waist, pulling her into my lap so she was once again straddling me, and her warm breasts flattened against my chest.

"What would you do to me," I murmured against her lips, "if you could?"

The wind blew, making the walls of evergreen shiver and undulate around us.

"I think if you'd let me," she whispered, "I might love you."

EIGHTEEN

VANCE

Of all the things I'd expected to tumble out of Emery's mouth, this was not one of them. I went still, hoping if I didn't move, if I didn't breathe, it'd let me process what she'd just said. But it didn't help. My mind refused to understand.

"Is it allowed?" she asked.

I swallowed even though my mouth had suddenly gone dry, and my voice was low and off-kilter. "Allowed?"

Her hands cased the sides of my face, and she stared into my eyes like they were bottomless. "You told me once not to fall in love with you."

My stupid heart wouldn't maintain a steady rhythm. As an attorney, I'd been taught not to ask a game-changing question during examination if I didn't already know the answer, and even though she'd basically said she loved me, I still felt like I was ignoring the advice. I didn't know how she'd respond. "Have you?"

Her smile was shy. "I have."

"Then," I drew in an enormous breath, "I guess I'll allow it." Her lips parted, maybe to scold me for trying to make light of this serious moment, but I wasn't finished. "On the condition you say it again."

Her soft laugh reached inside my chest and squeezed.

"Vance . . . I love you."

I wrapped my arms around her, crushing her to me, and it put my lips right beside her ear. I'd only said it a handful of times in my life. I'd held the words in, locked up tightly in my heart, but I should have known better. There was no countermeasure I could install that she couldn't outsmart, no combination she couldn't decipher.

It was surprising how easily the words rolled off my tongue. "I love you too."

And now that it was out there, the world seemed to stop. All that remained was the need to show her how I loved her. I tightened my arms behind her back, lifting and turning us so she was beneath me, making her soft brown hair splash all around her on the mattress.

Every plan I'd made was tossed aside and smoldered into ash in the fire enveloping us. Emery's legs wrapped around my hips, and her hands gripped my shoulders, and her wide, beautiful eyes begged me to bring us together.

So, I did.

She made a sigh similar to the one when I'd first kissed her, like she'd been in agony and finally found relief with me. I eased my hips forward, sliding into the snug heat of her body that gripped me like a vise.

Fuck, she was all around me. Everywhere. Which one of us was inside the other?

I kissed her as I pushed deeper, going until her hands tightened on my shoulders, signaling that was as far as she could take me. I dropped my forehead into the crook of her neck, breathing in the faint perfume she'd put on hours ago, and gave her time to adjust to the size of me.

I wished I could see us from afar right now, our naked bodies tangled together, lit by candlelight and the fireflies floating in the air under a moonless sky. Her heart was pounding. I could feel it with our chests pressed together. Did I own it the way she owned mine?

When she was ready, I drew my hips back and then eased them forward, and this action pulled a pleasureful whimper from her. It begged for more, so I gave it to her. I found a slow, steady rhythm that allowed me to move deep and really feel the sensation as I pushed into her body.

"Oh, God," she moaned as I sucked on her neck. "You feel so good."

I grunted in agreement.

Our kisses dripped with passion. Her fingers dragged down my back, gliding over the straining muscles as I exerted myself, rocking my body over hers, sliding inside her. It was wild to me that I'd spent all this time telling her every filthy plan I had, all the dirty fantasies of how I was going to fuck her, yet this wasn't anything like that. It was infinitely hotter.

Better in every way.

I'd had plenty of sex before, but never . . . a connection.

We were both sweating now, making our skin stick together as I thrust, and her body took the impact. My muscles were taut and strained, and my orgasm kept trying to creep closer, but I wasn't going to get mine until she had hers.

I hadn't made Emery come from penetration alone, so it seemed unlikely that was going to happen right now. I slid a hand under her ass, tilting her hips up, which allowed me to grind against her clit with my pelvis.

The cadence of her breathing changed abruptly, and her hand suddenly grabbed a handful of my ass. I grinned. This new angle was a winner. I drove into her, rolling my hips on the downstroke so she'd get pleasure inside and out, and when my mouth claimed her, Emery broke apart.

Her orgasm radiated through her body, and the rhythmic pulses deep inside squeezed at me. I froze and closed my eyes, trying to hold off, but she was writhing and moaning beneath me, and I was done for.

The explosion of pleasure detonated, sending a shockwave of ecstasy flowing through my limbs, all the way to my fingertips and toes. I moved, riding the remainder of her orgasm as mine began, and she shivered beneath my frantic kiss.

Shit, my orgasm was *intense*, and from the sound of it, hers was too.

She was still shuddering when I slowed to a stop, lodged deep inside her. I held my weight off her by rising onto my elbows, and it gave us a chance to see each other in the vulnerable aftermath of our climaxes. Her heavy eye makeup was smudged and her face dewy with perspiration, but—God, was she stunning.

She pressed a hand to my chest, perhaps wanting to confirm my racing heart matched hers, which it did. And then she peered up at me, her chest heaving and her eyes wide, acting like the world had suddenly changed around us and I was the only constant.

"That was kind of amazing," she whispered.

My smile was so big, it hurt.

It *was* amazing, and it was all because of her.

The day of Damon Lynch's retirement party arrived, and Emery wore the green dress Jillian had sent to her, which I found fitting. She'd be wearing his daughter's work when we cracked open Wayne Lambert's safe, discovered his secrets, and Emery finally got the revenge she rightfully deserved.

The Lambert estate was only a decade old, but it had been built to look historic and match the other houses in Cape Hill. Even though she'd been there before, she surveyed the estate critically from the back seat of the Range Rover while we waited to unload at the front door.

She was understandably anxious, but I took her hand in mine and reminded her how prepared she was. Thursday and Friday we'd done dry runs, and she'd been flawless. Even still, if at any point she wanted to abort, she knew to do that. She already had one strike on her record, and she'd lose everything if she got caught.

We were one of the first couples to arrive, and that was by design. I wanted Emery to make an appearance before disappearing upstairs early in the evening, giving her as much time as possible to work on the safe.

When the back seat door opened and she stepped out of the car, it was like she'd flipped the switch on her nerves to the 'off' position. Emery's smile was perfect and her eyes calm as we walked together up the stone steps to the front entrance. It was impressive how good she could be at playing a role.

Wayne and Serena Lambert were waiting in the foyer to greet their guests, and both sets of eyes lit up when they saw me. Wayne's because he wanted to discuss his progress with the board, and Serena's because . . . well, I was everything her husband wasn't.

Even when I was dating her daughter, Serena had hinted that she wanted to have an affair with me. She found reasons to get me alone when I was visiting Jillian or had been invited over for dinner. She always had excuses to touch me, such as standing too close and putting a hand on my arm while laughing.

Her attempt at flirting was annoying, and I wasn't interested. Even if I were—shit, my sex life was complicated enough at the time with Alice. I wasn't about to add another married woman into the mix, especially the mother of my girlfriend.

We pressed on fake smiles and shook hands with our hosts. Wayne's grip was uncomfortable and tight as he jerked me close. "I'll come find you later so we can talk."

"I'm sure you will," I said.

We were ushered deeper inside the house, only to be led out a door and onto the back lawn. A massive white tent had been erected there, complete with portable air conditioners to combat the summer heat. Most people wouldn't have bothered to send guests through their house, but Wayne wasn't going to pass up an opportunity to show off his place.

The entire Lynch family was already in the tent, and Duncan perked up as soon as he saw me. I swore under my breath as he got up from the table and headed straight for us.

"Do I need to steal his watch?" she whispered.

I doubted he wore one, and if he did… "He wouldn't notice."

So many of the guys I'd been 'friends' with during high school were douches, and Duncan was the king of them. The apple didn't fall far from the tree for most of the families in Cape Hill, and Duncan was just like his father. Arrogant. Entitled. Spineless. He treated women the same way he treated his income—disposable.

There was no one else to talk to, though, so I was forced to introduce Duncan to Emery and put up with his inane conversation about his favorite places to go rock climbing.

From the moment we'd made it on the Lambert property, I felt the ticking clock. Even if the party were a bust, it'd last a minimum of three hours. I wanted to give her as much time as possible to get the safe unlocked, but we also had no idea what we were going to find inside. If there were hard drives or other devices, it could take a while to copy them.

Thankfully, more people began to arrive, including Royce and Marist, which gave us a chance to escape from Duncan.

Marist had a hand draped over her belly, and I wondered if she were subconsciously trying to shield her future son from the wicked gods of Cape Hill. She had to know he'd be a future king, continuing the Hale lineage. My father was quite pleased he was going to have a grandson.

"I love your dress," Marist said to Emery.

"Thank you." She gave Marist a once-over. "And I still love your hair color."

Because Marist's hair was a dark green, and Emery had been fascinated with it when they met at the awkward family dinner last month.

"This is going to be great when Dad gets here with Sophia," Royce said with heavy sarcasm. "Not at all uncomfortable."

He was right, but I tossed a hand up. "What's he supposed to do? He can't *not* come."

"Hey, remind me again why Wayne's hosting this thing."

I gave my brother a pointed look. "You know why."

I'd pulled Royce aside two weeks ago, told him I'd been approached by Wayne about the vacant seat, and asked him for a favor. Take the asshole out for lunch to help get him off my back. I'd left out the part where I was being blackmailed, but since Wayne had such a grating and pushy personality, Royce believed the meeting would solve my problem and Wayne would leave me alone.

"How was your lunch?" I asked him.

He returned my pointed look. "You can imagine how it was."

When more people began to arrive and fill up the tent, the volume of conversations rose above the music. I turned to Emery. "Should we go find Tiffany?"

She gazed up at me and her shoulders lifted with a preparatory breath. "Yup."

Tiffany Lambert looked a lot like her older sister. She had the same honey-brown hair and heart shaped face, but she seemed more youthful and energetic than Jillian, probably because she didn't have as much pressure on her shoulders.

I wondered if people thought the same when they compared me to Royce.

We found her standing near the bar station surrounded by friends, and I motioned to her, making it clear I had something urgent to discuss. She nodded, excused herself, and came over.

"Hey, what's up?" Her curious gaze went from me to the woman at my side who she did not recognize.

"This is my girlfriend, Emery," I started.

Tiffany's eyes widened with concern, because Emery had her fingertips pressed to her temple and her eyes closed. "Is she all right?"

"No," I said. "She's had a migraine come on just now."

"Oh, no." Tiffany gave Emery a sympathetic look, even though Emery's eyes were closed.

"Do you mind if I take her in the house," I said, "and let her rest in one of the guest rooms until she's feeling better? I'd take her home, but I think the car ride would make it worse."

Emery's voice was strained, selling the lie. "I took some medicine, and it usually conks me out for a few hours."

Tiffany considered the request only for a moment before gesturing toward her home. "Of course."

We followed her up the path to the house, and Emery hung on to me like I was the only thing keeping her upright. She was so good at it, I had to remind myself she wasn't in crippling pain.

The staff member waiting at the back door listened dutifully as Tiffany explained one of the guests wasn't feeling well and she was escorting us upstairs to someplace quiet to rest. The house was supposed to be off-limits to the partygoers, but a Lambert could overrule that, and an excited thrill shot through me as the guy waved us through and we climbed the steps.

Wayne and Serena's bedroom was at the end of the hall, and it was flanked by the guest bedrooms. Either one that Tiffany selected would put us within fifty feet of her father's safe, and it was harder to keep my excitement at bay. So much of this was in Emery's hands, but I was here for her and knew without a shadow of a doubt she could do it.

I'd gotten the same feeling I did during the calm moments alone on my boat before a big race. We were going to win. No other outcome was possible.

Tiffany stood at the doorway to the guest bedroom that was decorated in blues and grays, and she asked it of me quietly, wanting to keep her voice down and not cause Emery more pain. "How's this?"

I matched her hushed tone. "It's great, thanks."

She went to the far side of the room and undid the sashes on the curtains, drawing them closed to block out the evening sun. I eased Emery down to sit on the bed and then bent to take off her shoes, helping her get ready to 'rest.' She set her purse beside her, but the duvet cover was silk and her purse was heavy, and when it slipped off and landed on the hardwood floor with a loud thump, my heart stopped.

All her equipment was in there, including her sophisticated and sensitive amplifier that couldn't be housed in its protective case because it was too big for her already questionably large purse. My gaze snapped to Emery, and behind her frozen expression, I saw the terror. She had the same thought I did, that if the microphone were damaged, she wouldn't be able to hear the necessary clicks of the wheels, and this was over before it even started.

I gingerly picked up her purse and set it on the nightstand, wanting to say a million things to her, but couldn't. I kept my gaze fixed on her as she lay down on her side, tucking her hands beneath the pillow under her head.

My voice wavered, wanting to break under the need to ask more. "Are you going to be okay?"

"Yeah." She knew what I meant because her expression was full of anxiety. "I hope so."

It spilled from me, carrying as much weight as possible. "Hey, I love you."

"Love you too," she said.

I couldn't stay here with her. The last thing I needed was Wayne to come looking for me, and I felt Tiffany's curious gaze on us. I'd dated Jillian for a year, and she'd never heard me say those words to her sister.

"She'll be more comfortable in the quiet," I said, "and probably asleep before we make it back downstairs." It seemed to convince Tiffany I wasn't a shitty person who was abandoning their sick partner in favor of a party. We exited, and I pulled the door closed behind us, hating that Emery would have to do this next part without me.

It had been years since I'd been in the Lambert house,

and it was strange to be back. Tiffany was quiet as we moved down the hallway, and I sensed there was something she wanted to say but didn't know how. When we reached the top of the stairs, she abruptly pulled to a stop.

"Your girlfriend's dress is beautiful." She stared at me like she knew a secret. "Where'd she get it?"

I blinked, evaluating how much to reveal. "A friend designed it for her."

Her smile was an enigma, but her knowing eyes gave it away. "Hmm. Her friend is very talented."

So, she did know what became of her sister.

"Yes," my voice was warm, "I think so too."

When we returned to the tent, cocktail hour had begun, and I made my rounds as required, but my thoughts were one hundred percent on the woman I'd left upstairs. I wanted to text her and ask if her equipment was all right but didn't dare disturb her, and we'd agreed not to leave any proof on our phones of the crime she was about to commit.

Instead, I visualized what she would be doing right now. Assuming her amplifier was okay, the first thing she'd planned was to double check the camera and sensors were still disabled in Wayne's bedroom. She'd logged into her system at work this afternoon and taken the whole second floor of the house down for 'maintenance,' which would conveniently end at two in the morning tomorrow.

And once she was sure the hallway was clear, she'd sneak into Wayne's room, don her gloves, and locate the safe.

Had she already done that? Was she on her knees right now, taping her amplifier and her graph paper to the front of the door? Fuck, I hoped so. I was jittery and sweating beneath my suit coat, making my dress shirt stick uncomfortably to my back. Being on the sidelines when so much was at stake was freaking killing me.

I'd been in the house when my father and Sophia arrived, so I'd missed the show of side-eye and murmurs of interest. Most of Cape Hill tolerated my father dating a woman half his age, or at least they did to his face, but it wasn't the big scandal tonight. It was Sophia attending the retirement party thrown for the man who refused to claim her as his daughter.

Damon Lynch and my father had been friends once, but what Damon had done to her was unforgiveable in my father's eyes.

Or so I thought, right up until the moment my father stepped in front of the microphone with a glass of champagne in hand. He held a piece of cutlery in his other, which he'd likely swiped from one of the place settings nearby. He tapped the edge of his knife against the side of his glass, signaling to the crowd to quiet so they could listen to his toast.

"Please forgive the interruption," he started. "I have something I'd like to share."

The music faded and conversations ceased. Macalister Hale was still the king of this town, and when he spoke, Cape Hill listened. It was the sinister smile creeping on his lips that told me he was up to something.

"This morning," he continued, "I asked Sophia Alby to be my wife, and she did me the honor of accepting my proposal."

The buzz from the crowd rippled through the tent, and my mouth fell open, only for me to snap it shut with a smile that was probably identical to his. I was sure some people's attention went to Sophia, but most gazes shot to Damon, who was frozen with a glass of champagne in his hand. He'd thought this was going to be a toast in his honor, given by the former chairman who'd installed him on the board.

Instead, my father had upstaged him.

The partygoers clapped politely, and a few even murmured out their congratulations.

"Are you making Damon pay for the wedding?" someone asked loudly as a joke. Or maybe they were serious, it was impossible to tell. Some people laughed genuinely, and others did it to cover their unease with the situation, but any humor died when my father's intense glare landed on the man who'd asked the question.

If looks could kill, that guy would have been vaporized.

The irritation drained off my father's face, and it returned to the cold, superior look he usually held. "Thank you."

He dropped the knife off at the table he'd borrowed it from and carried his champagne as he strode back to Sophia's side. I wasn't surprised when he passed his glass off to her because my father didn't drink.

I made my way over to them, but basically had to get in line. Evangeline Gabbart was the first to approach and gave them both a hug, and I watched with comical fascination as my father accepted it. They'd 'dated' briefly before he'd started seeing Sophia, but I knew better, and this stilted hug was further proof their relationship had been all for show.

When she moved on, I worked my way forward and thrust my hand toward my father. "Congratulations."

His grip was firm, but his smile was genuine and pleased. "Thank you. I regret I didn't get a chance to tell you before the announcement."

Because he'd called me twice today and I'd pushed them both to voicemail. I had too much to focus on this afternoon. I waved a hand, brushing his comment off. "It's okay. I knew you were planning it. You caught Damon by surprise, though," my tone went sardonic, "so I'm going to go out on a limb and assume you didn't ask his permission."

Tradition was everything to us Hales, and I wondered if this had been a hard one for him to forego.

"No, I asked Stephen Alby," he said.

This was news to Sophia, and she looked up at him in surprise. "You did?"

His face contorted. "I didn't necessarily ask. I may have just informed him of my plans."

She gave a short laugh and shook her head, as if saying, "classic Macalister behavior."

"Well, nice work on the announcement," I said, "and shaming Damon."

"I don't know what you mean." Only the evil victory lurking in my father's eyes said otherwise.

Dinner was served shortly after that, and I barely touched my food. My fingers itched to text Emery and see how she was doing, but I resisted the urge. Her empty seat beside me at the large, round table didn't help. Anxiety grew and weighed me down like a stone as time dragged on and there was no word from her.

"Is everything okay?" Marist asked me in a low voice when dessert was served. She was seated beside me. "You've checked your watch at least ten times in the last ten minutes."

I struggled to find a convincing lie, and so instead I went with the truth. "I'm worried about Emery."

She abruptly grabbed Royce's hand and put it on her belly. The baby was kicking, and it was surreal to see the grin break out on my brother's face. He was going to be a father soon. Didn't that scare the shit out of him?

Marist's attention went back to me. "Dinner's almost over. You could go check on her."

"Yeah, I think I will." I kept my tone steady, even though a swarm of bees were trapped in my stomach. We were rapidly approaching the safety threshold we'd set. Once dinner was over, the party could rapidly thin out and it would be obvious when I was missing.

My phone vibrated with a text, and I hurried to check the screen.

Emery: I'm still not feeling well. We might need to leave.

My heart dropped to the floor. This was her way of telling me she didn't have the safe unlocked yet.

Me: I'm on my way.

Maybe I said goodbye to my family, but my focus was scattered as I got up from the table and headed up the path toward the house. The guy in charge of keeping the guests out of the house remembered me and waved me up the stairs when I asked.

I didn't know where Emery was, and both bedroom doors were shut. It was possible she'd slipped back in the guest room to wait for me, but I hoped not. If there was any way I could help her—shit—I was going to try.

My thought was I'd go straight for Wayne and Serena's bedroom, and if anyone saw, I could claim confusion about which door I was looking for. But it didn't sound like there was anyone on this floor besides us. I hurried through the door, shutting it behind me, and then surveyed the room.

The sun was setting outside, but there were two long windows on one wall and the curtains were open, so there was still enough light to see without turning on a lamp. The shadows were long, giving the large, elegant bedroom an ominous feel.

In the far corner, I found Emery with her back to me,

sitting on the floor with the skirt of her green dress ballooned around her and her shoes and purse off to the side. The Lagerfield was identical to mine, except it was surrounded by wooden walls and the door at the front was decorated with silver knobs. It was a clever disguise to hide the safe inside a faux dresser, but it wasn't enough to fool my girl.

Her amplifier and graph were taped to the safe, and her paper was full of dots and crossed off numbers. Way more than I'd ever seen her use, telling the story of her struggle.

"Hey," I whispered, creeping toward her as I slipped my hand into my interior coat pocket and pulled out a set of gloves.

She turned to face me, and my heart broke. It sank so much it plummeted all the way to the first floor of the house. Her eyes were rimmed with red, and I could see the shiny streaks of tears down her cheeks. She'd been crying.

Her voice was shaky and rasped with emotion. "I don't think I can do it."

I knelt beside her on the floor, quickly sliding my gloves on, and put my arm around her to pull her up against me. "It's okay. Tell me what's going on. Is it the amp?"

She sucked in a short breath. "Maybe? I don't know. This Lagerfield sounds totally different than yours." She gestured to the paper, glaring at it. "I've tried so many different combinations. I wasn't sure if twenty-eight is right, or if it's twenty-nine, but I went through all fifteen sequences for each and none of them worked. I mean, I even started over to make sure the drive cam has four wheels like yours, and it does."

I felt utterly powerless, and I fucking hated the feeling. "So, where are you now? Is there another number you're questioning?"

She nodded slowly. "Seventy-three. It's sticky around that one, but the click leans more toward seventy-four. But, Vance,

I've been trying that. I went through the sequence using seventy-four and twenty-eight, and all those failed. I'm almost done trying it with twenty-nine, and if that doesn't work . . ." She looked utterly lost, and her chin began to wobble.

"Shh," I said softly, squeezing her tightly. "It's going to work."

I'd never asked the universe for anything before. I'd been too young to do it when my mother had lain dying in a hospital, so wasn't I owed a favor from the universe now? I needed this to work out, not for me, but for her. I couldn't care less in this moment about whatever incriminating evidence was inside the safe or what would happen to me.

I wanted this victory for Emery.

And Wayne Lambert deserved retribution for what he'd done to her.

She swallowed so hard, it was audible, and her hand reached out, twisting the dial to the right to start entering the combination. I held my breath as she spun back and forth between the numbers, and then she gripped the spoke on the wheel.

It didn't turn. She drew a line through the sequence she'd just tried, making her pencil scratch loudly across the paper.

"Try the next one," I said before she let the rejection get to her and shut her down.

It was a losing battle. Defeat clung to her expression as she cleared out the dial and started again. I watched the numbers as they went by, double-checking them against the next set on her list. She tried the wheel, but it didn't budge, and then she angrily swiped her pencil over the sequence.

My mouth was dry, and my heart pounded as she took a deep breath and began to enter the next sequence. She went slower than before, and my heartrate climbed with each number that ticked by. Back and forth the dial moved, painstakingly slow. She stopped on the final number and sat back, her hands resting on her knees.

"That's it." Her voice was coated with dread. "That's the last one."

If it didn't work, we were finished, and time suspended. The room became a vacuum.

She was paralyzed with fear, unwilling to handle the defeat of it not opening, and I understood that. I filled my lungs with air and decided I'd do this for her. I'd deal with the sensation of the wheel not turning, and the bolt staying in place.

If that happened, I had to believe we'd figure out a way to overcome this. I wouldn't stop until she had what she wanted.

I reached out, grasped the cold, steel wheel, and pulled with all the force in my body as if I could wrench it open with brute force. But that was unnecessary.

The wheel turned.

NINETEEN

EMERY

When the door to the Lagerfield cracked open, I nearly collapsed into Vance. My heart was banging in my throat, clogging my ability to breathe, and when the door moved, air swept into my lungs in a rush.

I'd done it. It took nearly two hours, but I'd manipulated the open of one of the most challenging safes on the market. It wasn't an individual effort, though. None of this would have been possible without Vance. He was the man I'd fallen in love with even as he'd warned me not to, and was literally my partner in crime now.

But there was no time to sit back and congratulate ourselves. We were way behind schedule. He had the same thought because he jerked the door all the way open, revealing its contents.

The interior setup of Lambert's was different than Vance's. The top section of this safe had been customized with a watch winding panel. There were eight watches displayed, separated into two rows of four, and each timepiece was housed in a circular mechanism. It would cycle every half hour, moving to mimic being worn on a wrist and charge the battery through kinetic energy.

In the center section were the velvet lined drawers, and Vance beat me to the first one. When he pulled it out, diamonds and pearls and various gemstones glinted in the low light. Serena Lambert's jewelry collection was extensive, and spanned the next two drawers, and I tried not to think about how a single piece from it could have covered months of rent for my family when we were struggling.

The final drawer had several compartments and was mostly empty, other than a silver handgun, two spare magazines, and a few pairs of cufflinks.

All the relief that had poured through me moments ago was beginning to dry up. The bottom section of the safe was a stack of assorted documents no thicker than a few notebooks. Where were the laptops or hard drives?

I grabbed a handful of paper off the top, being mindful of what we were doing. The plan was to put everything back exactly as we'd found it, so Lambert would have no idea we'd been here. Vance worried if Lambert discovered his safe had been penetrated, it might trigger a contingency plan, and who knew what that would unleash?

One of us was an attorney, but even a layman like me could understand the top document. The prenuptial agreement looked recent, and since Vance was a faster reader than I was, he got the gist first.

He gently pulled it from my grasp and flipped to the final page, staring at the black ink scrawled at the bottom. "Shit, he already signed it."

The prenup was between Jillian and Ansel, and his signature and the signing date adorned the bottom line of the contract. I tugged my eyebrows together as I read the neat printing. "Look at the date."

It was only a few days before Jillian had set sail on *The Trident*. Her signature line was blank, though. Had this been drafted without her knowledge? What if the night I'd broken into Lambert's safe was the first time she'd seen it?

"This is what spooked her," I guessed. She'd felt the walls closing in and wasn't going to be forced to marry a man she didn't love. Especially if she was in love with someone else, someone her family would never approve.

Vance set the contract aside, and we focused our attention on the next set of documents. They looked like email printouts, and the Barlowe Pharmaceuticals logo was in the signature line for some of them. The dates were from earlier this year, so well after my father's passing. I thumbed through the printouts, not finding anything of interest, and moved on. The next set was some sort of report. I scanned the dense text and saw the numbers in the columns, but nothing leapt out at me. It appeared to be clinical trial results of a drug Barlowe had developed.

"Any ideas on this?" I handed it over to him.

While he read, I stared at the safe critically. This couldn't be it. What if these papers were nothing more than sensitive documents Lambert hadn't gotten around to shredding yet?

I rose onto my knees and opened the top drawer, running my hands along the trays and beneath it, searching. He'd gone to the trouble of concealing this beautiful safe inside a fake piece of furniture, which I'd spent five frustrating minutes figuring out how to get open. My gut told me I hadn't discovered all this Lagerfield's secrets.

I moved on to the second drawer, sliding my gloved fingertips over the velvet lining and moving the necklaces around before putting them back in place. My search of the third drawer was just as fruitless.

He moved on too, sifting meticulously through the documents while I examined the final drawer. There was hardly anything to it since it'd been sectioned off into compartments and most were empty, but my gaze caught on the brush pattern of the velvet in the back corner. It looked like something had rubbed against it.

Holy shit. Did the thing have a false bottom?

I traced my fingers along the partition, and when I pushed down on the bottom, the spring-loaded panel popped open, revealing a small, secret compartment beneath. It was just big enough to store a folded stack of cash, or in this case, a USB stick drive.

I reached for him like I was worried if I took my eyes off the drawer, the compartment would disappear and the flash drive with it. "Vance."

Papers rustled as he set them down. He saw what I'd found, because he immediately went for my purse. He retrieved the duplicator device and the blank mini drive we'd brought, hoping for just this scenario. I plucked the drive out of the tray and plugged it into the available slot, and when the red copy light began to flash, excitement raced through my bloodstream. Whatever files were on here, they were explosive; I could sense it.

"How much longer do you think we can stay in here?" I whispered.

He looked down at his watch. "I've been gone awhile."

I nodded in understanding. When the drive was done copying, we'd need to go. He began to put the documents back in order while I peeled off the tape holding my amp and graph in place.

The red flashing light grew to two bars, meaning we were

fifty percent done.

I finished stowing my gear and gave a cursory glance at the watch winding section of the Lagerfield, and a strange prickling sensation washed down my arms. One of the watches was not like the others. Its gold face was dull, and the leather band worn, and it looked much too old to have a self-charging battery.

My heart pounded like a cannon being fired repeatedly.

I knew this watch, but it made no sense how it could be here.

Vance's question was rushed and worried. "What are you doing?"

I ignored him as I pulled out the black cuff, which was like a pillow that the watch was clasped around. It took me less than a second to undo the band. After all, I'd had years practicing on it. I turned it over, and my legs gave way, causing me to drop to the floor and a sob to well up in my chest.

I could barely get the words out. "It's my father's watch."

"*What?*" He couldn't believe it, but I didn't blame him. I couldn't believe it either. His shocked gaze darted from me to the watch in my hand. "You're sure?"

"My grandfather's initials are engraved on the back." Tears sprung into my eyes, but I blinked them back. I'd already cried once in this room, and I didn't want to do it a second time in front of him. "Why the fuck does he have this? And *how?* We buried my dad with it."

Vance had no idea what to say. He simply stared at the gold watch that was a perfect fucking metaphor for all the time with my father Lambert had stolen from me. Bile burned up my throat as liquid fire. "I'm taking this."

His eyes went impossibly wide. "No, Emery. I know you want to, but you can't."

"Fuck him," I snarled. "It's mine."

"Look at me." He put his hands on either side of my face, forcing my attention on him, and the smell of powdery latex from his gloves invaded my nose. His expression was pained. "If you take it, he'll know we were here."

"I don't care. It belongs to me, and this might be my only chance."

He hardened, maybe because we were out of time, and he had no choice. He needed to scare some sense into me. "Right now, if we get rid of that flash drive, there's nothing to tie us to this safe. If you take this, that's proof you committed a crime."

When I tried to look away, he wouldn't let me. He stared into my eyes with so much determination, it made the world stop.

"I know it isn't right," he whispered, "and it sure as shit isn't fair, but, Emery . . . you *can't*. Not tonight." He brushed the lightest of kisses across my lips. "I promise you we'll find another way."

I closed my eyes and let him kiss me again, and I was sure if he could give me the strength to resist the temptation, he would. When the kiss ended, he lingered, his forehead pressed to mine.

"Okay?" he asked.

I was far from okay, but I understood what he was asking. I had to trust what he'd said. We'd get another chance. I swallowed a breath and forced the word out. "Okay."

It wasn't difficult to fake looking ill as we left the party. My stomach was twisted in knots from the adrenaline and the emotional rollercoaster I'd been on, and I leaned on Vance for support as we waited for the car to pull up.

We didn't talk on the short drive back to his house. We were both too deep in our thoughts. He was probably wondering what was on the flash drive, but all I could see was the gold face of my father's watch as I'd struggled to put it back in Lambert's safe.

There was an uneasy feeling in the air as we got out of the car and went up the front steps of his family's mansion. The wind seemed cold and vicious as it rippled across my strapless dress and bare skin, like it knew we'd taken something we shouldn't.

Our feet carried us through the house, up the grand staircase, and into his bedroom. We sat together on the couch with his MacBook perched on the coffee table in front of us, and the copy of Lambert's flash drive clenched in Vance's fist.

"Ready?" he asked.

I'd been ready for ten long years to see what my father had been after, and now the moment was finally here. "Yes."

He plugged it into the port, gave it a moment to recognize the device, and then double-clicked. The window opened to display a few folders. One was titled Barlowe, and another Stockwell, but it was the Hale folder in the middle that Vance navigated the cursor to and clicked open.

It held a single .mov file, and the name on it was a random series of numbers. I couldn't tell anything from the dark thumbnail, and it didn't seem like he could either, judging by his confused look.

He didn't ask for privacy before clicking on it. Perhaps he felt I'd earned the right to see everything on the drive since I'd been the one to find it, or maybe he thought I'd understand it was a long time ago, and he didn't want me to think he was hiding secrets.

The video application launched, the screen filled with the black dialogue box, and then the footage began to roll.

The Hales' formal dining room was naturally dark because it was paneled in wood, but in this video, it was lit only by the candles in the five-arm candelabras that rested on the long, elegant table.

A woman in a corseted red ballgown sat in a chair with her back to the camera, and she was surrounded by tuxedoed men on either side. No one seemed to be aware of the camera, and there was a green leaf at the edge of the frame, like it had been hidden inside a flower arrangement.

"What is this?" I asked.

He stared at the screen with utter confusion. "I don't know."

Some of the men moved, blocking our view with their backs, but when they shifted out of the way, the woman was on her feet and turned to look up at the guy closest to her. I blinked, recognizing her even though she was younger and didn't have her pretty green hair.

Marist Hale held a glass of champagne, but it went untouched as the man looming over her spoke. I recognized him too. Vance's father looked more like his sons back before his hair had begun to gray.

As Macalister appeared to speak, nothing came through the laptop's speakers. Vance pressed a key repeatedly to turn up the volume, but it didn't make a difference.

"I don't think the camera captured sound," I said.

We watched in silence as Macalister continued to talk and Marist said nothing. Her eyes grew larger, though. Why was he lecturing her in front of all these other men?

Beside me, Vance said it like he was talking to himself. "I don't understand."

I didn't either. He wasn't on screen, nor was Alice Hale, and this clearly wasn't a sex tape—

Royce appeared behind Marist and worked to undo the strings at the back of her corset. He loosened them, sliding his hands inside her dress as Macalister took the glass of champagne from her and set it aside on the table.

"What the fuck?" I gasped.

She'd had her hands pressed to the front of her corset, holding it in place, so when she let go, the entire dress peeled down her body. It left her wearing only a pair of skimpy black panties and the layers of red fabric puddled at her feet.

Vance bolted up off the couch, but his horrified gaze was glued to the screen like he was witnessing a train wreck. On screen, his father held out a hand to Marist, which she reluctantly took, and let him lead her to the end of the table.

That was enough for Vance. He'd seen his sister-in-law basically naked, and now knew his father had too, and the information filled him with a desire to escape. His feet pounded on the floor as he began to flee, only to abruptly halt a few steps away.

When he slowly turned to face me, my breath caught. There was horrible recognition streaking through his eyes. Whatever we were watching, he understood it now, and that filled him with so much fear, it made my heart stop.

On screen, Marist sat on the end of the dining table and the men moved in to surround her, once again partially blocking her from view with their black tuxedoed bodies.

"What. Is. This?" I asked.

Vance stormed back to the table and slammed the laptop closed, then jammed his hands in his hair. "Oh, fuck. It's . . ." His gaze darted around, searching for the answer like he'd somehow find it in the air. "It was an initiation."

Like that explained it. I pulled my chin back. "An initiation for what?"

His mind was distracted, racing with thoughts. "For Royce to become a board member of HBHC." His gaze snapped to mine, suddenly giving me his full attention. "It was a really fucked up family tradition. I don't know the specifics because you only get those when you're about to be seated, and no one ever talks about it."

Ice moved in my veins. "But you knew about it, at least enough to recognize what was happening."

It looked like he was coming unglued. "I got a vague explanation that a new board member's wife would be subject to board approval, and there was some kind of ceremony for it."

I tensed my hands into fists. "And what if the board member is a woman?"

He gave me a dubious look. "This tradition started more than a hundred years ago. Women weren't allowed to be board members." He straightened, running a hand down his tie like he could easily wipe something so unseemly away. "The initiation doesn't exist anymore. Royce got rid of it as soon as my father lost his seat."

I didn't know how to feel about any of this. Vance wasn't a part of whatever fucked up tradition the rest of his family had followed, but . . . he knew about it, and it was hard to separate him from the association of it. I almost wished the video had been a sex tape between him and his stepmother.

That seemed somehow less scandalous.

I could figure out how to handle this information later and forced myself to move forward. "You said Lambert had stuff with you and Alice."

"He'd said she'd given him something, and my family wouldn't want it getting out. I assumed it was the affair. I never suspected it was *this*."

He dropped down beside me on the couch and scooped my hands up in his. The way he peered at me, it was like I was his only hope.

"This is so much worse." His voice was heartbreaking. "If it gets out, it'd be catastrophic, and I'm not just talking about for my family. Most of the board members on that video are still seated today. If Lambert leaks this, it'll nuke the entire board of HBHC, and without them, the company will be vulnerable to a takeover. If that happens, the bank my family built when America was still in its infancy will cease to exist."

The Hale family legacy would be destroyed.

I drew in a deep breath, withdrawing my hands from his hold so I could tuck my hair behind my ears, and focused on how we could prevent that from happening. Deleting the video we had wouldn't do anything, because the original was still locked inside the Lagerfield in Lambert's bedroom.

I was thinking out loud. "How do we know the only copy of this video is on the drive we found?"

He looked sick to his stomach. "We don't."

Meaning even if I broke into Lambert's safe a third time and erased the drive, we'd never be certain. I sat up straighter as the idea took shape in my head.

"Then we bargain for it." I reached out to cup his cheek and gazed into his blue eyes which were full of chaos. "That video isn't the only thing on here. There will be something we can trade; we just have to find it." I brushed my thumb over his lips, wishing I could brush his worry away that easily. I mimicked his gentle tone from when he asked me to put my father's watch back. "Okay?"

He blinked, and resolve filled his eyes. "Okay."

Vance wore a black suit with a gray striped tie, and he looked every bit the cutthroat lawyer ready to go to war. I matched him by wearing a fitted black dress with a keyhole cutout at the neckline. It was the classiest, most professional dress I owned. I added to the look by twisting my hair up into a bun and donned a pair of earrings that were a simple dangling bar of silver.

I was almost as nervous walking into the Lambert's house as I'd been last night, which was ridiculous. I didn't have to sneak around or crack his safe. Today we had the upper hand.

The gentleman who answered the door recognized Vance right away and informed us that Mr. Lambert was waiting for him in the study. We followed him, passing by the portrait of a happy family of four which had already been a lie when it was taken.

Did Lambert even miss his daughter? Or had the loss only affected his plans of gaining clout in specific social circles?

The study was painted in a subtle green and had warm, honey colored wood beams crisscrossing on the ceiling. One wall was built-in bookshelves stacked over cabinets, and a classic fireplace with moldings was centered on the opposite wall.

Lambert sat behind the desk that was angled out from one corner and faced two leather armchairs. When we entered, he pushed up to stand. His smile fell a notch when he saw me. My attendance purposefully hadn't been mentioned when Vance set up the appointment.

Lambert gestured to the chairs. "Please, have a seat. I'm

glad you called, Vance. We didn't get a chance to talk last night."

"You were busy," he offered, like it was the other man's fault and not his.

Lambert's smile was superficial. "Yes, well, I'm all yours today. Your brother seems to be warming up to me. We had lunch last—"

Vance lifted a hand to silence him. "We're not here to talk about that. There won't be any more discussion about an HBHC's board seat. That's no longer on the table."

It was like he'd just been told water was no longer wet. "Excuse me?"

Vance was relaxed, but still looked powerful and in control. "We've come to negotiate."

Lambert still hadn't recovered from the first statement, and color flushed to his neck. "Don't patronize me, kid. I'm not selling you what I have."

Calling him a kid was meant to diminish, but Vance let it roll right off him. He looked down at his hand and examined his fingers for hangnails because that was more interesting than the irritated man across from us.

This, of course, only made Lambert angrier. His eyes turned dark as coal. "Listen up, you little pissant, I'm not someone you want to mess—"

"Let's talk about EpiClick."

The older man's face contorted with confusion. "What?"

Barlowe Pharmaceuticals was a huge company and had developed hundreds of drugs over the last fifty years, but their crown jewel was an epinephrine rapid delivery system. EpiClick was literally a lifesaver because it was easy to use, even if someone were experiencing a severe anaphylactic reaction.

A sinister smile threatened on Vance's lips. "Don't you

find it interesting it doesn't have any competitors?"

Lambert rolled his eyes. He'd been hauled in front of a congressional committee last year and already testified about Barlowe's dominance in the market. "Seriously? You're going to waste my time with this? EpiClick has competitors, like AdrenaJex."

"Their reputation took a serious hit after their recall two years ago, as did their market share."

He spoke to Vance like a father lecturing an insolent son. "They put out an inferior product. How is that my problem?"

I had to press my lips together to hold back my evil smile. He'd walked right into it.

"Because you absorbed the partner company of AdrenaJex six months before the recall."

We'd stayed up until three in the morning trying to solve the puzzle from all the emails that were inside the Barlowe folder on the flash drive. It had been a deep rabbit hole to fall down, but at the end, we'd figured it out.

While Barlowe didn't own AdrenaJex outright, they'd bought a company called Maxlyn that manufactured the drug that went inside the auto-injection device.

"You caused the recall," Vance announced, "wiping out the competition, and when EpiClick controlled ninety percent of the market, you tripled the price."

It made me sick just thinking about it. People's lives depended on this drug, and the manufacturing cost for the entire system was only twenty dollars. But Barlowe's price had skyrocketed over the last two years and was now north of six hundred for a two-pack dose.

I'd expected Lambert to look guilty, but maybe he wasn't capable. He barely looked human as he raised an eyebrow. "You're awfully bold to come into my home and accuse me of something so utterly ridiculous, and to do it when you don't have even a shred of proof."

"You sure about that?" Vance fired back.

He hesitated for a microsecond. "You've got nothing."

"Maybe," Vance agreed. "Perhaps I don't have an email thread about adjusting the manufacturing process at Maxlyn, or how you were warned it might lead to incorrect dosing, and you signed off on it anyway."

So, Lambert was human after all. Worry seeped into the edges of his expression. We weren't bluffing, and now he knew it.

Vance's shoulders broadened as he straightened in his seat, looking regal and deadly. "As I mentioned, we came here to negotiate."

The tension in the room climbed, turning more hostile with every breath.

"What the fuck do you want?" he snarled.

"If you delete every copy of the video Alice gave you, right now, in front of me . . . no one has to know what caused the AdrenaJex recall."

Even though I knew it was coming, it crushed me anyway to hear him make this offer. A true deal with the devil.

If we turned what we had over to the authorities, it'd be months before there'd be any fallout, and Vance couldn't wait months. The video of the initiation was Lambert's poison pill. If he didn't get a seat, he'd take the whole fucking company down.

I despised the offer because it felt like everyone was losing. I'd given away the only thing I could use as revenge in order to save what was important to the man I loved. Barlowe would go on, profiting off their schemes, and Lambert was going to get away with it.

My hands clenched so tightly, my muscles ached. In fact, everything ached from holding on to ten years of rage and knowing now I'd never get satisfaction. I had nothing to show for it.

"And the gold Rolex you have," I blurted. "The one with the initials MJS engraved on the back."

Both men turned their attention to me. Lambert's expression was shock, and Vance's was dismay, but I pressed on. I wasn't walking away with nothing.

"That's a *specific* request." Lambert's eyes narrowed as he studied me. "What makes you think I have something like that?"

Because I saw it in your safe.

That was the moment I realized what a huge mistake I'd made.

The information Vance had offered to Lambert to trade could have come from a half dozen different sources. A disgruntled employee or a hacked email account, for example. But my father's watch? It had likely been locked away, hidden for the last ten years. The only people who knew it was in his possession were the ones who'd seen the inside of his safe.

Which meant I'd just confessed, throwing a grenade into Vance's carefully laid plans.

For once, I didn't have a good pivot strategy. I couldn't see a way out of the hole I'd dug, and my gaze flew to Vance, hoping he had a way to save us. But he struggled the same as I did, and I could see the wheels turning in his head, trying to think.

When it was clear I wasn't going to answer, Lambert put his elbows on the desk and leaned forward, his gaze locked on me. "If I had such a thing, why would you want it?"

I dry-swallowed. There was no going back now, so I went

all in. "It was my father's."

He had the nerve to let a *'that can't be right'* expression cross his face, but then a lightbulb must have gone on. He tilted his head, and his voice was curious. "Are you . . . Em Slattery?"

I flinched. My father had been the only one to shorten my name to Em, and I couldn't tolerate hearing it come out of Lambert's mouth. Bitterness flowed through my veins. "I was."

Because Em Slattery no longer existed. Emery Mendenhall had risen in her place.

"It wasn't David's watch." Lambert sighed, as if reluctant to reveal it. There was so much gravity in his eyes, I couldn't escape from him. "It was our father's."

TWENTY

VANCE

Wayne's statement landed like bomb, and it was so deafening, we sat in the brutal silence of its aftermath. Had he just said Emery's father was his brother?

Holy fuck. That would mean Wayne Lambert . . . was Emery's uncle.

She was motionless for so long, I wondered if she was broken, but then it burst from her in the same tone I'd expect her to shout, *'how dare you.'* "What are you talking about?"

He laced his hands together and rested them on the desktop, taking his sweet fucking time to explain. "After my mother died, my father remarried and had two more children. David came first, and I don't just mean that literally. Your dad was everything our father wished I could be, and let's just say the only thing your grandmother wanted for me was that I didn't exist."

Emery stared at him with dubious eyes, but she didn't tell him to stop talking. There was just enough pain in Wayne's voice, it was hard to ignore.

"By the time I was seventeen," he said, "I'd had enough.

I wanted more, and no one was going to help me as Michael Slattery, Jr. so I left. I went to Boston, bought a new life as Wayne, and started over."

He sat back and looked around the room, clearly impressed with all he'd accomplished. He thought of himself as a self-made man, but was he? He'd found himself an heiress and married into the Barlowe fortune.

"I met Serena one night on campus when I returned her lost wallet, and that was that. We were married a year later."

Emery sneered. "Let me guess. You stole her wallet before 'finding' it."

It was an assumption, but a correct one judging by Wayne's half-smile. "When I came to Barlowe, it was heading downhill and barely turning a profit. It was like no one cared about making money." He shook his head. "I took over, did what needed to be done, and turned the company around. Barlowe would be *nothing* without me." He paused, letting disdain fill his face. "And once I'd built this spectacular new life and amassed a sizeable fortune—your father appeared and demanded a part of it."

Her mouth dropped open. She wanted to defend her father, but she seemed too shocked to find the words. Or maybe, deep down in her heart, she knew there was a kernel of truth to what he'd just revealed.

"David had ... how should we say it?" Wayne lifted a hand like he'd pluck the word from the air. "A moral flexibility, that I found useful. He got me things I needed, and in return, I paid him enormous sums of money."

Her back went rigid as she sat up straighter. "What? That's not true. We were—"

"Broke?" he lobbed at her. "Yes. That tends to happen when you gamble all your money away. By the time he approached me, David was in deep to some unsavory people, and when he got sick, that made it worse."

Her eyes were glassy, but the tears rimming her eyes looked to be from fury. "You mean, when he got cancer and you turned him away from the one drug trial that might have helped? God, he was your own fucking brother!"

He tensed, and his expression turned angry. "That wasn't my choice. He was stage four. There was no way this drug was going to help him. And even knowing that, and despite how he'd threatened to expose me," his hand clenched into a fist, "I *still* tried. I did everything in my power to get him on the list, but I wasn't the CEO at the time. I was overruled."

Whatever emotion he might have had, he crushed it back, and the ruthless version of Wayne Lambert reappeared.

"When he broke into my home," he said, "that was the final straw. I had to protect what I'd built, and I'd be damned if I'd let David come in and take everything away from me a *second* time. He went to prison, and for his silence, I paid off his debts so his bookies wouldn't come after you or your mother."

Her hand flew to her mouth, but it was too late to stifle her gasp.

Maybe she'd only gotten one version of the story—the version her father had told, which left out several key details and put all the blame on Lambert. She'd grown up idolizing her father, so perhaps she'd only remembered the good and had been unable to see his flaws.

But if what Wayne had said was true, this changed things. How could it not? The last ten years she'd held on to this rage that might have been misplaced.

I wanted to know what was going on in her head right now. To reach for her and offer some kind of support, but instead I sat glued to my chair like a fucking idiot. I was inept at dealing with my own emotions. How could I help with hers?

Emery retreated inside herself, and the woman who emerged was unrecognizable. It had to be a coping mechanism. She leveled a cold, detached gaze at the man across from us. "How did you get the watch?"

"Who do you think paid for his funeral?" he asked. "I had them remove it before they closed the casket."

Her face was an emotionless mask, but her voice broke. "Why?"

"Our father acted like his Rolex was expensive and special, but once I had money, I learned the truth. It's the type of watch a poor person thinks a rich person buys. I keep it as a reminder of where I began and how far I've come."

That could be true, but I suspected he'd also taken the watch as a final *fuck you*. The resentment he had toward his half-brother was obvious.

"You want to negotiate?" he asked. "Fine, let's do it. My offer is you do not repeat what we discussed today, including anything about EpiClick or the AdrenaJex recall. In exchange, I'll hand over the watch and write you a check for five million dollars."

I jolted. "The video Alice gave you—"

"Will be a separate negotiation." His irritated gaze swung toward me. "I'll get to you when I'm finished with her."

It was suddenly difficult to breathe. The room grew smaller, and my heart tried to beat its way out of my chest. By splitting us up, it put him in control, and . . . did she understand what he was doing? How he was asking her if saving me was worth more than five million?

I stared at Emery as a dark voice in my head whispered that she'd never had money before. When we'd been in Monaco, she'd been fixated on how much everything cost.

She'd grown up struggling, and this amount could be more than she'd make in her entire life.

That was why I tried not to take it personally when she hesitated.

"No," she said finally, and I exhaled.

Displeasure smeared across Wayne's face. "Ten million."

The room went quiet, but alarms blared in my head, and for the first time in my life, I wished my father were here. He'd warn me Emery was emotionally compromised and we should walk. Better to not close a deal than make a bad one, he'd say.

Her chest rose and fell with her rapid, uneven breath, and her gaze went to the floor, too overwhelmed to look at either of us. Or maybe she needed to focus on fighting the temptation to consider his offer.

Her voice was small. "I want you to delete the video."

"That's not part of my offer," he snapped.

My father's voice was loud in my mind. *Get control. Weaken his position to bargain.*

It surged out of me. "Turn that down because I'll match it. I'll have ten million wired to your account first thing Monday morning."

All that did was throw more chaos at her, and Emery's wild eyes found mind.

The idea of paying ten million dollars to the woman I was dating didn't sit well with me, but what choice did I have? It was only money. And it was well spent if it would secure her decision to protect my family.

"This is my final offer, and I suggest you be smart and take it." Wayne's voice was colder than a nor'easter in winter. "You keep your mouth shut for the watch, fifteen million, and the promise I won't turn you both in to the authorities for breaking into my safe."

The fear that splashed across her beautiful face flipped the world upside-down. Everything was slipping away.

"You don't have proof," I spat out.

"Maybe not yet, but I'll find some, Vance. Nobody's perfect."

We'd worked hard to cover our tracks, but it was possible we'd made a mistake and he'd find some evidence we'd been in his safe. And if he didn't? I fully believed he'd fabricate it.

It meant she'd go to prison and never be allowed to work in her field again. It meant *I* could go to prison, just like my father had.

The room grew even smaller, and time slowed to a crawl. Emery said she loved me, but—

Did she love me enough to turn down fifteen million dollars and risk everything?

It was so much money, and even though I could match it, I couldn't compete with the rest of his offer. A dark thought took hold in my heart, growing too big to ignore. I'd been betrayed before, and I'd be a fool not to consider the possibility that her feelings for me were not as strong as she made them out to be. She'd demonstrated time and time again how skilled she was at playing a role.

She looked at me with her trembling chin and her face full of turmoil, wordlessly begging me to tell her what to do.

My mouth was bone dry, but I attempted to speak anyway. "Don't."

I saw it in her eyes the moment she made up her mind, and I failed to live up to the Hale family motto. I was about to lose.

She took in a shallow breath and set her gaze on her uncle. "I accept."

Bile crawled up my throat at his revolting, victorious smile.

"Good. I'll go fetch the watch and my checkbook in a moment." His attention shifted over to me, and he was so smug it took every ounce of strength to stay in my seat and not punch his fucking face. "I no longer see a need to negotiate. Best case scenario for you if anything leaks is the mutual destruction of our companies, but let's be honest. That won't happen. There'll be an investigation and maybe a significant fine for Barlowe, but we'll weather the storm. I doubt the same is true for HBHC."

I hated that he was right.

He tipped his chin down and commanded it like he owned me. "Get me what I want, or I'll leak the video, and then there will plenty of space for me—every board seat will be available."

Wayne had slid her check and her father's watch across his desktop, told us to leave, and Emery hadn't looked at me since she'd taken them. As we left, she put the check in her purse, but her fingers remained wrapped around the watch. It was more precious than the fortune Wayne had scribbled out to her, and more important than me.

On some level I was aware that wasn't fair, but I was too angry with the situation to see reason. She'd sold me out.

The car was still waiting for us outside in the circle drive, and I opened the door for her out of habit. She finally lifted her gaze to meet mine, showing that she was a riot of emotions, but I didn't care if she was worried or felt bad about her decision. It was done, and now I had to deal with it.

"Vance—"

My voice was clipped. "No. We won't talk until we're home."

She could go with whatever reason she wanted to for why

I said that, but I didn't care if my driver overheard our conversation. I shouldn't speak to her until I had a grip on myself. Otherwise, I might say something I'd regret.

She nodded and ducked into the car.

The entire ride was tense. We sat on our separate sides in the back seat, and she stared out the window, but her fingertips traced over the edges of the watch. Her world had come apart today. All the anger she'd been holding on to was no longer necessary but had nowhere to go, no way to dissipate.

Don't think about her right now.

I needed to focus on my own problems. I was going to have to tell Royce about the video—there was no way around it. I wouldn't be able to convince him to put Wayne Lambert on the board otherwise. He was the last person he'd want, and not just because Lambert was a dick. HBHC's board had been nothing but white men for far too long.

I was running out of time, too. I'd foolishly pinned all my hopes on Emery getting me out of this mess, not knowing how bad the situation really was. The secret video wouldn't just damage the company either. What it would do to Marist . . . My stomach roiled at the thought.

How the fuck was I going to tell Royce?

My stepmother's secret recording was bad enough, but giving it to Wayne was exceptionally cruel. Alice had found another way to torture Marist, even after her death.

I hated her. My father had done terrible things, but he'd believed in a warped and twisted way what he was doing was for the greater good. Alice's motivations had been to hurt or destroy. She hadn't been born a Hale, but she'd played the game the hardest.

And look where it got her.

The car had barely come to a stop in front of the house

before I threw open the door and marched up the front steps, not waiting for Emery to follow. I just assumed. I heard her quick footsteps behind me as she tried to keep up.

I pushed open the door, strode across the foyer, and up the grand staircase. I hadn't spoken to her in the car to try to cool off, but all it had done was make me angrier. At Alice, at Wayne, and at myself for not being good enough to outsmart him. And I was pissed with how quickly Emery had accepted his offer.

By the time we reached my bedroom and had the door shut, it boiled over.

My voice was harsh. "Do you understand what happens now? I have to tell my brother that Lambert has a video of him and his wife, and they . . ." I couldn't bring myself to say the rest. "Fuck, Emery. Think about what this is going to do to them."

"I know, but it won't get out. We'll stop him," she said. "We'll figure out a way."

"Really? Because it seems to me like you sold my only way out." There was a meanness growing inside me that I was powerless to fight. "Jesus, was it even hard for you? You barely hesitated."

She flinched. "I get that you're upset, but do you have any idea what that was like for me? I'm a fucking mess right now. If he had us arrested, we could both go to—"

"And whose fault is that? I know I wasn't the one to tell him we'd been in his safe."

The hurt in her eyes was like I'd buried a knife in her belly. "I made a mistake," she said, "but don't act like this is all on me. I'm not the one with the video of that fucked-up family tradition—which you wouldn't even know about if it wasn't for me. Remember? You thought it was a video of you fucking your stepmom."

Fire heated my face.

She sucked in a breath and ran her hands down the sides of her dress, smoothing out nonexistent wrinkles. "Look, you might not believe me, but I took that deal to save us."

"Okay." My tone was condescending. "So, the money had nothing to do with it?"

She sighed loudly and her gaze went to the ceiling, too irritated to look at me.

"Yeah, I thought so." I was bitter, looking for a place to direct it. "So, spare me the excuse you were trying to save us. Just be honest that when you couldn't get your revenge, you realized his money would do just fine. I mean, it was over so quick, I can't help but question your motivations."

She froze. "My motivations?"

"You're a great actress when you want something, and I'd be an idiot not to consider that this," I gestured between us, "is all an act."

She stared at me in disbelief. "What are you saying?"

"You know what I'm saying."

Her eyes went narrow, and her face hardened. "No, I don't. Explain it to me, Vance. Tell me why you think I'm lying when I've told you I love you."

Pressure had been building to a level I couldn't manage, and it suddenly erupted. "Because it can't be true!" My shoulders tightened up to my ears and my hands balled into fists. "None of this is real." My anger burned out, leaving my tone cold. "We were supposed to be partners. If you loved me, you wouldn't have sold me out."

Her mouth dropped open, and more hurt splashed across her face. "You know what? I love you whether you want to believe it or not. That's how love works. But frankly, it's pissing me off that I keep having to tell you this is real for me. I don't know what else I can do to prove it to you." She tilted her head. "It's almost like you don't want it to be. Is that it? Would that be easier for you if it were a lie?"

I closed my eyes and pinched the bridge of my nose. "I don't know how to do this."

"Yeah, I can tell," she said dryly. "When you asked me to put my father's watch back, you promised me we would find another way. So, I'm asking you the same thing right now. We can work together and find another way."

"No," I said. "There's nothing you can do now because it's over. You made sure of that when you took his money."

She inhaled a sharp breath, and her posture stiffened. I hadn't meant our relationship, but the longer my statement hung, the worse it got. I knew I should apologize and clarify, but I . . . didn't. The words wouldn't come.

Her chin lifted and she gazed at me like I was a coward. "Fine." She spun on her heel and marched away from me.

"Where are you going?" I demanded.

She didn't look back as yanked open the door. "I've got work to do. Goodbye, Vance."

TWENTY-ONE

VANCE

Monday morning, I went in to the office because I didn't know what else to do. Royce and Marist had gone over to her parents' house for dinner last night, preventing me from getting a chance to speak privately with my brother. I could have forced him to find time, but subconsciously I was relieved to have an excuse to put it off.

I dreaded the conversation like a prisoner marching to the gallows.

And I'd spent all of Sunday evening regretting how I'd left things with Emery. I'd picked up my phone several times with the intention of calling her, but wasn't sure what to say, and told myself it'd be better if I waited. She needed time to process all the revelations Wayne had dumped on her, and I needed time to figure out what the hell my problem was.

I loved her. Why was it so hard to accept that she loved me?

It was impossible to focus on work, and after an hour of sorting my thoughts, I finally picked up my phone and sent the message I should have sent yesterday.

Me: I'm sorry. Can we talk?

Time ticked by with no response; the message hadn't even been read.

After three hours, I began to worry. She was usually quick to respond. Was she hard at work on a job? There'd been a few times during practice when she'd been so focused on listening to her headphones, I'd accidentally startled her.

The image struck me of her sitting on the floor in front of Wayne's safe with her gorgeous green dress pooled around her. If we'd had more time, I would have told her how beautiful she looked, or how amazing she was, or . . .

I checked my screen, seeing there were no messages from her I'd missed, and she still hadn't read the text. I scowled. It was now the longest we'd gone without talking since we'd started dating, and I hated it.

It was just after lunch when her text finally rolled through.

Emery: Can't talk right now. Will call later.

Her clipped response made my heart beat slower, and the rest of the day dragged as a result. At four-fifteen, I sent a text to Royce, asked how late he planned on staying at the office, and if he wanted to share a car going home because I needed to talk to him about something.

He came back and said if nothing else came up, he could be ready in an hour.

I was glad not to be stuck at the office until late, because my brother's job was demanding and he often didn't come home until well after eight, but my relief ended when Marist appeared at his side in the parking garage. It wasn't personal—I liked my sister-in-law quite a bit, but it was going to be a tough conversation, and telling them both would be infinitely harder.

He'd called for a limo, and I climbed in, taking the rear-facing bench, and flashed a smile in greeting to Marist. She wore a black suit with a red top beneath, and once she was seated, I watched her fasten her seatbelt over her belly.

"How was your day?" I asked while we waited for Royce to get settled.

"Long," she answered. "You?"

Truer words had never been spoken. "Yeah. Same." I watched her scrub a hand low on her lap belt, and saw her eyebrows pinch together. "You okay?"

"Yeah," she said, although her tone suggested otherwise.

Royce picked up on it instantly. Whatever email he'd been reading on his phone was ignored, and he looked at his wife with concern. "What is it?"

She hesitated. "I don't know. Maybe I'm having contractions, but they feel just like they did last week, and those were nothing." She shot me a look like she needed to explain herself. "I'm not due for another week, and you're usually late with your first."

"How far apart are the contractions?" he asked.

She waved a hand. "I can't time them. They're random." He wasn't convinced, but she took his phone from him and tucked it into his suit pocket. "I'm fine. You said Vance wanted to talk to you, so maybe give him your attention for five minutes."

"That's okay," I said automatically. Maybe this should wait until later.

But Emery's voice filled my head, reminding me that time was finite. I needed to man up and stop putting things off.

I shifted in my seat, taking a deep breath.

"Actually, no," I said. "This can't wait. It's about Wayne

Lambert and how he wants a seat on the board."

My brother made a face. "Is he still giving you shit about that? If you want me to make it clear to him he's not being considered because—"

"Oh," Marist said abruptly, pitching forward and wrapping both arms around her stomach. Her eyes were wide, but it seemed to be more surprise than pain.

Royce went on high alert. "What's wrong?"

She slammed her eyes shut, her whole face scrunching, and this? This was definitely pain. Stuttering breath was dragged in and out through tight teeth. She reached out, clamping a hand on her husband's knee. "Contraction."

We held our breath, not wanting to use any of the air Marist might need, and when her eyes finally blinked open and her face relaxed, my gaze darted to my brother. He was looking at the watch on his wrist, and his cufflink shaped like Ares glinted back at me.

She sounded embarrassed, like she had any control over it. "That one was really intense." Then she looked down at stared at her lap in disbelief. "Royce?" Her tone was calm and even. "Uh, my water just broke."

I'd been in the labor and delivery waiting room of Mass General for twenty-five minutes before my father and Sophia arrived.

"Traffic was awful," she said.

My father gave a dark look, as if he'd ordered it otherwise and the flow of cars had willfully disobeyed his command.

We said hello, sat together on the uncomfortable chairs, and made the requisite idle chitchat while waiting for a text from Royce with an update on Marist. I'd expected my father to be impatient. To act like this whole thing was an inconvenience for him, or for him to storm into the delivery room and demand Marist speed things along.

But he really had changed. I'd witnessed it for the first time last year in a different waiting room in this hospital, when Sophia's boating accident had sent her to the emergency room. He'd been worried about someone other than himself, and that worry had stripped away his shields. He'd made his first attempt to connect with me, and it had been so disorienting, I'd frozen.

Today, he looked excited. Like there wasn't anywhere else he wanted to be but here, waiting for the birth of his first grandchild. I saw him as merely a man, not the cunning and ruthless creature intent on winning the game, no matter the cost.

I'd lost the chance to talk to Royce. He was about to be a father, and I wasn't going to shatter this happy moment or cause any stress over the Lambert news. A voice inside my head reminded me he wasn't the only person Wayne wanted me to convince to put him on the board. My father could make it happen. I needed to stop avoiding him. He would undoubtedly be the biggest asset for strategy, or the biggest weapon to deploy.

Maybe both.

"Is Emery going to be joining us?" Sophia asked, interrupting my thoughts.

"Oh. Uh, I'm not sure." I glanced at my phone. She hadn't called or texted since this afternoon, and it was hard to think she was doing anything other than blowing me off. Didn't I deserve that?

I must have been making a face because Sophia leaned toward me in her chair and lowered her voice. "Did you guys break up?"

"No," I said quickly. "I don't think so." I frowned. "It's complicated."

It didn't seem like he'd been paying attention, but I should have known better. My father was so observant. His icy blue eyes turned toward me.

"Do you love her?"

It was a simple question, but my mind went blank at hearing it come from him. He'd been emotionally shut off and avoided talking about feelings after my mother died, but Sophia had reactivated that part of him. I still wasn't used to this new, old version of him.

He'd asked if I loved her, and my voice was strong and sure. "Yes."

He considered it for a moment, probably crafting all the ways he saw this as a failure or how Emery was unworthy of me, but his expression remained thoughtful, not critical. "Then it's not complicated," he said. "You're a Hale, so you win at all costs, and that includes her heart."

I nearly fell out of my chair. Where was the lecture about how this didn't fit into the plan he had for me? He was the last person I expected to get unsolicited advice from regarding my love life.

Sophia's smile was pleased as she gazed up at him, and he returned the same look, full of love and a smile hinting at the corners of his mouth.

Her focus turned back to me. "Does she love you?"

This conversation was weird and uncomfortable, and I put my hand on the back of my neck, massaging the tired muscles there. "Yeah. She does."

"So, what's the issue?"

I lifted my hand, signaling it was difficult to explain. "I don't know." But that was a lie. I knew exactly what the problem was. "I have a hard time trusting people."

I didn't miss the way she glanced at my father, and she wasn't wrong to assume he was mostly to blame for that. But she must not have known about the file her fiancé had collected on Emery because her question was straightforward. "Has she given you a reason not to trust her?"

"Yes," a familiar voice came from behind me. "But I found a way to fix that."

I turned to see Emery standing a few feet away. Her hair was pulled up in a haphazard ponytail, and she wore leggings and a t-shirt. Gone were her provocative clothes and sexy makeup. She looked weary, but her eyes shimmered when she saw me, and my heart swelled. It propelled me up out of my chair.

"What are you doing here?"

"I went to the house, and Elliot told me Marist went into labor. He said everyone was at the hospital."

She glanced past me to my father, and I could tell what she was thinking. She was embarrassed about how she looked, but that was unnecessary. She looked amazing to me no matter what.

She jerked her head toward an empty corner of the waiting room. "Can I talk to you?"

"Yeah, of course." I took her elbow and guided her toward it, using that as an excuse to touch her. As soon as my fingers grazed her skin, warmth spread through my body.

"Sorry I look like hell," she said as soon as we were out of earshot. "I'm running on four hours of sleep and wearing clothes from yesterday."

"What? Why?"

"Because I came straight from the airport. I took a redeye to Miami last night."

Confusion hit me. "What's in Miami?"

"A six-a.m. flight to Aruba."

Holy shit. My voice dropped to a whisper. "You went to see Jillian?"

"I did. After I left your place yesterday, I started thinking about Lambert's deal. He escalated so quickly, and it felt . . . off. Like he was trying to distract by separating us. It made me wonder if we'd missed something. So, since she'd also seen what was inside his safe, I went to see her."

I pulled in a slow breath as I realized what a fucking idiot I'd been. I should have gone with her. Hell, we could have taken my family's jet or chartered a private plane. We were supposed to be partners, and I'd made her go it alone.

"How was she?" I asked.

Emery's smile was quick, but it lit her eyes. "She's doing good. They're really happy together."

She grabbed my hand, pulled me down so we could sit in the chairs nearby, and then told me the whole story, how Jillian and Lucas were in love and had been planning for months to run away together. He'd helped her buy a new identity, train for the long open water swim, and then faked the fight to make sure no one suspected them.

When Jillian saw the prenup already signed by Ansel, she freaked out. There was a storm rolling in the next night, so they moved up the timetable. She said goodbye to Tiffany, set sail, and when *The Trident* was far enough out, she'd put on a wetsuit, left everything behind, and jumped.

"She said swimming in the storm was really hard," Emery's

voice softened, "but the reward at the end was worth it. Lucas was waiting for her on the beach."

He'd dropped her off at a bus station and stayed behind in Cape Hill until *The Trident* was found adrift, everyone believing she'd gone overboard. Then he set sail for Aruba, stopping in Atlantic City to pick her up.

"She found the collateral she was looking for in her dad's safe," she said, "and it wasn't on the flash drive—she didn't seem to know about that. It was in the papers we'd looked through."

She reached into her purse and pulled out a clear plastic zipper-top bag that contained several folded sheets of paper.

"What's that?"

She held the bag gingerly, as if it were priceless. "These are pages from a secret Barlow manual on how to manipulate clinical trial data to get favorable results—a practice they've been using for *years* to increase the reported efficacy of their drugs." Her gaze dropped down to the plastic protected pages. "This is what Jillian took from his safe, and the only thing she carried with her when she left Cape Hill to start a brand-new life. It's the collateral to stop her father from revealing she's alive in case he ever finds out."

Sound faded until it was just us. "And she gave it to you?"

Emery swallowed hard and nodded. "When I came clean and told her who I was."

I still struggled to wrap my head around the idea she was Jillian's cousin. It was clear that had been a difficult conversation for her, and once again I was angry at myself that Emery had no choice but to do it without my support. "I should have been there with you. Fuck, I'm sorry."

She seemed to accept my genuine apology. "I wished you were there. I want us to be partners in this, all the way to the end."

"I do too."

"Then that means you have to trust me. When I tell you I love you," her voice was stern, "I need you to believe me."

"Emery, I swear I'm done with that bullshit. I know it's as real for you as it is for me—I just got scared." I drew in a deep breath. "I once told you that if you didn't need sex to survive, you hadn't been with the right person yet." I needed to put it out there, get it all off my chest. "What I didn't realize was up until now, I'd never needed anyone else to survive, and it was only because I hadn't found you yet."

She blinked back the unexpected tears that leapt into her eyes and shoved the papers enclosed in plastic forward.

"This is what you can use to bargain for the video."

I stared at the packet, stunned. This was what she meant about proving her love was real. She'd done everything she could to save me.

"Despite his revelations," I said, "Wayne Lambert is not a good man."

"No," she agreed.

"And this is more proof Barlowe is shady as fuck. You could use it to take them both down."

It was all she'd wanted for so long, but she shook her head. "I've spent ten years trying to get my revenge, and I don't want to lose any more time to it. I'd rather have you."

I ignored the packet she was holding and put my hands on the sides of her face, pulling her into my greedy kiss. Whatever was decided, we'd do it together.

But our lips had barely met before a shadow fell on us and someone cleared his throat.

"Royce and Marist have invited us to their suite to meet their new son," my father said.

Emery separated from me, perhaps embarrassed to be caught kissing in front of him, but there was a strange, pleased look in his eye. Maybe he was just riding the high of knowing the Hale family name was going to continue, but I got the feeling it was more than that.

As if he were happy to see I was happy.

I stood from my chair as Emery put the documents back in her purse, and when she was done, I helped her up and laced our fingers together. He hadn't said specifically if she were invited, but it was implied.

I'd expected the new mother to be the one glowing, but instead it was Royce. After we'd gotten our passes from the receptionist and were led back to Marist's suite, we found my brother standing beside his wife's bed with a blanket-wrapped baby in his arms and an enormous smile on his face.

Marist's family was there too, standing on the opposite side of the bed, and her parents stiffened when we came in. My father's presence made all the Northcotts uncomfortable, but Royce was oblivious.

"This is Tobias Eduard Hale," he said, gently angling his arms to proudly show off his sleeping baby to us.

Emery might have made a soft sigh, but it was drowned out by Sophia. "Oh, my God, he's so cute!"

She wasn't wrong. My nephew was pretty cute with a full head of hair and a tiny, curled fist pressed against his temple. I watched as Royce gingerly passed Tobias off to his in-laws. Had he given them this first privilege because they'd named their son with Hale family names? My father had to be pleased about that.

"Are you going to hold him?" Sophia asked her fiancé. "Because I might die seeing you with a baby in your arms."

My father's gaze was pinned on his grandson, his

expression full of satisfaction. "Yes, I intend to hold him."

We watched dutifully, waiting for our turn after the Northcotts. I leaned closer to my father.

"When we're done here," my voice was hushed, "would you mind stopping by the house? I have something I need to discuss with you."

Did he suspect this was the conversation I'd put off for years? His shoulders rose as he took in a breath. "Of course."

It was late when my father arrived at the house, late enough that Elliot had gone to bed. Not that my father needed an escort. He still had an access code and could come and go unannounced in the house he'd lived in for the first fifty-five years of his life.

He wore the same black Balenciaga suit he'd had on at the hospital but looked less intimidating to me than he had in the past. I was waiting for him in the foyer, my belly full of apprehension but also a weird feeling of excitement. I was ready to admit to my mistakes and take some power back from the guilt that had plagued me for years.

"Thanks for coming," I said, turning into the salon and not giving him a chance to argue.

There was a liquor cabinet with a set of glass tumblers and few bottles that hadn't been touched in years, and one that was brand new. It was the same brand of scotch my father drank once a year in remembrance of my mother. I turned two tumblers upright, unscrewed the cap on the scotch, and poured a finger's worth in each glass as he quietly observed.

"No," he said when I extended one, offering it to him.

"You sure? I think Mom would have today, would have wanted to share one with you. You're grandparents now."

His expression didn't change, but shit—my words hit him like a sledgehammer. He didn't hesitate in accepting the glass. "Perhaps you're right."

"Good. You're going to want it after this conversation." His posture stiffened, but I motioned toward the door. "We should talk in the office."

He carried his untouched drink as we wound through the house, and when he came into the office, his curious gaze immediately went to the Lagerfield in the center of the room.

"Yeah," I commented. "We'll get to that in a minute. But first, I need to say something that's long overdue." I took a sip of the scotch, letting its smoky flavor roll over my tongue. It wasn't a tactic to stall. I'd done it to lend gravity to the next thing I was going to say because I wanted him to hear that it was genuine. "I'm sorry I had an affair with Alice, and I'm sorry it's taken me this long to apologize for it."

He kept his intense gaze fixed on me as he took his first sip of his drink and considered my statement. He lowered his glass. His words were simple, but there was nothing simple about their meaning. "Thank you."

His acknowledgment plunged the room into awkwardness, and surprisingly, he broke first.

"I understand," he said, "better than most how manipulative Alice can be."

"Don't," I said. "She didn't take advantage of me. I knew what I was doing, and so did she." I'd lived so much of my life following his orders, and even though I no longer did, it was hard to stand up. "You made sure everyone under you didn't have any power. It's why Royce came after your board seat, and it's why Alice and I had the affair. It's not an excuse, and yes, I did it intentionally to be cruel—but it was a way for me to take back some of the power you held over my head."

The muscle along his jaw flexed, and his fingers tightened on the glass, but otherwise he didn't react. This was the part where I expected him to get angry. He would rain down harsh words in a frigid voice and destroy something I cared about with surgical precision as punishment.

But his gaze didn't fill with fire. The tension in his body didn't erupt and cause him to surge forward. He just stared at me like a statue holding a decorative glass of scotch.

"I am aware," he said slowly, "I am not blameless. There is much of my life I would do differently if I could, and I would have started with how I treated the people I cared about." His chest lifted, and he squared his shoulders to me. "I forgive you and would like to move beyond this." He took another sip of his scotch, then stared at the amber liquid in his glass. "When your mother died, a large part of me went with her, and though I've started healing . . . I am *not* healed. I don't believe that's possible until I've repaired what I can of what I've done to you and your brother." His tone shifted, becoming more hesitant than I'd heard in ages. "Will you let me try?"

"Yes." The instant it was out, I felt different. Lighter. The heaviness of my guilt wasn't completely gone, but it was a fraction of what it had been.

He looked pleased, and perhaps he felt lighter, too. "Excellent."

I finished my drink, set the glass down on the desk, and turned my attention to the Lagerfield. "The good news is we can start right now. The bad news is, what we just discussed? That was the easy part."

Had that made him anxious? If so, he didn't show it. His

gaze followed mine to the safe. "This is about Ms. Mendenhall, I presume."

"Yes," I said, "and no." I put my hands on the back of the chair I'd sat in every night while watching Emery practice, and turned it back to its original position, angling the chair toward the fireplace. I gestured to the one opposite it for my father to take a seat. "I need to tell you a story."

When he sat, I began by telling him about the malfunctioning alarm sensor and the pretty sales rep who'd asked me out to lunch. That I'd suspected she had ulterior motives early on, but I was willing to play along because I was intrigued by her theory that Jillian had faked her death. I explained what we'd discovered and then how we'd confirmed our friend was very much alive and well, free from her life in Cape Hill.

He didn't ask questions when I talked about Emery's plot to get inside Wayne's safe and why she wanted to do it. How she'd spent ten years believing he'd stolen the final months she would have had with her father before he'd died, only to learn her father and his gambling addiction shared much of the blame.

"Wayne Lambert is blackmailing me for a seat on HBHC's board," I announced. "He didn't go to Royce, because the board would be openly hostile to him if he did. I don't think he went to you because you scare the shit out of him." My tone was bitter. "I was the easiest Hale to target."

My father stayed calm and detached, focusing on evaluating the problem. "What does he have on you?"

"Nothing, actually." My heartrate climbed, and my breath quickened. "I'd thought it was a compromising video of me, but it's . . ." I inhaled a long, deep breath. "Alice put a hidden camera in the dining room, probably in one of the flower arrangements she'd had done for the party."

His mind worked so much faster than mine, so it already sensed the answer, judging by the dread in his voice. "Which party?"

"The one celebrating Royce's promotion to the board."

One moment he was sitting, and the next he was on his feet. "Have you seen this video?"

"Enough of it," I said, "to recognize what was going on, and the faces in the room. I stopped watching when Marist's dress came off."

He moved so quickly as he strode the room, it was almost too fast to call pacing. He retreated deep into his thoughts, traveling a tight circuit across the rug before stopping and putting his hands on the back of his chair, leaning over it. He squeezed so tight, his knuckles turned white.

"Fucking Alice," he uttered. It was so rare that he swore, but it was entirely appropriate. "I'm going to destroy Wayne Lambert."

"I figured as much, but how are you going to do it without burning all of HBHC in the process?" I rose from my seat, leveling my gaze at him. "How do you do it without hurting Marist?"

He looked uncertain, but only a moment. "I'll find a way."

I nodded, hoping he'd say that. "I have an idea, but I need your advice." Because my father wasn't just a master at chess, he excelled at all kinds of strategy. "You're always two steps ahead, and no one knows how to play the game better than you." I brushed back the bottom of my suit coat so I could rest a hand on my hip. "A while ago, you came to me when you needed help executing your plan with Sophia. I'm asking the same of you now. Will you help me?"

He didn't blink, didn't hesitate. "Absolutely."

TWENTY-TWO

LAMBERT

Serena hadn't slept in the same room with me for months, unfairly blaming me for Jillian's death. Had she forgotten I'd lost a daughter too? My frustration with my wife was at an all-time high, and a big part of that was because I couldn't do anything about it.

I'd taken Barlowe from a struggling, marginally profitable company to a multi-billion-dollar empire. We were a household name, the gold-standard for several drug lines. But no matter how much money I made, or new drugs the company developed and secured FDA approval for under my leadership, I'd never be able to leave her.

Not without fear the Barlowe family would cut me off.

I couldn't cement myself as a Cape Hill elite until my network was a spiderweb. I wanted the security that I wouldn't unravel if one strand was clipped.

So, I stood outside the door to the guest bedroom Serena had claimed as hers, drank my whiskey, and stewed in my irritation. It shouldn't bother me. We didn't love each other anymore, but we'd stayed partners. Yes, we'd both had multiple affairs over the years, but there was something so disrespectful about how she shut me out. I was good enough to share a child with, but not the grief over losing one.

I was halfway to my empty bedroom when my phone vibrated with a text message.

Unknown: I know who you are, Michael Slattery.

It stopped me in my tracks. That name hadn't been uttered in thirty-five years . . . not until last week. Did David's daughter think she could blackmail me after I'd already paid her fifteen million? Christ, the apple didn't fall far from the tree. Greedy little bitch. She was going to regret—

My phone rang, the call coming from the same unknown number, and I smashed my finger on the screen to accept it.

"Listen up," I spat out, "because I'm only going to say this once—"

"Hello, Dad."

All the anger in me flipped onto its side, turning into suspicion. This was a trick. A voice actor or a computer application that sounded exactly like her because it couldn't be Jillian. My little girl was dead. I'd accepted that awful truth, unlike Tiffany and Serena.

"I'm calling to tell you," the eerie, familiar voice continued, "I've done what you said I never could. I started over with nothing and am building a new life. Just like you did—only better because I'm not doing it at the expense of others."

"You're not her," I snapped.

"You want me to prove it?"

Her tone and inflection were well done. Pitch-perfect Jillian, and a tentacle of worry, mixed with hope, wrapped around me, dragging me down. I could picture her clever eyes and cunning smile on the other end of the line.

"When I was twelve, you and Mom had a big argument about whether or not I needed to wear a life-preserver whenever I went sailing with you. You were on my side and finally convinced her to let me make the choice."

My heart stopped. There was no power in my voice. "Jillian?"

"I think about that a lot. It might have been the last time I was allowed to make a decision in my life."

She was *alive*.

I turned, hurrying down the hall to tell Serena. "Where are you? Are you all right?"

"I'm fine. A lot better than you're going to be soon."

My hand froze on the doorknob. "What are you talking about? Tell me where you are, and I'll send someone to get you." I frowned. This was too important to trust to anyone else. I needed to see her with my own eyes. "I'll come get you."

"No, it's too late for that. I'm not telling you where I am, and you have much bigger things to worry about. I found some Barlowe paperwork at the house before I left, and you should be aware I turned it over to the FBI this afternoon."

I let go of the doorknob like it had burned me and backed away from the door. "You did not."

"Oh, I did. I imagine they're working on getting a warrant to raid the house right now. It's why I'm calling. You need to make sure Tiffany isn't home when it happens. Mom probably knows what you've done, but don't traumatize my sister."

"Stop it." I used anger to mask my fear. "I'm sure whatever you think you found, the FBI isn't going to be interested in it."

"I saw the prenup, Dad. Even after I told you not to because I was *never* going to marry Ansel, you had the lawyers draft it, and then he fucking signed it. Ask yourself what else I might have seen in your safe."

Fuck.

If what she was telling me was true, I was in deep, deep shit. I couldn't catch my breath, and the room began to sway. I'd never had so many emotions overwhelm me at once.

The betrayal by my own daughter, after everything I'd given her, was exceptionally cruel. "What have you done?"

"You won't hear from me again, and don't look for me. I'm throwing this phone away. Goodbye, Dad."

Before I could say anything, the call disconnected.

I didn't sleep that night. I doubted I would have been able to even if I'd had the time. I'd woken Serena up, told her to pack a bag, and sent her and Tiffany to the house in the Hamptons. I didn't care what story she had to use to convince our daughter. I just needed them gone so I could focus and not worry about them.

I called Mitchell, because I had done my best to cultivate a relationship with the president of the United States. We didn't have the kind of friendship where I could call him in the middle of the night, but I would try anyway. If the FBI had opened an investigation into me or Barlowe, I hoped I could press him to give me some time, or at least a heads-up. The FBI was supposed to be independent, but the president still had influence.

Mitchell's private phone went straight to voicemail. I sent a text for him to call me as soon as possible, but it went unanswered.

My next call was to Sovereign Systems. I had a contingency

plan on file with them, but it took forty-five minutes to get in touch with a person who had a fucking clue what I was talking about, and even then, he was unsure if they could get things in motion in the next few hours.

I couldn't wait that long. The FBI was partial to early morning raids. They liked to maximize the embarrassment by catching their targets off-guard and asleep, and in the most unflattering situation possible.

"Do you only have one goddamn truck?" I asked the guy when he said it'd be several hours before it would arrive at the house.

"No, sir. It's the middle of the night, so we're having difficulty putting together a team to staff it."

"I don't give a fuck," I growled. "Whatever it costs, just get it done."

I went through the house, collecting anything that had the slightest chance of having evidence on it. I stacked laptops and boxes of files in a pile in the entryway, waiting for the security transport truck to arrive. Once it was here, I'd clean out the safe. The most damaging information was in there, and if agents showed up before the truck, at least I'd have a few days while they brought an expert in to open it.

I'd be long gone by then.

A little after five a.m., security at the front gate called to tell me a truck had arrived and was requesting permission to enter the grounds. I hurriedly told him to send them through.

The gray armored truck was large and aggressive looking, with its bulletproof glass and heavy plated exterior. It was overkill for a job like this, but the sooner I handed off custody of my assets, the safer I became.

A warrant did not extend to the contents of this truck.

Once I signed off, it'd drive to the marina, unload

everything onto *The Trident*, and as soon as I boarded, I'd set sail for Cuba. I had a secondary passport just in case, and Cuba didn't extradite if things got really out of hand.

I was not going to prison.

Two men got out of the cab of the truck, and two more were in the back, and all four wore the bland Sovereign uniforms, complete with gray caps and thick, black Kevlar vests. It belayed a bit of my fear. In addition to moving sensitive material, Serena had millions in jewelry. Some of it she hadn't ever worn—it was an additional form of currency if needed.

None of the men were quick to move, and their lack of urgency was infuriating.

"Well?" I demanded, flinging my hands toward the open front door and the stack of items they could start loading.

The biggest guy, who seemed to be in charge, lumbered toward me, carrying a lock box. "Hey, boss. Where do you want this?"

He followed me upstairs and set it on the floor of my bedroom, and I made him wait in the hall while I unlocked the safe and hurried to load the contents inside the container. I haphazardly dumped handfuls of necklaces and bracelets in, rattling against the metal sides of the box. Once I had every drawer and secret compartment emptied, I closed the lid and engaged the lock with a four-digit code I set. Only I'd be able to open it once it arrived at the marina.

"I'm finished. Put it on the truck," I barked after throwing open the bedroom door.

The guy gave me a look like he didn't appreciate being ordered around at five in the morning, but I didn't have time for pleasantries. My pulse was pounding as he carried the box down the stairs, and my heart beat even faster as I stood on the front patio and supervised the crew loading the back of the truck.

It was still dark out, but light was breaking on the horizon. Sunrise wasn't far off, as was the opportunity for me to survive another day unscathed. I'd reinvented myself once before. If I had to, I could do it again. It'd be so much easier this time because I had money and assets I could leverage.

"Is that it?" the big guy asked.

At the same time, another member of his team approached and passed me a clipboard to sign over custody, except he wasn't paying attention. He let go before I had the thing in hand, sending the board and its pen tumbling to the steps.

"Goddamnit," I muttered, bending at the same time he did, both of us reaching for the pen. It was irritating, and our hands collided.

The big guy watched our fumbling with disinterest.

"Awful lot of truck for a few boxes," he commented.

I glared up at him, wanting to tell him to mind his business, but refrained. I was about to sign over everything to him, and even though he wouldn't be able to access the lock box, I'd be wise not to be an asshole. The smaller guy had finally wrangled the clipboard and awkwardly handed it to me, uttering a feeble apology.

"I'm moving some valuable pieces," I said, scribbling my signature on the line, and shoved the clipboard back at the idiot who'd dropped it. "I appreciate the care you'll give them during transit." I squeezed out a wide smile. "And there will be a little something extra for each of you once everything is safely aboard my ship."

"Sounds great, boss," the big guy said. But he was weirdly indifferent.

As if early morning runs to a mansion in Cape Hill were normal and boring for him. It got under my skin, but I kept my mouth shut. He hadn't a clue who I was and didn't respect me the way he should.

Instead, he nodded to the rest of his men that it was time to go and climbed in the back of the truck with a teammate, pulling the doors closed with a loud thud. Relief poured through me as the engine rumbled to life and the final guy hurried to the passenger side of the cab, the clipboard tucked under his arm. He had a slight build, and as he opened the passenger door, an unsettling feeling overtook me.

My phone rang in my suit coat pocket, and I pulled it out, tapping the screen to accept.

The man on the other side didn't wait for me to greet him; the security guard just began talking. "This is Robert at the front gate. Sir, federal agents just entered the property. They have a warrant."

I kept my gaze locked on the slight man as he tossed the clipboard inside the truck. That document ensured I'd protected myself. So why did I have this horrible sense of dread?

The clipboard guy must have known I was watching him because he was halfway into the cab when he turned to look at me. He smiled, yanked off his hat, and chucked it into the truck, making his long brown hair spill out around his shoulders.

Those bulletproof vests were so bulky, and the uniforms masculine, I'd just assumed the whole crew were men. Plus, I hadn't paid any attention to them, hadn't bothered to really look at their faces. If I had, I would have recognized my niece much sooner.

Now, it was too late.

The world began to close in around me as she waved goodbye, then turned her middle finger up at me. I stood with my feet glued to the ground in shock, staring at her offensive finger and the oversized wristwatch she wore dangling on her arm.

That had been my watch up until she'd taken it off me during our fumbling over the clipboard and pen. Just like the contents of that truck had been mine until I signed over custody.

She'd cracked my Lagerfield safe in a few hours. It'd take her *much* less time to crack the simple lock on the security box Sovereign had provided. Everything inside was hers to keep, destroy, or turn over to the authorities.

In the blink of an eye, my fortune had been stolen from me.

When I took a step toward her, she jerked the door closed, and the truck lurched forward. I'd given them instructions to hurry and go out the back gate, and the driver was intent on following them. Maybe the rest of the team had no idea who she was or what she had planned, but I did.

I chased after the truck as it sped off, screaming for it to come back so loudly my vocal cords felt like gravel had been dragged across them. It was futile. The gray beast of a truck carrying everything I needed to start over grew smaller and disappeared behind the line of trees that obscured the back exit.

I was out of breath and out of my mind as I pulled to a stop. I could hear the cars barreling up the front drive, and a single thought repeated in my head.

I was fucking doomed.

TWENTY-THREE

EMERY

I tried to decline the invite to the Vegas Vault show, but Vance insisted we go.

"Don't you want to defend your title?" he asked.

I did, but I hadn't practiced much during the last seven months. After everything that happened with Lambert, I'd needed a break. I'd resigned from Sovereign, but left my relationship with them open-ended, willing to freelance if a particularly tough open required someone like me.

I enjoyed the challenge, but I didn't need the money from it—Macalister had seen to that. His father offered to personally manage my new wealth. I'd helped save him, his family, and his company, he'd said. It was the least he could do.

The only investment he wasn't in charge of was the brand-new design label I owned, a little outfit in Aruba. Jillian was family, who'd given me the only piece of collateral she had, and then even more help when I asked if she'd call her father.

Funding her label was the least I could do, I'd told her.

It'd been Macalister who'd made sure the documents made it to the right people at the FBI, but we'd needed to warn

Lambert about the raid to trigger his contingency plan. Our best chance at swiping the flash drive was if he moved it, and I'd been so relieved when he called for the armored truck.

Vance's plan, refined by his father and executed by me, had worked perfectly.

During the drive away from Lambert's house, I'd explained to the rest of the crew there wouldn't be a bonus waiting for us at the dock, only FBI agents. I asked for ten minutes alone in the back of the truck. I'd give them five grand each to take a smoke break and look the other way, and all three of them agreed.

It'd taken me much less time than that to override the lock on the safe deposit box and get inside, which was ironic. I'd warned my boss more than once how easy the boxes were to crack. I'd grabbed the USB stick, tucked it in my pocket, and relocked the top so no one would know I'd been inside.

And as I'd predicted, there were agents at the marina, executing a search warrant on all three of the Lamberts' boats. He'd been so good at getting away with things, he believed time made him invincible, when what it had really done was make him sloppy.

Two days after the raid, he was pulled over by the Coast Guard on a boat full of supplies and a passport and was arrested for trying to flee prosecution. He'd sit in prison until his trial, and likely a long time after that.

He deserved it, but rather than feel happiness or a sense of justice, all I felt was sadness for Tiffany. She'd carry the same shame Vance and I did, the guilt of being tied to someone else's mistakes, for the rest of her life.

I stood at one of the roulette wheels in the casino and fiddled with the name badge slung around my neck. Vance had stepped away to use the restroom, but he'd been gone a while, and I was beginning to wonder if I should go look for him. My boyfriend had a habit of making friends with half the people he met, and while that was amusing to me, sometimes I wanted him all to myself.

I was nervous. I was giving a demonstration in fifteen minutes to the master safecrackers in attendance, and he'd offered to help. So, where was my partner to help calm me down?

"Hey," he said in a rush, materializing out of thin air. "Sorry, I got sidetracked."

He brushed a hand through his hair, making the ends wild, but it only added to his appeal. In the months since we'd erased the flash drive, we'd grown inseparable. With my goal completed, I would have been adrift without him.

There'd been so much I'd put off in my pursuit of taking Lambert down, but now I had time and money, and Vance encouraged me to live my life. He was teaching me how to sail, and we talked about sailing his yacht together to Monaco for this year's Grand Prix.

Which meant we were talking about our future, and for the first time, I couldn't wait to look forward. I had everything I wanted, especially because I had him.

"I bet on eighteen while you were gone," I said, using his birthdate. "Turns out you're still unlucky."

He wrapped an arm around my waist. "I don't know, Emery. I still feel pretty damn lucky." He dropped a kiss on the side of my neck, sending warmth buzzing through my system. "How about you?"

"I'm nervous," I admitted. I'd practiced the presentation enough times in front of him he could probably give it if anything went wrong, but that didn't do much to help my nerves.

His look told me I was being silly. "You're going to do great."

Then he linked my hand with his and we strode toward the hall, funneling in with the rest of the certified safecrackers who'd been vetted to watch the demonstration, as I'd be giving away trade secrets. I recognized several faces in the line, mostly people I'd competed against in previous years.

We bypassed the man at the door who was checking IDs, and then confirmed everything was set up properly for my demonstration. The donated, older model Steadfast safe had been parked on a raised platform, serving as a temporary stage, along with a table where I'd stowed my tool bag beneath. Chairs were placed in rows in front of it, and as people began to move in and claim seats, I made small talk with them.

Us safecrackers were a motley crew, and it was nice to be with my peers.

But when the lights dimmed, anxiety fluttered in my stomach. The pressure was nothing compared to the agonizing hours with Lambert's safe, but it was always hard working with an audience watching.

Well, except for Vance.

He joined me on stage and glanced at his watch, giving me the signal it was time and wordlessly asking me if I was ready. I nodded and took a deep breath as he strolled to the microphone.

I'd given him my biography to use for the introduction, and when he delivered it without glancing at any notes, it reminded me how gifted he was at public speaking. His performance was natural and captivating. If he did decide to go into politics, he'd do well. But like me, he wasn't sure yet what path he wanted to take, and that was okay. We had time to figure it out.

Before he gave me the floor and exited the stage, he flashed his gorgeous smile, which quelled a big chunk of my anxiety. Without words, he reminded me I had this, and he was here for me.

I turned my attention to the Steadfast. As far as safes went, it wasn't exactly sexy. The design was a simple black rectangle, trimmed with a thin white frame around the door. The electronic keypad was centered over a silver handle, and I started off the presentation by discussing the different areas of attack. I could go after the hinges or the battery in the keypad. Or I could come at it from the front, the side, or the back, and then I gave the pros and cons of approaching from each angle.

Finally, I got out my drill, focused on the door, and began my attack.

While I was drilling, Vance went into the crowd and held the microphone up for anyone who wanted to ask a question. I would pause my drill to answer, sometimes changing a drill bit or giving the motor some time to cool down.

It didn't take me too long to penetrate the outer layer of the door, and I threaded my wire camera through the hole. The viewfinder of my borescope was mirrored on the screen beside the stage so everyone could see what I saw, and they watched as I located the white cable loop. I dug out my vice grips from my bag, clamping the cable off, and drew back the bolt.

When I pushed the handle, the door swung open, and there was a smattering of applause. I let out a relaxed breath and turned to face the audience, feeling pleased with my success. "What other questions do you have for me?"

A guy in the front row raised his hand, and Vance strode over when I nodded toward him.

"Yeah, hi," the guy said. "What's that?"

He pointed back to the safe with a puzzled look on his face. I followed his gaze and my heart skipped. It was habit not to look inside, and this safe had been donated, so I had assumed it would be empty.

But it *wasn't*.

The interior configuration was similar to Lambert's with a watch winding section, and there was a single piece in one of the spots, sparkling under the stage lights. I pulled the cuff out to examine it and stared at the beautiful watch where the oval face was ringed with diamonds. The word *Cartier* was printed beneath twelve o'clock.

This was a woman's watch, and clearly meant for me. My focus snapped to Vance. When he'd disappeared 'to the restroom' earlier, he'd really been placing this watch inside the safe.

He stood in the center aisle of the chairs, wearing an enigmatic smile. Maybe he wasn't sure how this would go over with me, or that I might not like the watch he'd probably spent tens of thousands of dollars on.

But, oh, I did.

My pulse quickened and the audience faded until it felt like it was just us, all alone in this enormous space.

"Is this for me?" My voice was tight because not only was the watch gorgeous, but there was also meaning behind it. He wanted me to start making new, happier memories.

He lifted the microphone so everyone could hear. "You can still steal mine anytime you'd like." A few people chuckled, but his gaze didn't waver from me. His eyes gleamed. "By the way, there's something on the back. Go ahead and read it out loud."

I turned it over to see the tiny printing there and looked down to read the inscription. "What would you do to me if you could?"

"Well, Emery, I think I'd marry you."

I blinked in stunned surprise, and glanced back at him,

only to find he was no longer standing.

Oh, my God.

He'd directed my focus flawlessly, so I hadn't seen him move. He was down on a knee with the microphone in one hand, and a ring in the other.

All the air in the huge room disappeared. I went weightless, but he held me tightly with the way he peered up at me. His expression was full of love and hope.

"I want us to spend the rest of our lives together." His tone was teasing... but also completely serious. "What do you say? Is that allowed?"

I didn't have to think about it. My answer was automatic. "Yes, Vance." I matched his playful yet serious tone. "I'll allow it."

An enormous grin burst on his face as he climbed to his feet and then charged toward the stage. I met him halfway, of course, because we were partners. I leapt into his arms and his lips crashed into mine because neither of us could stand another second apart.

When we'd first met, I'd thought we'd never work. I couldn't see a future for myself, and certainly not one for him that included me. I'd never been so happy to be wrong. We'd each worked to unlock the other person's heart, and I knew we'd solve anything else life threw at us.

Because we'd do it together.

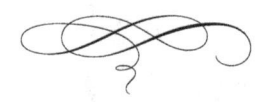

MORE BY NIKKI SLOANE

THE BLINDFOLD CLUB SERIES
It Takes Two
Three Simple Rules
Three Hard Lessons
Three Little Mistakes
Three Dirty Secrets
Three Sweet Nothings
Three Guilty Pleasures
One More Rule

THE SORDID SERIES
Sordid
Torrid
Destroy

SPORTS ROMANCE
The Rivalry

THE NASHVILLE NEIGHBORHOOD
The Doctor
The Pool Boy
The Architect

FILTHY RICH AMERICANS
The Initiation
The Obsession
The Deception
The Redemption
The Temptation

THANK YOU

Thank you so much to my husband for brainstorming this book with me every waking minute and helping me push through to the end, even when we were on our first vacation in more than two years. I am so lucky to have you—you're the best partner in the world!

Thank you to my friend Aubrey Bondurant for being there to motivate when deadline pressure started getting to me. If we hadn't taken our writers retreat when we did, I would still be writing this book.

Thanks to my editor Lori Whitwam for working so tirelessly to ensure the book was as good as possible, especially given the ridiculous timeline you were given. You're amazing!

Thank you to my publicist Nina Grinstead and the gang at Valentine PR for all you do!

Thanks to the readers, reviewers, authors, book bloggers, TikTokers and Bookstagrammers for all the love you've shown this series.

ABOUT THE AUTHOR

USA Today bestselling author Nikki Sloane landed in graphic design after her careers as a waitress, a screenwriter, and a ballroom dance instructor fell through. Now she writes full-time and lives in Kentucky with her husband, two sons, and a pug who is more slug than dog.

She is a four-time Romance Writers of America RITA® & Vivian® Finalist, a Passionate Plume & HOLT Medallion winner, a Goodreads Choice Awards semifinalist, and couldn't be any happier that people enjoy reading her sexy words.

www.NikkiSloane.com

CPSIA information can be obtained
at www.ICGtesting.com
Printed in the USA
JSHW031309130622
26961JS00002B/122